CHAINS IN THE SKY

CHAINS IN THE SKY

CARL R. MOORE

Cover design: Stephen Zimmer

Additional texuring detail on cover image: Madeline Dee Moore

Cover art in this book copyright © 2020 Stephen Zimmer & Seventh Star Press, LLC.

Editor: Stephen Zimmer

Published by Seventh Star Press, LLC.

ISBN Number: 978-1-7362781-3-0

Seventh Star Press

www.seventhstarpress.com

info@seventhstarpress.com

Publisher's Note:

Chains in the Sky is a work of fiction. All names, characters, and places are the product of the author's imagination, used in fictitious manner. Any resemblances to actual persons, places, locales, events, etc. are purely coincidental.

Printed in the United States of America

First Edition

Acknowledgements

I would first like to thank my family, Sarah, Madeline, and Isabel, who will always be foremost in my heart. Next, I would like to thank Stephen Zimmer and Holly Philippe of Seventh Star Press for making this book a reality—your work and your skill are deeply appreciated. I would also like to thank Fran Cathcart, Rich Shea, Sean Hasey, Ed Stevens, Lew Richards, Zac Rathke, and Julien Bouget for being like brothers. A special extra shoutout goes to Rich for consulting on boats and nautical terms. I also must show appreciation to Alejandro Castro-Reina for advising on the Spanish language and Aran Mull and Tom Blassman for the many conversations about writing and the fantasy genre. I thank Daniel Dark, Dean Harrison, Sara Deurell, and the many writers from Imaginarium who have been an inspiration and an influence. I would also like to thank Frank and Martha Moskowitz, Josh and Theresa Alexander, and Lauren Newell for playing the songs that help me stay sane. There are many more whom I am not able to name here, but who have been great inspirations—I feel I could populate the entire borough of Brooklyn with the list. To all of you, thank you.

"The heart knoweth his own bitterness; and a stranger doth not intermeddle with his joy."
—Proverbs 14:10, King James Version

1

"Over here! I'm over here!"

Ray Barrs ran for his granddaughter as she hung onto the gunwale. Rain hammered the *Faustina's* deck, and the boat lurched to the side as he took hold of the girl's wrists, hauled her over the edge, and looked in her eyes.

Death had made them cloudy, and pus flecked her irises like foam in a sickly sea. *Ada's in pain,* he thought, *she's in pain, and I have to make it stop.*

The girl squirmed as he carried her across the deck. She fell out of his arms like a fish escaping a net and flopped around on the wet planks.

Ray's heart pounded in his chest, and as he caught his breath, she got control of herself and stood. She balanced easily, though the boat rocked on the waves, and stepped toward him.

"Ada?" he rasped.

Her voice was as thin as a sliver of rain. "Grampa, please," she started, then her words distorted as if she were choking on them. Her legs lost their firmness, and she crumpled when the next wave hit.

"Ada!" he cried. He reached for her hand but failed to grasp it. She began to slide backward, screaming once more as she went back up over the gunwale.

Something was pulling her—a slither in the shadows that vanished into the waves.

***

Late that afternoon, when he arrived at the marina, the sun had returned. It cast a red-orange glow promising serenity and warmth. Tourists sat outside the bars and cafés, enjoying their drinks in a pleasantly drier eighty-degrees.

Ray docked the little Defiance fishing boat he'd named *Faustina*, climbed in his truck, and drove home. He said nothing when he passed his wife at the kitchen table, and he ignored the foil-covered dinner left on the stove. When he reached the bedroom, he stripped to his boxers, sprawled across the bed, and fell asleep.

***

He awoke that way at three in the morning. Heading downstairs for a drink, he found Bonnie watching television.

"I'm sorry," he said.

"It's okay, you were tired," she said.

"It won't happen again."

"Really? You mean you won't go back out?"

"I mean I'll use the guest room next time."

"Oh," she said, then turned back to her infomercial.

Ray made good on his promise and went to the guest room to catch a little more sleep. When he closed his eyes, his mind flashed with dreams of New York, images scrolling like messages from some imprisoned place in his heart.

He saw the townhouse he and Bonnie had rented in Windsor Terrace. He saw himself holding Beth as a baby, the detective with his little girl on his knee on the steps. He was giving his wife a break, letting her sleep in after her late shift at *Buca's Bar & Grill*. Back then, the recipe for smiles called only for sunshine and a stoop. When the clouds moved in front of the sun, well, that didn't matter much when there were songs to sing.

That was one dream, and he wished he could stay in it. But then the other interrupted—the one where he was walking across John Ferretto's courtyard. He couldn't stop his feet from moving, and couldn't stop his eyes from seeing.

He began to fire his gun. The shots from the mag he used up on Ferretto's son Joey echoed in his skull. Then it was Johnny himself, suffocating in Ray's headlock. Then he was shooting again, the don's daughter and granddaughter. The entire family. Fini.

When he woke, he showered off the nightmare's sweat and prepared for another day on the water. Catching his reflection as he toweled off, he noticed his skin was raw and sunburnt. Years of lifting weights and the strains of police work had packed his body with muscle, but now he looked thin and grizzled.

His chin was covered in what had become more than a little salt-and-pepper stubble, and the guys on the force would have made fun of the gnarled hair inching down his neck. He picked up a razor, then put it down. "Screw it," he muttered as he went to the bedroom and threw on a tank top and some jeans. He went on to the kitchen where he gulped a coffee, then snatched his raincoat from the hall, and headed out the door.

When he arrived at the marina, he gave the boat a thorough check, making sure the extra gas tank was full, and then joined the half dozen other fishing vessels setting out into the sunny day.

By noon he'd eaten the wrapped sandwich he'd bought and finished all of his coffee. He let out a line and pulled in a few mackerel, which he held up when another boat passed close. He had no reason to try and pretend to people he didn't know that he was fishing and assigned the deception to guilt about Bonnie knowing what he was really up to.

A tingle touched his spine when the sun finally began to set. Each time he looked in the darkening water, he wanted to see her face. He wanted to see its pale, magnified reflection. He imagined her dead eyes rising toward him, dead yet elated that he'd returned for her and never given up.

"I didn't give up on your mother, either," he said aloud.

He remembered the day the preacher came into the precinct

and dropped off his card.

"Are you Detective Barrs? I'm Reverend Abe Calderwood," he'd said. "We run an alternative counseling service through our ministry."

The Reverend had the usual salesman smile, but his card simply read *Assembly of the Blessed*. He had an athletic build beneath his sport coat and a strong grip in his handshake. It fueled Ray's urgency to stay on the road to look for Beth as if it were a sign for a clean start.

He searched for her in every damn motel from Pensacola to Tampa until the smell of crack cocaine became as familiar as a Christmas ham. He even saw her once outside a bar but lost her by the time he parked. He checked the nearby motels again, twice, and left behind his number along with the preacher's card.

That had been the last straw, because the next time he came around, Beth had left a note with the baby in her bassinette:

Adopt her. I'll sign whatever, just leave me alone.

Ray and Bonnie Barrs did as she asked and adopted their granddaughter. Raising Ada was supposed to be a redemption of sorts, and for the first ten years of her life, it had been.

Then came the fall. One minute she was fishing for red snapper, the next she was over the side of the boat. Hours of agony followed, then weeks. Neither he, nor the Coast Guard, nor the damn coterie of volunteers had been able to find her.

How could her life jacket end up on the deck after she went over? He'd put it on her himself that morning. It didn't add up, just stumbling over the port side on a clear day. You didn't need the skills of his profession to know something was wrong, that it had been no accident.

Which was why he would never give up.

Moving back to the wheel, he tipped his course from due west to west-southwest. He looked over his left shoulder and saw black clouds moving north. Whatever bull people spouted about red skies at night and a sailor's delight, rolling thunderheads needed no rhymes.

When the lightning began to strike, he threw on his raincoat and kept the *Faustina* pointed into the wind. It wasn't a hurricane, but it was damn near a gale. The gusts rattled the door to the pilothouse and rain flooded in around his feet. The waves were stirring but not enough to risk capsizing. He set the wheel, kicked open the door, and moved out onto the deck.

The boat quaked and lightning flashed as he peered over the gunwale into the depths. As if mocking him, a racket came from behind. He whirled around and saw her climbing over the opposite side. "Grampa!" she cried.

He ran toward her, boots sliding on the flooded planks. Her blonde hair looked soaked and stretched, and her face twisted with panic.

As she ran to meet him, a pair of tentacles whipped across her body. One clung to her ribcage, while a second slithered through her hair and wrapped around her neck. Her screams heightened in pitch and she extended her hand.

Ray reached out and grasped her cold flesh. He felt a sting as a third tentacle suckered onto his thigh. Peering over Ada's shoulder, he saw an oblong creature covered in scales. Its head looked like an ant's, and a pair of cellophane-thin flaps draped over its thorax. As it climbed over the gunwale, he couldn't tell if they were fins or wings. Underneath, its abdomen was swollen, and the brown coloring gave way to a transparent film that looked like an egg sack.

The sack contained recognizable shapes. The figures were too large to be fetuses, though most crouched like they were. Some wore the vestiges of clothes, and the decayed flesh gave an impression they were experiencing a process that was the opposite of gestation.

"Grampa no!" Ada screamed as the creature's tentacles pulled her closer.

Ray tore the suckers from his leg and charged. A hole opened in the creature's sack, and an egg slid forward. The egg, in turn, opened from the middle and sucked Ada in with flatulent gulps. The creature blinked its bulbous eyes as if daring him to follow as it leaped back into the sea.

A wave crashed against the hull, causing the *Faustina* to tilt. Ray barely kept his balance as he stumbled back to the console and corrected his course. The storm raged for hours, battering the boat late into the night. Ada never returned, and he limped back to the marina beneath a starless sky.

2

"It was me," said Bonnie. "I asked him to come."

Ray looked from Tolly Crespo to his wife, then back to the detective. "What's this? Some kind of intervention?"

"Sure, the kind where we pour a pair of scotches and talk," said his old colleague. "Whattaya say, bud?"

"Okay, but outside," said Ray.

They moved to the back patio of the ranch house and sat at the umbrella table with their drinks.

"She says you take the boat out every day," said Crespo. "Every day, no matter what."

"I got somethin' I gotta do," said Ray.

"Look, I know retirement ain't all it's cracked up to be. But you gotta consider what you still got, gotta consider *who* you still got."

Ray sipped his scotch. At the base of the hedge along his yard, he saw the hornet's nest was back. *Bastards are back and thicker than ever,* he thought. "Look, Tolly, I understand what you're trying to do," he said. "And I appreciate it. But, you see, it's like… it's like you don't understand."

"Don't understand what?"

"What's been happening out there. What I've seen."

"Maybe I'm the only one who does," said Crespo. "Thirty years on the police force, twenty in homicide, I think I'm the one who does."

"I'm not talking about Tampa turf wars here."

"You think it was any worse back in Brooklyn?"

"The fuck's Brooklyn got to do with it?"

"Only that we should both know better. Only that we both understand," said Crespo. He finished his scotch and put down the glass. "Ray, I'm tryin' to tell you, I've seen things, too. I've seen things that are there but shouldn't be. Things that exist but shouldn't exist at all."

The detective squinted against the sunlight, a distant look in his eyes. Ray considered how sure he was that he had been seeing his dead granddaughter, and that maybe Crespo was telling the truth that he had experienced something like it.

"If that's true, and you do understand, then you wouldn't be trying to talk me out of what I'm doin'."

"I'm not," said Crespo. "I'm tryin' to tell you that you might be in over your head. My advice is to let this one go. But since I know you're not gonna, why don't you give this guy a call?" Crespo handed him a piece of paper and stood. "Thanks for the drink," he said.

3

The guy on the other end of the line said to meet him at the *Motel Roger Jones,* ten miles east of Pensacola. Although Ray had never heard of it, when he pulled up, he knew the kind of place well. A once respectable split-level motel that used to entertain vacationers, it was now a mold-stained heap of concrete with a dried-up pool. He was surprised he hadn't checked it back when he was searching for Beth.

He parked in the second spot as agreed. The black Taurus pulled up beside him, and they lowered their windows.

"Stay where you are, we can talk like this," said the man.

His black hair styled in a high flat-top, he sat with his seat pulled close to the wheel due to his diminutive height. Ray turned to look at him, but the man faced forward, staring at the decaying motel.

"So, this is the deal," he said. "I'm Satan, the fallen angel."

"Excuse me?" asked Ray.

"You know, Satan."

"Sure, pal. I'm outta here," said Ray. He started raising the window.

"That's not the way to get Ada back," said the man.

Ray lowered the window again.

"Oh, did I get your attention?" he asked. Now the man turned and tucked a smile into his poorly sculpted goatee.

"How do you know about Ada?" Ray asked.

"I know lots a' things by virtue of who I am."

"You expect me to believe you're Satan?"

"That's me."

"Like, from Hell?"

"Actually, I'm from New Jersey."

"If Satan's from New Jersey, where's God from?"

"Connecticut."

"I think you need help. I don't know who told you about Ada, but that's it," said Ray, reaching for the gear.

"Okay, okay, look," said the man. "I was just kidding, God isn't from Connecticut. But I really am from Jersey. I work in car rental, and I lost my powers… well, most of them. The Fallen Stars, they hate me. But for humans, I can still do a thing or two."

"And what is it you think you're gonna do for me?" asked Ray.

"First, how about you walk over to that pool there and take a look inside."

"What's that got to do with it?" asked Ray.

"Just go on and have a look, then we'll talk."

Ray's years in law enforcement told him everything about cooperating with this greaseball was a mistake. Yet he also knew that if any situation called for rule-breaking, this was it. Having already put everything on the line, he had to take the gamble.

He made like he was straightening his jacket as he checked the shoulder-holster securing the .40 caliber. Next, he opened the door, stepped out, and strode to the pool with a quickness that startled his friend in the Taurus. *Best way to thwart an ambush was to preempt it with an ambush of your own.*

Yet nothing could have prepared him for what he found when he reached the pool's edge.

The thing leaned against the wall closest to him, which is why he hadn't seen it when he'd driven into the lot. It huddled in a heap of broken pipes and oily puddles. Scales covered its blob-like body and were missing in places, revealing raw, shriveled skin. Three legs extended from one end of it, arranged in the points of a triangle, and on the other, there was a gaping fissure full of large, rotted fangs. A socket interrupted its middle, housing a half-open eye. The thing looked strong but sick like it had lain starving for a while.

Ray saw the greaseball's reflection in one of the puddles as he stepped up beside him.

"Could be all yours," he said.

"Is that… Is that an alligator or somethin'?" Ray asked.

As he spoke, the thing sprung to its feet and snapped its fangs. A sticky wad of saliva hit Ray in the neck. He resisted pulling the gun, the thing couldn't jump high enough, though its mouth kept snapping with a force he guessed would easily break him in half.

"Believe it or not, that's an angel," said the man. "I acquired it in another, unrelated transaction."

Ray tried to shake off his shock. He turned to the pudgy man who called himself Satan and said, "All right. How are we gonna move it?"

4

The rental van's side had a painting of a marlin leaping from a sun-streaked sea. *Florida* read the caption. Ray wondered how the artist would feel about the catch that occupied the cargo space.

The thing was thumping away when they first pulled out of the lot. It smacked the wall so hard, Ray worried the metal would be dented from the inside. They'd also left the winch they'd used to haul it out of the pool tied around it, and now the pulley ricocheted around. He was afraid it would break the back window.

But the thing settled down when they merged onto the highway. Ray heard a shuffle, the slow scrape of scales, then nothing. It was Sunday evening, and traffic was light as they glided through the humid drizzle toward the marina.

Ray looked at the little man as he drove with his seat pulled all the way up, legs barely reaching the pedals. The AC was broken, but he didn't have a drop of sweat on him, and every hair in his flat-top was stiff and in place.

"So, you know what this is, right?" asked the man.

"Excuse me?"

"This exchange, you know what I get in return for getting the girl back?"

Ray felt his pulse quicken. He didn't care who this little shit thought he was. Even if his mongrel gator could help, it was Ray who was making this happen. He had half a mind to throttle the greaseball.

Instead he asked, "How much do you want?"

"I don't want money," said the man. He took his eyes off the road for a moment and looked at Ray. His pupils glinted with a faraway light, a pinch of platinum that seemed to pollute his gaze with something alien and poisonous.

Worst of all was the way his body sat forward, driving, while his face was completely turned to Ray, staring wrongly.

In the presence of this awful pose, Ray felt a tremor shoot through his spine.

"What is it then?" he asked.

"Your soul will be mine," said the man, "for eternity."

Three hours before, Ray would have laughed at the lunatic. He didn't now. Instead he looked through the window at the cloud-covered sky and the gray ocean beneath.

"All right. I give you my soul," he said. He realized then he was holding back tears.

A hand lifted from the steering wheel and gave his shoulder a squeeze.

"Relax," said the man, still staring. "It's a trade, not a gift. Take comfort in the art of the deal."

"I'm not buying a used car," said Ray.

"Hey, I said I work in rentals," said the man. "Would it help if I gave you my card? I go by the name of Sam Luzzy here on Earth."

Satan pulled a business card from his pocket and reached over, but his hand was batted away.

"Just get us to the fuckin' marina, you little shit," said Ray. His voice crackled beneath a sob. He refused to look at the man, but heard him emit a throaty chuckle.

"Here we are," said Satan as they glided down the ramp.

5

Ray drove the *Faustina* south-southwest, full throttle. He should have kept an eye on the GPS, but somehow felt he knew where he was going. He glanced at the scaled thing crouched in the back by the motor. It appeared to be in some sort of stasis.

The little man had whispered to it before letting it waddle on board, covered in a tarp. He spoke in words Ray didn't understand, in a language he couldn't even guess at. He had then walked back to the van and climbed inside.

"See you later," Satan had said. He'd grinned and waved, too, like they were old pals.

Ray turned due south as a last flash of sunset broke through the clouds. After a half-hour, he cut to trolling speed and heard a scraping on the boat's port side.

The tentacles appeared, then the ant-head. The thing pulled itself over the side, its abdomen more swollen than the last time. The mottled bodies showed through the translucent flesh. Those toward the back had decayed more, gone to black slime and bone. There were newer ovals toward the front, one of which contained the distorted form of Ada, tucked in a fetal position.

"I got you, I got you," cried Ray, setting the wheel and running toward her. He wanted to rip through the filmy flesh and pull her out, but a tentacle whipped against him and knocked him to the deck. It bashed him once more on the head and darkness flooded his eyes.

***

Ray came-to, choking on rain. The storm clouds had returned and soaked him to shivers. He heard screeches and hisses and saw the beasts locked in combat.

The scaled thing's massive jaws clamped onto the tentacled ant's thorax. Its teeth chewed while the ant made an awful clicking sound. Green-black blood spurted from its wounds as it scuttled in circles. It lashed with its tentacles, ripping scales off its attacker. Together, they collapsed into a trough of bloody water that flooded the deck.

Ray didn't reach for the pistol, worried that if he fired, he might hit Ada. Instead, he crawled back to the pilothouse and locked himself in, while the tangle of jaws and tentacles wrestled across the deck.

The two beasts smashed against the door, first denting it, then, on a second blow, knocking it clear off. He decided to chance the pistol this time. He drew and aimed, but saw that the ant-thing was in retreat. It scuttled back to the gunwale, turned once, and rose on its hind legs. Parts of the mottled bodies hung out of its shredded abdomen as it clicked and hissed, then one fell out as it dove back into the waves.

"Ada," Ray cried.

She stood, her body covered in bruises, cuts, and torn skin.

"Grampa, I'm cold," she said.

Ray stepped through the broken doorway and approached the shivering child. As he drew closer, he noticed her eyes had changed. They were no longer gray, but a clear, healthy blue. When they embraced, her flesh was freezing, and her heartbeat absent. But her *eyes, her eyes had changed, and he knew she was with him again.*

6

Ray jogged across the marina's parking lot to his old Chevy Silverado. Bringing it around, he wrapped Ada's shivering body in a blanket and set her in the cab.

"You're safe now," he said.

He left her once more to check that the boat was securely docked. The deck was still a mess from when he had heaved the wounded angel over the side, as Satan had instructed. He threw another bucket of seawater over the blood, scales, and bits of bone.

Anyone who saw it would assume he'd been fishing, he told himself. But the color was not that of any fish's blood, and the stench even worse.

When he returned to the truck, he took what felt like his first full breath since he'd met the man at the motel. Keeping a hand on his granddaughter's shoulder, he drove out of the lot and onto the highway.

Ada hadn't spoken since she'd said, "I'm here." Her hair looked gnarled and savage, and her body carried a hint of the odor he'd smelled on the boat.

He was afraid for her, for what must have been unbearable suffering. He almost pulled over when they first came off the exit ramp, just to hold her and tell her everything was going to be all right.

Before he did, she leaned her head against the hand on her shoulder. It was the kind of gesture she made when she was younger, and it reminded him of trips to the amusement park. Those were full, fun days that ended with a belly full of ice-cream and a cozy nap on the way home. He'd taken it then as a sign of a world made whole.

Now the gesture kept him steady on the road, though it felt slightly odd. He listened as she mumbled something, repeated strange words—"Abaddon... Abaddon."

She was still mumbling when he pulled in the driveway. He carried her into the house, through the kitchen, and was about to take the first step onto the stairs when Bonnie appeared in the living room doorway.

She looked at the mumbling girl. "I see," she said, and turned away.

Ray brought Ada up to the bedroom and laid her on the bed. He pulled a bottle from the dresser drawer, poured himself a scotch, then went to the window and watched the weeping clouds.

7

That week he stayed in the guest room and Bonnie slept on the living room sofa, aided by television and a new bottle of prescription pills. Ray decided he wouldn't ask what they were, so long as Bonnie didn't ask about Ada. On the third day, he fried pancakes and made everyone come in the kitchen.

Ada sat in her Disney bathrobe, lifting one bite after another in a straight line to her mouth.

"Is she going to go to school?" Bonnie asked.

"She might need to rest a while," said Ray. He carried her upstairs after breakfast and put her back to bed.

"Maybe you *should* go to school," he said as he stood in the window drinking. "It's August and school will start soon."

"Okay," Ada said flatly. "Will you take me shopping first?"

"Of course I will," he said. "We can get you some new clothes."

"We need to," she said. "They take your clothes in Abaddon. They take your clothes and your skin."

Ray clutched his glass a little tighter. "I don't understand," he said.

"No," she said, "there's no way you could. It's nice to be back though. Sorta. Can we go see my mom?"

He moved to the bed and sat down. "I still haven't heard from her," he said.

"We have to find her," she said. "I need her. I need her if

I'm going to stay here."

***

When school started that fall, there was talk of a special needs class. They said she could keep up academically, but there was an issue with communication. Was everything okay at home? *Absolutely fine,* Ray wanted to say, *she's come back from the dead and lives with her grandparents. One's an alcoholic, the other addicted to painkillers, hence the false name and address.*

But when he mentioned the social worker's concerns to Ada, she just said, "Okay, I can start trying."

The next day she made friends with a girl named Marissa and they started doing running club and having play dates. The minute her friend went home, she joined Bonnie on the couch and watched TV. They sat for hours like a pair of ghosts and Ray came to realize that not disturbing them was part of the unspoken agreement.

On the weekends, Ada insisted they look for her mother. Grampa was a retired policeman, didn't he have ways to find her? "Yes, of course," he said, but he'd promised her he wouldn't.

"You promised *you* wouldn't look," said Ada, "but I can look. You can drive me."

Ray supposed she was right, and they started driving around to nearby towns. Sometimes they stopped to eat at a diner or watch a movie, and Ada liked to photograph houses with his phone while he drove.

"We could live in that one, or maybe that one," she said.

"You wanna move?" he asked.

"I mean for when my mom's back. See, I drew a picture of a house."

The drawing she held up was no crayons-with-yellow-sun caricature. It was a pen and ink sketch of a small house set behind grassy dunes, as if on a beach.

"That's pretty good, honey. Maybe you'll be an artist when you grow up."

"No," she said, shaking her head. "I'd rather take pictures. I only drew this house 'cause I had to. Maybe I'll be a real estate agent."

Ray chuckled. "That's pretty specific," he said.

"I need someplace to go," she said. "I need someplace where I can stay."

"You can stay with me," he said.

"Not always," she said.

"Always," he said. "As long as you like."

"You don't understand," she said. "I just wish I could see my mom. I just wish she could spend a little time with me."

He reached over and stroked her hair. It felt almost normal. But one night she turned to him and used the voice that sometimes said other things: "My mom made the deal she had to make. But that's okay, because you were an absent fuck her whole life."

He ignored the jab. "What deal?" he asked.

"The one she made with *them*," she said.

"Who are you talking about?"

"*Them*, but that's what you don't understand. There's another place besides where I was, another place where I don't want to go, but I have to."

"Ada, where were you?"

"I think you already know. The place down there. But there's another place, and it's not at all like they say."

8

That winter, the frequency of his dreams increased. They varied, but usually started with Ray rising from his bed like something pushed his body against his will. Step, step, step, his feet carried him toward the mirror like they weren't his own. A burning sensation came over him as he walked, flooded his flesh like liquid flame.

When he got close enough, he saw his face had turned to ash. He took a sudden fall (though it felt again like he was pushed) and began writhing on the floor, nostrils and lungs full of burning smoke. He wanted to pass out in his sleep, anything to make it stop, but it would not.

When he awoke, he sometimes saw Ada beside his bed. Her hair was gnarled like when he'd first taken her from the boat. She was eleven years old now and had her thumb in her mouth. She took it out to say, "See what you've done?"

In some of the dreams, he stumbled down the stairs, trailing flames and sloughed flesh until he rolled up to Bonnie's feet. She sat drooling in a wheelchair in front of the TV while her husband burned on the carpet beside her. The stroke had mostly paralyzed her, but she moved her eyes toward him, just for a second, to show she could, then rolled them back to the screen.

9

When spring came, he took Ada in the truck and started driving further west.

"We ought to try Mobile," said Ray. "I remember she used to go there with her friends."

Ada shrugged. "If you think she's there," she said.

They tried the usual motels and rooming houses. He even had the girl wait in the car while he asked around at some bars. When the sun began to set, he turned around and said they could get something to eat on the way home.

They stopped at a diner just west of the city where Ada ignored her food and stared at a church across the street. There was a group sitting on the lawn in folding chairs, listening to a reverend preach. The older folks outnumbered the younger two to one, with a few babies thrown in. Ray saw there were still a number of women Beth's age. He admitted that if she had cut her hair and put on some weight, he might not even recognize her.

Ada appeared to be staring at one woman in particular. She wore mirrored sunglasses and had a white kerchief tied over her head. Ray squinted. *Could it be her?* He turned to Ada and asked, "Should we go over?"

But when he looked out the window again, he saw that the reverend had already crossed the street. He was walking hand-in-hand with the woman in the kerchief. Ada put her face close to the glass. "It's her," she said.

Ray slid out of the booth and stood. The bell on the door jingled, but only the reverend came through. Ray recognized him as the man who had come to the police station all those years ago. He offered his hand as he approached and grinned beneath his dusting of short gray hair. Although smiling, the reverend didn't instill hope like the first time they met. This time he seemed like a salesman who had sold him broken goods and taken him for a sucker.

"Abe Calderwood," he said.

"Yeah, we've met," said Ray.

"I regret I don't recall your first name, Mr. Barrs."

"Shame," said Ray.

The reverend took a step back. His muscles tensed beneath his sport jacket.

"I want to talk to my mom," said Ada. She held her hand against the window. The woman outside put up her own so that they were palm to palm but for the sheet of glass.

"Honey, I think you should come with me," said the reverend. "If you come with me, you can see your mom. All the time you have left, you can spend with her."

The reverend was speaking to the girl, but his eyes were on Ray. He kept his arms ready at his sides, like they were about to draw six-shooters. The waitress paused mid-step, gripping her coffee pot, and the patrons in the booths stared.

"Here's what you're going to do," said Ray. "You're going to go outside and tell my daughter to come in. Then you're gonna cross the street and never come near my family again."

The reverend snickered. "Still a fool after all you've seen? The girl is coming with us. She will spend her remaining time with us. When the time is right, we will contact you. The Lord Jarwhal hath little patience for fools such as—"

The reverend's teeth crunched as Ray's right hook smashed his jaw. Calderwood collapsed, then reached for the pistol in his jacket. Ray let him draw before he kicked his wrist and snatched it up. He held up his old badge for the sake of the diner's patrons, then planted a second kick in the reverend's gut, causing him to vomit.

"They're coming with me," said Ray.

The reverend looked up. He had bile on his chin and the cobalt flecks in his eyes flashed. "They shall destroy thee," he hissed. "And thy daughters shall belong to them, no matter what thou mightest do."

Ray wanted to obliterate the man's face. It didn't matter anymore, he would obliterate him and he would obliterate *them*, whoever the hell *they* were. He aimed the pistol between the man's eyes.

"Grampa, no!" cried Ada.

Ray snapped from his spell and turned to the girl.

She had come out of the booth, and behind her, he saw his daughter. She was moving away from the window and was halfway across the parking lot. She kept going, looking back over her shoulder as she went, tears streaking her face.

"It's no use, she can't come," said Ada. "And it's time now, and anyway, I got something I wanted, so it might as well be time now, Grampa. You might as well take me yourself."

For a moment, the slight smile Ada had when she had first seen Beth blossomed again. It was the one from her younger years, that full day-at-the-fair smile. It stayed on her face as she gave Ray's hand a squeeze. She then turned to the reverend and gave him a hard kick in his already broken jaw. "Remember that," she said. "Remember it forever."

When she turned back to her grandfather, the smile was gone. "Let's go now," she said.

10

They drove back to Pensacola through an afternoon downpour. Ray grimaced as he spied the girl riding beside him. Her thin arms hung awkwardly, elbows dangling at right angles. When she turned, it was her head only, and in a way he'd only seen once before.

"It's better this way," she said as rain hammered the cab. "It's better they take me now."

"What do you mean *them*? Who are *they*?"

"The ones in the sky," she said.

"Who do you mean?"

"Not the ones down there. Not anymore. They're for you now. Don't you pay attention to your dreams? I'm going to another place."

"What place is that?"

"The place in the sky."

***

That night, Ray dreamed he was burning in his bed while all around he heard fluttering, scraping, and buzzing. His mouth opened and his molten tongue uttered the word, "Abaddon!"

When he awoke, he saw that it was still only 2:00 a.m. and he was alone and drenched with sweat in the guest bed. He stood and poured himself a scotch in hopes it would help him go back to sleep. When he moved to the window, he saw the rain had lightened only a little, and now swept in damp gusts against the house.

Finishing the whiskey, he added three aspirin and lay back down. A second dream seized upon him as soon as he closed his eyes. It was deep, clear, and distant. In it, he could smell the sea. But it wasn't Florida's salty warmth this time. Instead, it was Brooklyn's cold, smoggy air, with only a hint of the North Atlantic's brine.

"Do you know who he is?"

It was Tolly Crespo's voice. It sounded different because they were thirteen. They stood on a basketball court between Prospect Park and the Gowanus Canal. The boy who stood opposite was tall and lean. He was thirteen, too, and wore a two-hundred-dollar track suit and had black, gel-slicked hair.

"I don't give a fuck who he is," said Ray. "He stabbed my fuckin' ball."

Crespo lowered his voice. "You shoulda let him win."

"Fuck that," said Ray.

The boy in the track suit smirked. "It's just a basketball, Ray-Ray."

"Don't call me Ray-Ray," said Ray.

"What's the matter, you wanna get burned? You like to run to the fire?"

"You gotta pay for the ball," said Ray.

"You want me to pay for a fuckin' ball? Come on, Ray-Ray, it's not like it's your sister." He held the knife under the slashed ball and shook it. "Help, he's gonna cut me! Oh wait, he already did!"

Ray stepped closer. "I ain't got a sister," he said. "But you do."

But Track-suit ignored him and kept shaking the ball. "Help! Help! Someone save me!"

"Yeah, your sister's Bianca," said Ray. "I always forget cuz she looks like the fuckin' mailman. Next time she comes over I'll tell her sorry."

The other boys on the court laughed, but Track-suit lost his smirk. He dropped the basketball, but held onto the knife.

"Jesus, Ray, do you know who he is?" repeated Crespo. "He's Joey fuckin' Ferretto!"

"I don't give a fuck if he's Abraham Lincoln," said Ray.

As he spoke, Ferretto thrust the knife. He thought he had the surprise, but Ray pivoted as he had planned and clipped the kid's arm under his elbow. He grabbed the kid's wrist and bent it back until he squealed in pain and dropped the knife.

"What? You're gonna fuckin' stab *me* now?" shouted Ray. He kept hold of Ferretto's arm and slammed him on the court. The wind left his lungs and he gasped for air. Ray hit him once more in the jaw, then reached in his pocket, pulled out a crumpled wad of cash, and removed two twenties.

"That's for the ball," he said. "Now get the fuck outta here."

***

When he awoke, his heart was thumping and he lay in a cold sweat. The dream had at first seemed distant, but now that he had returned it was as if he brought the memory back with him.

Had that been the first trouble with the Ferrettos? Had it led to what happened after? He had enough new troubles without dredging up the old ones. Sitting up in bed, he brushed the sweat from his forehead and thought to get another drink, an ice water this time. He'd managed to get on his feet when he saw Ada standing in the guest room's doorway. She was pushing Bonnie in the wheelchair.

"I'm sorry, honey," he said. "I had a bad dream. What are you doing? I thought your grandma was asleep."

But as he drew closer, he saw that his wife's eyes were open, but not awake. Open, but completely still.

"I found two empty pill bottles on her lap," said Ada. "Let's lay her in bed now, then you can take me to the marina."

They dressed Bonnie in clean pajamas and tucked her in on the king-sized bed. Ray wondered when they had last slept there

31

together. He also wondered when it was he had realized that she knew what was coming. Maybe the pills were just a way to keep from dreaming about it. Feeling something rise in his chest, a choking sob, he closed his eyes and tried to stave it off. *You failed both of them, Beth and Bonnie, just another professional at not being there, a real classic. Maybe that's why you don't mind the flames and the destructive dreams. Maybe those are for you what the pills were for her.*

He gritted his teeth and opened his eyes. Such thoughts were for those with the luxury of time. Gazing once more into his wife's eyes, he brushed back her hair and gave her a soft kiss. He reached for the bottle on the nightstand, poured and drank a bourbon, then followed Ada out to the driveway.

11

Clouds crowded the sky as he steered the boat southwest. The spring day was unusually cool, and he kept the pilothouse's new door closed and wished he'd brought a heavier jacket. Ada stayed out on the deck, her rigid form sprayed by the breaking waves. She kept looking up as they sped out, and when they reached a place where the clouds darkened, she put up her hand.

"Stop," she said.

Ray killed the engine and stepped out on the deck.

"Too deep to anchor," he said. "We'll drift."

"No, we won't," she said.

As she spoke, streaks of lightning shot through the clouds. They crisscrossed in interlocking chains. An icy wind swept over them, pushing away the waves and keeping the boat in one place. The streaks of lightning multiplied until their flashing lines appeared to bind the clouds and roll them away like curtains.

"You removed the chains of the abyss," she said, "only to trade them for chains in the sky."

A bright light shined down on them. Ray held up one hand and peered through his fingers. He saw flying objects, which as they came closer, looked like malformed chariots.

Wheels spun on the sides, led by what looked like harnessed comets. In some, he glimpsed what for a few seconds were the heads of horses, and in others, the heads of human beings.

In the chariots' cars stood other strange figures. They had

long hair, copper and gold locks flowing over elegant faces. Their skin looked like amber, alabaster, and ebony. They wore armor, and their eyes glowed cobalt blue, and their stares were like eagles focused on their prey.

Ray turned to Ada. He opened his mouth to warn her, but saw that she had come very close and spoke before he could. "I'd rather they take me now," she said. "Because of what Beth did. She sold herself, too."

Ray felt a shiver shoot through him. "You mean, she sold her soul?"

"Hers and mine."

"To the Devil?"

"No, the opposite."

"You mean the reverend?"

"I mean who he works for."

"But why?"

"She thought she was saving us. He convinced her they'd take me from you and bring me back to her. It was the angels from up there. They arranged my accident, and my rescue. Like bait. You're a fisherman, right? They made me into bait so they could catch another soul. They arranged it with the little man that he could have you, too, if he gave them back their kin."

"That thing he called an angel? I threw it off the side of the damn boat!"

Ada shrugged. "Maybe the little man was a liar."

Ray thought of the greasy bastard with the flat-top hair who called himself Satan. He thought about what he'd said about the art of the deal when he gave his soul in exchange for the wounded angel.

"When I fell off the boat that day," she went on, "I learned what it was like to drown. Yet it was nothing compared to what was to come, the wings and the fires, their crunching shells and their insect whispers, and the searing pain.'

"Because they told me how things really are, the demons I mean, in Abaddon. They said they wished to torment me forever, but that privilege belonged to others, that I was to go up, and what's above is even worse than what's below."

She took hold of Ray's wrist, and with a strength inhuman, thrust him down to the deck. She glared at him with a face pale and terrible, and he glimpsed in her eyes the immeasurable affliction she had endured. "Don't you understand? They were watching us for a reason. They were already watching us, and I was going one way or another. My mother did what she could, and now here you are, Grampa. I hope you understand this is the last chance you'll ever have."

And then, for a moment, she gave a wisp of the old smile. "I guess I'll have some memories for a while," she said. "A few good memories, because of what you did. After that, the pain will blank my mind. Better take your last try, Grampa. Better take your last shot, because the pain will blank your mind where you're going, too."

"Because I'm going to Hell," he said, "And you're going to—"

Before he could finish, the first of the chariots threw out a chain that spiraled around the girl's torso, strapping her arms to her sides. A second chariot came in close and hovered like a helicopter, wheels spinning so fast he barely glimpsed the bodies that made their spokes. Ray squinted against the glare as armored men threw more chains around Ada. Their jaws were stern and their blue eyes glowed. They whipped the chains around her, shifted the positions of the spinning wheels, and carried her upward.

Ray rose to his feet and mustered enough breath to call her name, "Ada," he cried, "Ada!" But she did not answer. Instead, he heard faint, crystalline voices, blurred by the whirr of the wind—*She is ours! She is ours! Let the swarm carry you to Abaddon, for the girl belongs to Our Lord, and forever she shall wear His chains in the sky!*

12

The *Faustina* limped into the marina early the next morning. He couldn't remember what happened after Ada vanished. He'd only dreamed of black water, shark fins, and thunder.

He landed the boat and hired a kid to help him get it into the storage house. After, he climbed in the Silverado and sped home. To his surprise, he found Crespo sitting on the bench by the front door. He offered Ray a beer and a sandwich he'd made in the kitchen.

"I let myself in," he said. "That old key you gave me still works." Crespo grinned beneath his sunglasses, their light brown tint a complement to his still blonde mustache. Throw in his triceps and chest, and you might be surprised to learn the guy was pushing sixty. If it weren't for the comb over and archipelago of brown spots on his forehead, he'd say his old colleague had aged well.

Ray ignored the sandwich and took the beer. "Not hungry," he said.

"Doesn't sound like you," said Crespo.

Don't feel like me, Ray thought, though he said nothing.

They moved to the back patio and poured whiskies to go with the beer. Summer weather was creeping into the spring with all of its cruelty. Greenbriar crept up his fence in the breezeless humidity like its vines would choke off his world.

Bonnie was dead and Beth and Ada had vanished. He felt

like he was looking not just at his own death, but the obliteration of his entire family.

"You look like you've seen a ghost," said Crespo.

"I wish," said Ray.

Crespo nodded like that made sense and poured him another drink.

"Do what you gotta do today," said Crespo. "Finish the bottle and sleep. Then, when you're done, call me. I'm here for you, you know."

Crespo's expression was meant to look sympathetic. Instead he looked like an aging porn star smiling over a stale joke. He patted Ray on the shoulder, and Ray nodded again, like he'd take his advice just to get the man to go away.

***

That night he didn't finish the bottle, but he did sleep. When he woke, he forced himself to do some calisthenics on the bedroom floor. After that, he went down to the basement, dusted off his weight bench, and lifted. He felt like he was slamming the eighty-pound barbell against himself, beating back the image of Ada's body rising into the sky. The wheels and wings churned in his mind, the sea and sky were a storm that wouldn't quit. Like the dreams of the winter before, they infested him and wouldn't let go. Like a child saying goodbye to belief in fairy tales, he again bowed to the knowledge that there were so many things worse than death.

As a detective, he'd known this for years. It wasn't as much the body with the shotgun hole that pained your heart as the look on the mother's face as you dragged her dead son out of the bathroom. It was your partner pushing her back a little too hard, and the rookie who wasn't supposed to let her get that close apologizing like it made any difference. And then, of course, the screaming, the inevitable and goddamned screaming.

She is ours! She is ours! Forever she shall wear our chains in the sky!

That wasn't what they said, but that's what he was hearing

now. He slammed the weights harder and harder, trying to make it stop. Finally, with his arms ripped to near paralysis, he went upstairs. This time he did grab the bottle of bourbon and drank it down an inch and then another. The heatwave broke, and an April downpour flooded the windows while thunder sounded from the south.

And now the storms will never cease, he thought as he heard a knock on the door. "It's open," he said. He roused himself from the table and moved down the hallway. At first, he assumed it was Crespo coming back. But if the asshole let himself in before, why would he knock now?

He felt dizzy from the whiskey as he opened the door. Instead of Tolly Crespo, he faced a slender wraith of a figure in a black hooded sweatshirt. The figure pushed past him and squashed its way across the carpet in soggy sneakers. He followed it into the kitchen, where it pulled a pair of glasses from the cupboard and filled them with water.

"House is still clean 'cause Mom made it that way," she said as she sat down. "And I guess you were never home to trash it."

Beth pulled down her hood. She was soaked to the bone in her tank top and jeans. The tattoos from her drifter days looked renewed by the rain. They reminded him of arguments about money and questions about drugs and why she was home so late. Still, he had to admit, it beat the damn prairie dress she was wearing when he saw her with the reverend.

Ray sat down across from his daughter and did not raise his voice when he spoke. "Everything we did, we did for you," he said. "Jesus, we moved down here to keep New York from messing you up."

"Don't matter if we went to Greenland or China," she said. "We still woulda been messed up."

Ray looked at her. This was new. He tried to study her face through the haze of booze and the storms raging inside and out. "So it's we now?"

"Yeah, but you're still an asshole. You killed mom and you screwed me up. But we went along with it. Because it was easier, and you had a steady check."

It dawned on him then that the whole prairie dress thing hadn't been real. Not just the clothing, but that whole damned downward-facing demeanor she had in the parking lot. Lightning flashed in the window and lit her tattoos again. He felt the first inward glimpse of happiness since the night he'd lost Ada.

"You ditched the reverend," he said.

"Technically, he excommunicated me. But the feeling was mutual. You never really get away from them though, not really. But I'm impressed you tried to help."

He detected the slightest warmth in her words, though she didn't smile. There was a little connection, like when she was a teenager and even though she'd already been arrested and they'd screamed at each other, they settled down together after and watched *Scarface*.

"I always tried," he said.

"Sure, whatever you say. So here's the deal. The reverend got you a plane ticket to LaGuardia."

"Excuse me?"

Beth slid an envelope across the table. He lifted the edge and saw the boarding pass.

"So you avoid me for twelve years and now you wanna go back to New York? You wanna to back to Brooklyn and play house?"

"No, just you," she said. "You're flying out of Tampa tomorrow."

"What the hell are you talking about? I'm supposed to just take off? I'm supposed to just trust you all the sudden? Just like that?"

"If you ever wanna see Ada again, yeah," she said.

Her eyes said it all, that she was doing this for Ada, too, and that there was still a chance for her. Ray knew enough about bitter deals to see that his daughter had swallowed one whole, and now it was his turn to have a bite.

Lightning flashed again and lit up her flesh. Among the menagerie of tattoos, he picked out a fat, muscular, monstrous thing. He remembered the fangy smile beneath its horns when she first got it. He wondered back then if it was supposed to be some slob of a boyfriend or even a pimp.

But now he knew what it was. "*You know what this is right?*" said the man with the fucked-up tilt to his head. It was Satan, as in the Devil.

Ray clasped his daughter's wet but warm hand. "You have to go," she said. "You'll find out the rest when you get there. That's all I can say." She stood and left the kitchen. He heard her sneakers squish down the hall and the front door slam behind her.

Ray finished the glass of water as well as the bottle of bourbon, then took four ibuprofen and caught some sleep before his flight.

13

Landing at LaGuardia was always fucked up. You came in close to the water like the city was saying, "Now you're gonna fuckin' drown." Not "Welcome to New York" or "I heart New York" or any of that shit. Instead, it said, "We're gonna fuckin' drown you while you're still in your seat, in this filthy fuckin' water." But the wheels screeched on the tarmac just in time, and you started taxiing toward the gate.

You waited for the city to say, "Just kidding!" by way of apology. Instead, the plane just rolled up to the gate like an old subway car and said, "Now get the fuck out."

His phone buzzed the second he was in the terminal:

```
my name is Riel. meet me at Dawn
Bar, 61 Lawton Street, off Grand.
```

Ray shouldered his duffle and slipped to the side past the taxi line. *Can't this asshole just meet at a sports bar?* he thought as he got in one of the black gypsy-cabs they told you not to take.

He gave the driver the address from the text and they headed south on the BQE. Lawton was fairly far east on Grand, in Bushwick bordering on Ridgewood. Last he knew, the area was about a hundred blocks of failed gentrification.

He'd helped out a narc there with a series of coke busts back in the aughts. It was sad and a little funny to watch a tased hipster call his daddy in L.A. to explain he'd become a felon. But the real gangbangers out of Jansen Projects and even pretty East Williamsburg were ready to rock-and-roll in half a second. He'd seen a uniformed officer get shot on Knickerbocker over a stolen bicycle. The little shit fled on foot. He was armed with a fashionably shitty Glock-9. The piece was later seized in a raid on a gun dealer, along with half a dozen assault rifles. The kid died in the firefight.

"I'll get out here," said Ray when they reached Grand and Leonard. After handing the driver seventy-bucks, he started walking east. Warehouses, bodegas, and shit hotels still abounded between the high rises and luxury condos. Brooklyn was a playground for some and a dungeon for others. For some, it was both.

In Ray's case, it was a shrine to his occupation. He had left for the sake of his family, though everybody else thought it was for other reasons. Abel Harding, the douchey young prosecutor looking to make a name, took it personally. "We could have protected you," he said. He texted Ray a picture of fourteen-year-old Giselle Ferretto's corpse. But it never bothered Ray. If Ferretto chose to shoot his grandkid before he met his maker, it had nothing to do with him.

He passed a row of bars and restaurants east of the warehouses. The first was a joint with a wrought iron door called *Portcullis*, then a windowy spot full of colored lights and pool tables called LP & Harmony. Further down, he came to a sign that read *Schwarzbier*, an attempt to make a dive bar look crafty. But after that, all illumination reverted to the glow of streetlights.

A trio of old factory buildings interrupted the spread of the restaurants. Their broken windows and corroded bricks were a little more than the gentrification wave could handle. An icy spring breeze blew across the pavement, spreading trash and dulling the thump of music from the bars. Ray resisted shivering, but felt cold to the core.

He reached Lawton and took a left in a vestige of a residential neighborhood. He remembered Maspeth from decades back, a strange holdout of duplexes that wasn't quite Ridgewood or Williamsburg.

The buildings stood cramped together, too old for driveways. Like tiny islands of pre-war domesticity, they were flooded by industrial buildings, then by industry's collapse and the rise of the projects. Even now, he saw a few pale faces on the porches, squat bodies in faded denim and flower print dresses. Like semi-translucent deep-sea fish, they were New York City's denizens of the deep. Once a week they ventured to the filthy *Hamm's Food* for groceries. Once a month they migrated to the barely operating post office off Bushwick Avenue to collect their dead relations' government checks.

But it was also an eye in the storm of rising rents, so between two yards full of torn plastic toys and trash, *Dawn Bar* stood flanked by low cement walls painted black. A sign with a soft orange sun glowed in its narrow windows, and a gargantuan bouncer dressed in black held the door for Ray as he stepped through the arched entrance.

A low bar lit with track lighting that matched the sign in the window lined the far wall. A half a dozen patrons, skinny guys in ankle-hugging jeans and girls in tiny black skirts, sat sipping cocktails served by a crop-haired androgyny in a turtleneck tank top.

It was the type of place that was too cool even for itself. Ray planned on ordering a water instead of a drink that was five bucks more than the hood's already absurd prices.

Not that he didn't want the booze. He'd scotched his way up on the plane, and it took everything he had to accept what he was here for, to banish the feel of Beth's hand in his and the sight of that fat monster on her arm. He felt like he could hear its voice—"There are things worse than death. Not just your death, your entire family's. Forever you shall wear His chains in the sky!"

"Are you Mr. Barrs?" The man was sitting at one of the low, square tables. He raised his eyebrows but did not stand. He wore a jacket and slacks and motioned with his rail-thin arm toward the opposite chair. "Please, sit down," he said.

"You wanna tell me what this is about?"

"Mr. Barrs, you know what this is about by now. The question is whether you're worth the price. Are you worth the price?"

The fact he already hated the prick tugged him away from the emptiness he'd felt since the night of the storm. "Dunno, is that glass of ice with a straw worth the price?"

The thin man smiled. "It's a Manhattan," he said. "Would you like one?"

"A whiskey's fine," he said. "If you're buying."

The thin man nodded and waved to the bartender. The place didn't have waitstaff, but a little dude with the man-bun scampered over, took his order, and brought the drink right back. This thin asshole must be a well-tipping regular. But there was something about him that was both familiar and despicable. Ray couldn't quite place it.

"I am authorized to make you an offer," said Thin Man. "We have need of a bounty hunter, of sorts."

"What, you startin' some kind a' reality show?" Ray asked. The whiskey was smooth and lent its glow to the bar's low lights.

"We are looking to settle an account," said Thin Man.

"You're looking for a collector? Most smalltime gangsters are DIY, though you do look kinda slight."

Thin Man smiled again, and this time Ray placed it. His eyes had the same blue flecks as Reverend Calderwood's. Like tiny jewels in the amber light. And the way he crooked his head, like that nut from Jersey who called himself the Devil. And like Ada, too, after he'd brought her back.

"It is not so much a concern for hiring 'muscle' as you might call it. We also need someone who understands discretion."

"Who the hell's we?" Ray asked.

"You saw us once, in the storm," he said.

He shot the rest of the whiskey and the buzz kicked harder. "Look, I got family stuff goin' on right now. But if that reverend thinks it means I wanna work for a small-time gangster, you can tell him think again."

But Ray knew even as he spoke that Thin Man wasn't buying it. He wasn't even buying it himself. He knew too much now, and messed-up as it was, he was hanging onto this chance as the only way to do something for Ada, Beth, and Bonnie.

Thin Man crooked his head again, as if to say, *are you finished?* He took a sip from his Manhattan and went on: "We are offering you a fifty-thousand-dollar retainer. You will likely need it to cover you expenses. Another hundred thousand will be paid when the job is done."

"No offense, Mister… I didn't catch your name?"

"Riel," he said.

It sounded biblical to Ray, like the last syllables of the name Ezek*iel*.

"Okay, Riel, thing is, I'm not really hard up for money. I got my pension, savings, a house."

"For now maybe. But you may need more. And that is only a part of your compensation. We are also offering something else, something only we can offer."

"And what is that?" Ray asked.

Riel nodded, looking past Ray's shoulder. Ray turned and saw Ada step out of a door behind the bar. She walked across the room, pale as when he'd seen her ghost on the *Faustina*. She looked at him once with her ethereal eyes, then vanished into a narrow corridor by the side window.

"As you know, she is ours," Riel continued. "But we can give her back to you, in a manner of speaking. Not unchanged, not exactly, but in a better place than she is now."

"Where is she now?" Ray asked.

"Heaven," he said. Riel looked at him, a thin man with a thinner smile. "Do we have a deal?"

Ray gritted his teeth. He wanted to call for another whiskey, make it look like he didn't believe in this shit. But he knew the thin man was serious. He looked into the man's blue flecked eyes and asked, "What's it like in… *Heaven*? What does she do?"

"What does she *do*?" Riel countered. "Why, she serves. She

is in several choruses on the pavilions. She also waits on the pleasure of His Saints and Angels. I saw her in a chariot wheel belonging to one of Gabriel's knights."

"What do you mean in a wheel?"

Riel grinned. "It is a sign of some prestige to adorn a chariot with the souls of the innocent. Only His most favored are allowed the indulgence. Would you like to see where she rests?"

The thin man held out his phone. Ray glimpsed a photo of an immense wall riddled with alcoves. He saw something in them, but pushed the phone away before the image was clear.

"Nevermind," he said. "I'll do it. Tell me what I gotta do."

14

An hour later he took the backpack Riel gave him and left. He headed west, then south, until he reached the Bushwick Inn, a discreet hotel four blocks off Grand Street. As he climbed the stairs to his second-floor room, he heard porn movies piping through the walls. Yet for a place with hourly rates, the Bushwick was in startingly decent shape. It had minimal cigarette burns on the rug and a blue tile bathroom that reminded him of a road trip he and Bonnie had taken through Mexico.

Which you'll never do again, he thought. *Where is her soul now? Do they have Oxycontin in Hell?*

He locked the door and emptied the backpack on the table. The contents included a brick of cash, what looked like a sheathed dagger, and a folder full of photographs. The photographs showed corpses that were naked, headless, and bruised. He had no forensics team to verify it, but the necks looked torn, not cut. Riel had told him it was a demon. He'd laid it out just like Sam Satan Luzzy had. *"We're interested in the victims only insofar as they will lead us to the trophy,"* he had said. *"The demon's heart will please Him greatly and give our regiment prestige."*

Sure, just like children in chariot wheels, thought Ray. He looked at the dagger next, unsheathed it and studied the blade. It was wide as a Bowie knife and sharpened on both sides for the first foot of its length. After that, it tapered half as long again, wickedly angled to its tip. *"Bullets can wound the demon,"* Riel had said, *"but you'll have to use this to kill it. Stab it anywhere first, but you'll have to cut off its head after. The blade is made from Oorinic steel, contains materials that are more than rare. Do not lose it or let it get stolen. To replace such a weapon is nearly impossible."*

Ray sheathed the dagger and looked back at the photographs. The victims had nothing in common but the neighborhood. This odd stretch of Metropolitan where Bushwick, Williamsburg, and Ridgewood met. They found a few further south, by Woodhull Hospital in Bedstuy, and one up in Queens. But the first five were clustered within a few square miles of Grand and Graham Avenue.

What the hell kind of killer's MO is two strippers, an undocumented cook from Nicaragua, and an Italian grandmother? Apparently, demons had motives of their own. According to Riel, the police were trying hard to stave off the press, and definitely had leads they wouldn't discuss. He'd have to go over to the precinct at some point and see if the old team would do him a solid and let him look at what they had.

In the meantime, he'd take a ride down Grand Street and see where the article from the *Brooklyn Crier* said Sadie Sparkle danced. The photo showed blue glitter on her breasts where they weren't covered in blood. Her head was so destroyed it reminded him of the famous photo of Mary Kelly's corpse where it lay shredded on her bed. But ol' Jack only went for the soft parts. Whatever did this could crush a skull like it was a beer can.

Ray slept for the rest of the night and half the next day. When he woke, he ran for coffee and called *Fazio's Auto World* up in Queens. They agreed to drop off a rental at the hotel, and Ray returned to his room, where he did calisthenics and showered to the strains of the echoing porn.

He toweled off then donned the leather blazer he'd bought years ago in the Russian boutique on Orchard Street. It had been stashed in his closet back in Florida and now covered the .40 cal in its shoulder holster well. The dagger went in the motorcycle boot under his jeans. When he reached the club, he'd have to leave the gun in the rental car, but he might be able to grease a door man's palm to keep the blade.

He took a quick look in the mirror on the way out to see if anything screamed cop, but no, his salt-and-pepper beard had grown out, and his hair was getting a little shaggy. Between the boots and the blazer, he looked biker meets mob-guy. Just another middle-aged wallet looking for a lap dance.

Parking was another luxury perk offered by the *Bushwick Inn*. The kid in the baseball cap and tats in the barred booth at the checkout desk would "keep an eye" on your car for an extra twenty bucks a night. That meant he'd make sure petty punks didn't strip it, steal it, or break the windows for whatever was in the glove.

He had given the kid two hundred for the week and pointed at the old Crown Vic. "That one," he said, wondering if the tip would make any difference for a ride that actually did scream *cop*. The kid took his money and gave a nod. It was probably horseshit, but it might work if he thought there was more money to be made by keeping the bargain.

But the Crown Vic had survived the first twelve hours just fine, and he drove it north, made a right onto Grand, and started rolling east. Not quite a mile from the hotel, he turned south again onto Elmstead, an empty avenue that stretched across an old railyard along the Newtown Creek. He killed the lights, locked the pistol in the trunk, and walked the quarter-mile back to Grand Street.

He was just east of the row of bars he'd passed the night before, and a little south of where he'd met Riel. Here the battered warehouses and former factories hadn't been converted to lofts yet, and the trash in empty lots made bestial silhouettes behind the fences. Most of the streetlights were broken, but another block on he saw the white lights of a diesel gas station that served traffic off the BQE.

As he drew closer, he picked up another glow further off, a crimson haze in the Brooklyn drizzle. *La Vela Roja*—the club where the dead girls had worked.

15

The bouncer wore a significantly shittier leather jacket than his own. Its rips and tears belied his calm demeanor. The guy was borderline on confidence, though if he dropped the beer belly, he would have the build of a heavyweight boxer. The sloppy goatee and odor of vape pen indicated he'd moved into a life of leisure, of sorts. He felt the dagger as he patted Ray down, but just as quickly took the two-hundred bucks he slipped him not to fuss about it.

As he moved inside, Ray reminded himself it would be important not to give the man a reason to kick him back out just as quickly as he'd taken the tip. He sat down at the bar, ordered a *Corona*, and did his best to look starry-eyed over blue-lit breasts.

"You don't look like a trucker," said the bartender as she pressed a lime into his beer.

"I'm not a cop," Ray answered.

"I didn't ask if you're a cop," she said.

"You were gonna," said Ray.

"How do you know?"

"Because I look like I might have coke."

"Do you?"

"No, just here for the ladies."

"Sure," she said. "But don't get a dance now. You should wait for my friend, she's hot." The bartender didn't smile once, and her black hair fell across her face as she turned to her work.

Ray felt a tap on his shoulder and turned to see a girl with caramel-colored hair and dark brown freckles squeezing her breasts together. He slipped five dollars in her thong and said thanks. She asked if he wanted a dance and he said no, then waited until she walked off before he turned back to the bartender.

"So your friend's really that hot?" he asked.

"Do you really not have coke?" she answered.

Ray grinned and finished his beer. The bartender handed him another straightaway despite a few frowns from what he assumed were regulars. When her friend did appear, she had company in tow.

"Lenora, damn girl, where's my tequila?" The girl had sandy-blonde hair and wore a white, fake-fur jacket.

"Why do you think you get a tequila?" the bartender asked back, though she had already started pouring a round of shots. "Do you want one?" she asked Ray.

Ray nodded. "Thanks," he said.

She handed out the shots and they toasted and knocked them back. The sandy-haired girl introduced a kid in skinny jeans and pleather jacket as Fenton, a friend of Kev's, who was apparently the other skinny hipster decked out in denim beside him. Ray scanned the bar as the girls danced and the tequila warmed his belly, taking note of where the bald bouncer pretended not to watch him from where he stood by the curtained-off VIP lounge.

The sandy-haired girl stepped closer. She nudged his shoulder as she slipped off her jacket and skirt, leaving only a G-string and pasties. He realized it was as much the wryness in her grin as her supple physique that made her friend give her sardonic sales pitch.

"I'm Bobbie," she said. "Are you a friend of Lenora's?"

"We haven't actually been introduced," he said.

"That's okay, she just bartends anyway."

The joke was meant to get her attention, but Lenora was looking at her phone, hair hanging all over her face like some horror movie ghost. Even with the club's sound-system thumping, he picked out the shriek coming from the video she was watching. Ray had just enough of a buzz to lean over and look.

"Damn, look at these penguins beat the shit out of each other," she said.

"I'm Ray," he said as she showed him the bloody birds.

"Oh, Lenora. Sorry. Hey are you gonna buy a dance with my friend or what? She didn't say hi cuz she thinks you're cute. And you gotta order another drink, too."

"Sure," said Ray.

"Hey, what's with the old man?" asked Fenton. "You guys lookin' to jack somebody?" The kid cracked a wise-ass grin and gave his buddy a knowing look like the line was from some asinine movie they liked to watch after bar hopping all night.

"Take it easy," said Bobbie. "He is kinda cute, and not exactly out of shape."

"She doesn't really think that," said Lenora, not looking up from her phone.

Bobbie ran her fingers along Ray's forearm, then looped her arm around his, and batted her eyelashes theatrically. The old-fashioned gesture belied the cobra tattoo that rippled up her leg and over her stomach. "So do you want a dance?" she asked.

"Sure," said Ray.

"It's fifty plus your drink," she said.

Ray turned back to Lenora, who already had another *Corona* and lime on the bar. He gave her twelve for the beer and tipped her twenty. She took the money without looking up.

"Lenora, seriously," said the one name Kev. He leaned in close in his *Volvo* t-shirt and denim vest. "Make sure you lose this dude before the after-party. They'll think he's a cop."

"Shit, check this out," said Lenora. "This bum's beating the crap out of an MMA fighter."

She held up her phone for the others, but Ray was already following Bobbie back to the VIP lounge.

16

"Gotta tip the bouncer, too," said Bobbie, nodding at Bald Man.

Ray gave him a twenty and smiled. He wondered if the guy would pat him down again after the lap dance if he had a tent in his jeans. *Nah, probably go straight for the blade.* By the look on his face, all pretense was off. He'd have started shit already but was letting Bobbie make some cash. *Or maybe you could just "jack" me and take the dagger and my cash. If you don't know what that means, just ask the rough-and-tumble gentleman in the Volvo t-shirt.*

Bobbie led him behind the curtain. The bench stood against the wall, was covered in chipped black paint, and lit by the glow of red track-lighting. "Have a seat," she said as she hung the jacket and skirt she was still carrying on a hook. She proceeded to remove the G-string, which, unless the pasties counted, left her wholly naked.

Ray chuckled. "Ain't that against the rules?" he asked.

"Oh, yeah right," she said. "Now listen, you don't touch. I touch you."

She had the body of an athlete but hadn't let herself go like the bouncer. For a moment, Ray's mind stung itself with a grandfatherly urge to ask if her parents knew where she was. A ridiculous notion, Bobbie was clearly well over thirty.

She batted the eyelashes again as a bass-thumping club tune thundered to life through the sound system. "Gonna stick my ass in yo' face," she giggled. "I'll put a condom over here in case we need it." She pulled the square plastic wrapper from her jacket pocket and set it on the bench.

"What happened to no touching?" he asked.

She laughed again, took his hands in hers, stepped back, and did as she promised. "Decide after this song. It's $700 for a quickie."

Fucking Brooklyn, he thought as she danced. He'd worked the neighboring precinct fifteen years and shown up at his share of strip clubs. But prostitution busts were rare. That was more a midtown Manhattan thing. He associated strip clubs with follow-ups on some idiot who drew a gun in the parking lot and shot somebody over a beef. That and the occasional drug bust during his narc days.

A lot of uniformed guys didn't mind being "taken care of" by the girls in exchange for unspoken protection. He had to admit as Bobbie wrapped his arms around her thighs and let loose with the full contact, if he were that kind of cowboy, this would be a good night.

But you're here for something else, he thought. Look at you, hanging onto the old bravado and a little drunk, trying to let the ghosts of good times kill the pain. He looked past the dancing girl and saw little bare feet scuttle past the curtain. They were Ada's, and she was answering a haunting with a haunting. The ghosts of cruelty were here, too. *I saw her in a chariot wheel… It is a sign of some prestige to adorn a chariot with the souls of the dead.*

Ray stood up, keeping Bobbie's hands in his. He whispered over her shoulder without pushing her away. "How about just a dance," he said.

"Well, okay," she said.

The second song started and he wondered how much of the seven-hundred she was going to get anyway if he didn't speak up. If he asked about the dead girl now, it would be an obvious kind of *quid-pro-quo* and blow his cover. And speaking of blowing, how much of his retirement had he spent in two days like it was bottomless?

He assumed Riel already thought he'd given him too much

and would renege somehow on the rest of the cash. But he didn't care what happened after. He needed to know Ada was not suffering, not in Hell, or Heaven-Hell, or whatever the fuck these grim revelations were taunting him with.

"Let's get a drink after this song," he whispered.

Bobbie seemed to be in a trance now. Their hands were locked, crisscrossed over his stomach. They swayed eerily to the pounding music, like a slow dance to a fast song. It occurred to him that, though lost in thought, they were hanging onto each other and committing the ultimate infraction by beginning to both feel good.

"You don't have to be a bitch about it. I'm fucking paying you."

The words came from the booth beside them. Ray turned to the partition, a slab of wood like the bench, also covered in chipped paint.

A slap accented the drumbeat. "What fuck was that? Fuck you!"

He recognized Fenton's whine and knew what was coming next. He let go of Bobbie's hands and slipped past the curtain. Even rounding the corner, he was a few critical steps closer than the bouncer, which experience told him made all the difference.

The girl in the next booth had already yanked back the curtain. It was the one with the caramel hair who'd first approached Ray at the bar. Fenton was too coked to know what he was doing and had a hold of her wrist. He'd reared back with his other arm and was ready to go the extra mile. He was drunk and high enough to piss his skinny jeans over whatever deal had gone bad.

Ray grabbed his arm mid-swing. "Take it easy, son," he said.

Fenton spun around, incredulous. "What? What the fuck? Get off me, you old fuck. You look like a fucking retired principal!"

Ray kicked his feet out from under him and punched him once in the jaw before he hit the floor. "You look like a bullying victim," he said. "Now pay the young lady what you promised her."

"But she didn't—"

"I don't give a fuck what she *didn't*. Pay her."

The kid had just managed to stand up when Bald Man appeared. He'd already let it go too far, which Ray assumed was intentional. *This is how he's gonna throw my ass out, too,* he thought.

Bald Man picked Fenton up and slammed him against the wall.

"Hey look man, wait, I'm sorry," the kid said. "You know, I fuckin' know people here, all right?"

The two dancers headed for the bar and he heard Bobbie calling for Fenton's friend Kev. As Bald Man twisted the kid's wrist, another man entered through a door at the end of the line of curtained booths. At first Ray thought it was two men, the way his head and hands looked they were floating in front of a shadow. But when he came closer, he saw the man's back was hunched and slanted and looked as if it hovered behind him.

His left shoulder was higher than his right, and he wore an expensive but disheveled suit beneath a long leather jacket. Ray caught a whiff of something awful, like charred human hair and fetid breath. In his dizziness, he thought he glimpsed something else in the doorway, a flash of sinewed flesh the color of dried blood.

The hunched man stepped slowly up to Fenton. His lips parted, but his teeth were clenched as he went through the kid's pockets and pulled out his wallet. He took out all of the cash then returned it. "Remove him," he said.

Bald Man took the kid by the shoulders and dragged him along the floor. "Hey, what the fuck," the kid protested. But the bouncer's grip was like a vise.

When Ray looked again for the hunched man, he had vanished. Though a few of the patrons had turned toward the commotion, the music never missed a beat. They returned to their drinks and the apparition-like dancers swayed beneath the blue lights. He moved back to the bar where Lenora was trying to get Kev to calm down.

"Your friend was a douchebag anyway," she said, then turned to Ray, "He's lucky you got to him before I did." She poured him another shot of tequila to go along with the round she had just poured the others. "Come on, let's drink," she said.

Ray nodded and let out a nervous laugh. Kev was whining to Bobbie, who had him by the arm, and was also trying to calm him. Ray couldn't make out his words, but Lenora just laughed and raised her glass. "Hell it is," she said. "To Hell!"

They clinked glasses. Ray peeled a twenty off his roll for Lenora's tip, then counted out two hundred for Bobbie.

"Thanks," she said, pearly smile promising there was more dance for more cash.

But Ray just ordered another pair of shots.

"No thanks, I'm good," said Bobbie.

Ray shrugged and downed both.

"No point in fucking around," said Lenora. She cracked the slightest grin.

Ray chased the tequila with a swallow of beer. He had told himself he was going hard so as not to look suspicious in the club, but now he wasn't so sure. Now he let the booze bring tears to his eyes but wouldn't wipe them, wouldn't even close them for fear of seeing his dead wife's eyes staring back at him.

Who do you think you're saving now?

No, he swallowed the liquor and shook it all off. Having a good time was part of his "deep cover", wink-wink. He could take a breath now that he'd made an impression of sorts.

Even Kev had finally calmed down by this point. "I guess Fenton *can* be a douche sometimes," he said. "I just thought he'd at least have a clue his first time here, instead of spouting shit about people he knows. Now he's probably all pissed and won't answer his texts."

Ray put down his beer. "You're texting him?" he asked.

"Well yeah," said Kev. "Just to see if he's all right."

"And he's not answering?"

"No," said Kev.

Damnit, he should have seen it. Ray looked at the front door, but there was a different bouncer there now, a big blonde lug with a beard.

"Did you see which way he went?" Ray asked.

"No, actually, why?"

"Damnit," said Ray. He jumped up and ran to the back of the club, past the VIP booths and through a doorway.

17

La Vela Roja's back hallway had a fresher coat of black paint than the dance-booths. More red track lighting lined the ceiling, and a single electric candle of the same color glowed on a corner shelf, giving form to the club's name. A door hung open on the left, revealing a small bathroom, and an archway opened into a larger room on the right.

Ray stepped through the archway into a makeshift lounge with a pair of plush chairs and a black leather sofa that looked like a "casting couch." Cigarette butts lay in the ashtrays on a coffee table surrounded by empty glasses and bottles. Along the far wall, a stairway descended through the floor, and to his left, there was a large steel door.

As Ray turned to the door, he heard footsteps trample up the stairs behind him.

"The hell you doin' back here?"

It was the bald bouncer, closing with him fast. The question belied Bald Man's grin as if he'd expected Ray to show up. Ray grabbed the doorknob and twisted but found it locked. *Right into the asshole's trap,* he thought, as he turned to block the first punch.

Bald Man didn't worry about accuracy and slammed his fist into Ray's left elbow. The blow felt like a sledgehammer and his bones crunched. Ray answered with a fast right hook. Bald Man didn't duck close to fast enough, and his jaw gave off a crunch of its own.

Both men staggered back from their initial blows, Ray toward the arch and Bald Man toward the couch. In an attempt to be sly, Bald Man tried a quick kick at Ray's knee while swinging a left-right combo with his fists.

But the fool had fallen for Ray's trap this time. He leaned in just a little like he was going to draw the blade Bald Man knew was there. You could use a weapon without pulling it to buy time, and this guy was already slow.

"Fuckin' A," Ray heard behind him as he grabbed the big man's ankle with his left hand. The man's body tilted, his punches swiped air, and his poorly planted left foot stumbled. Ray hit his face three times in a row. Blood spurted from his nose before his head hit the floor.

"Whoa, you beat the shit out of Louie," came the voice again.

It was Lenora, standing in the doorway. She'd come back after him with the other bouncer. But while her smile betrayed not a little adoration for the mayhem, the blonde lug beside her was all shock and rage.

He grabbed Ray by the collar of his jacket before he could fully turn. Though this lug was faster than big Louie had been, Ray could have twisted out of the attempted hold. Instead, he allowed himself to be restrained, in hopes it would get him kicked out the back faster.

But strangely, when the bouncer had a hold of him, he didn't head for the nearest door. Ray assumed the lug could unlock it and hoped he would toss him into the rear parking lot. He expected a few payback jabs for the sake of the damage he'd done to his buddy. But instead, the lug pulled Ray back into the low-lit hallway.

"Sorry dude," said Lenora. He took in a faint scent of coffee and jasmine as the lug dragged him past her. He made a bit of a show of it as he shoved Ray through the club and out the front door.

"Just get the fuck outta here," he said as he gave him a final push onto Grand Street.

18

It took all Ray had not to turn and pummel the guy into the wall, then to the ground, then kick his ribs to splinters. He took slow, deep breaths as he headed west down the Grand toward the truck stop. When he was sure he was out of the bouncer's sight, he looped back around to Vanders Ave. A rusty fence overgrown with weeds lined the club's rear lot, and he moved along it until he reached an overturned dumpster where he took cover and watched the back door.

Has to be the door off the lounge, he thought, *the one they kept locked.* A single bulb shined above it. That and the gas station across the street were the only light sources on the north side of the block.

The rest of the parking lot was overcome with shadows. He made out a few cars, an old Dodge and a newer Lincoln. He watched and waited, though he had lost time and the emptiness mocked him. He felt like he had on the Faustina when he'd hooked and lost a marlin and gone back and trolled the same waters, even though he knew nothing would bite and his day was done.

The icy spring breeze rustled again among the filthy weeds as the after-midnight hours turned into the early morning hours. *That kid Fenton's dead and you know it, he's dead and Hunch Man isn't coming back. Kick the bouncer's ass while he's closing up and distracted, while he's having a beer and gloating.*

After, he could go back to his hotel room and get the little wannabe drug dealer at the desk to get him two bottles of Oxycontin. Take both and go to sleep like Bonnie, go to sleep forever, OD so hard he'd be numb even to the flames and faces of his family in Hell.

"But I'm not in Hell."

The girl's voice was crisp against the wind. Ray saw her standing in a patch of weeds strewn with cigarette butts and plastic bags. She looked alive, three dimensional, but in black and white, like an image out of an old movie.

"I'm not in Hell, I'm in Heaven," she said. "I never sleep there, it's always bright. But those little holes aren't the worst part. They make our backs ache but it's not the worst thing. I hate the beach more. They make us go to a cold beach and gather these silver shells. The angels eat something inside the shells. They're trapped under the freezing surf in the sharp sand and when we dig them up, our fingers get cut and turn blue and hurt. They cake up with ice and throb and if you're slow, you're one of the last ones there and they mock you from their houses on the shore, and you're crying and freezing and unable to die, and—"

"Ada stop, just stop! I'm gonna help you, I promise, I promise I'm gonna help!"

"Who ya talkin' to?"

Ray turned and saw Lenora. She stood on the sidewalk on Vanders Ave. Bobbie and her other friend Kev were with her.

"No one, I'm sorry, I… I went to another bar and came back."

"Dude, we're closed, it's like five in the morning."

Ray looked up and noticed the sky had turned lighter. He was sitting against the overturned dumpster, blood from where the bouncer burst his lip all over his shirt and jacket. Apparently, he'd fallen into a scant but refreshing sleep. He knew somehow the visit from his granddaughter had been real, because it was Beth who was in his dreams, and Ada was haunting him like a ghost.

"Sorry, guess I missed last call," he said.

"It's okay, plenty of liquor stores still open. Who were you really talking to, who were you gonna help?"

"Nothing, no one, I didn't recognize you, I was just asking—"

"If I need any party favors? Think we're good, dude. Hey, by the way, you're not kicked out permanently. Shit happens. If you come back just apologize and it's all good."

"You want me to what?"

Lenora grinned. "Ha. Didn't think so."

"Hey, Lenora, come on, let's get outta here," said Bobbie. She was shivering under the faux fur coat, legs still bare. "Club gives me the creeps when it's closed."

"All right, sure," she said. "See you 'round, old man."

They started walking north again, turned to cross toward the gas station.

"Hey wait," Ray said. "You guys need a ride?"

Lenora turned. "You got a car?"

19

At first, Kev whined about Ray coming with them but changed his tune when he let him drive the Crown Vic. "This is so classic cop," he said. "What is it, eight-cylinder? You got a radio in this thing?"

"It's just a rental," said Ray.

He sat in the back seat passing a bottle of Jim Beam with Bobbie and Lenora. Lenora was trying to hold her phone steady while she took a video. "Kiss her again," she said.

Ray kissed Bobbie while she pulled his hand under the fake fur jacket. She whimpered porn-movie style as he moved from her lips down her neck. He moved his hand lower and she raised her leg, showed the camera the shallow crease of skin just below her belly.

"Okay good, you can stop," said Lenora. She laughed as she swigged the whiskey and locked her phone.

"Gimme that," said Bobbie. She took her own swig then fixed her jacket.

"It's perfect, I'm gonna send it," said Lenora.

"Hey, no Internet," said Ray.

"Don't worry, I'll tell him not to post it," said Bobbie.

"Who the fuck is *he*?" asked Ray.

"Just some rich guy in Manhattan. He pays to pretend I'm his fiancée cheating on him. I send him the videos. It's weird but the money's good."

"Oh, so everyone gets a cut?" asked Ray.

"Haha, old man," said Lenora. "Have a bump."

She put some powder on her knuckle and offered it to Ray. He took it along with another pull from the bottle.

They'd picked up the car in the lot by the Newtown Creek and driven south on Morgan until they hit Broadway. He lost track of where they were while they made the video and the bump didn't help. He recognized Bushwick Ave and Halsey when they crossed them and ended up on at an old brewery turned lofts on a dead-end called Jessup Street.

"That was fun," said Kev.

He finished off the whiskey and said he'd go get more. Lenora led them into a square brick building and up five flights of slanty stairs into an exposed brick loft that took up an entire floor.

The hardwood floor was rough, and she told Ray to keep his shoes on so he didn't get splinters. The place was startingly neat, other than a mountain of clothes spilling out of the closet at the far end. She flipped on a projector that cast a horror movie onto a white bedsheet hung over the bricks. The movie was something from the nineteen-eighties that involved a madman with a meat cleaver, but he couldn't name it.

"Shit, we're out of blow, too," said Lenora.

Bobbie went to the fridge and found a six-pack of *Modello*, which she brought back to the futon in the middle of the room. They sat in a row like they were going to watch the movie, but both women just stared at their phones while Ray sucked down three beers in succession so that his head went from swimming like a happy kid at a campground to diving like a world-class Olympian.

Kev came back with the liquor and more blow. Somehow, they ended up by the counter in the kitchenette. Kev had a new buddy along with him, a kid with a ratty mustache whose name Ray didn't catch. They stood around in the kitchen cutting lines and playing songs for each other on their phones. Most of the bands were from Europe and Ray had never heard of them.

The movie was still playing in the background, and the cacophony had Ray's head reeling as if in a storm now. The two guys and Bobbie went to the futon, stripped down to their underwear, and played cards.

Ray stayed in the kitchenette with Lenora. The stimulants cut away the liquor's haze and he took in how muscular her limbs were. Her jeans hung shallow on her hips and looked almost masculine beneath her studded belt. He studied the shape of the bulge in her pocket and said, "Let's see your knife."

Lenora smiled, pushed back a lock of her black hair. "What is this, stop and frisk?"

"More like show and tell."

Lenora rolled her eyes. "Whatever," she said. She reached into the bulged pocket and pulled out a butterfly knife. She flipped it open casually and rolled it between her fingers, showed she could move fast if she wanted, but didn't have to.

"You don't wanna just get some pepper spray?" he asked.

"What, so I can piss 'em off before they try to rob me?"

"Fair enough," he said.

"Now your turn," she said.

"What do you mean?"

"Show and tell. Your turn to show what you're hiding."

"Why, are you selling videos too?"

Lenora shook her head. "No, I mean the weapon in your fucking boot," she said.

That's when Bobbie appeared. She had put her jacket and heels back on. "Hey, Nora, I'm outta here," she said. "Those guys cheat at cards and they're too coked to screw."

"Yeah, they suck," said Lenora. She gave her friend a hug goodbye.

"What about you?" Bobbie asked Ray. "Change your mind about the seven-hundred?"

"Afraid I'm a little light," said Ray.

"Too bad," she said. She pecked him on the cheek like he was her long-lost uncle and headed for the door. By then, the two guys were up and dressed. They muttered something about breakfast at the Mexican bakery and followed Bobbie out.

Once they were gone, Lenora hopped up on the stone counter, dangling her legs over the edge. She took the whiskey from his hand, pulling him toward her as she did.

"So let's see it," she said, nudging him with her knee.

Ray pulled up the leg of his jeans and drew the dagger from his boot. He held it between them, saw the reflection of her full lips and dark eyes in its blade.

"It's a seax," she said.

"The hell's that?" he asked.

Her reflection smiled. "An old kind of dagger," she said. "Design looks like northern Germany or Frisia, maybe early Norse. It's weird, the grain looks authentic, but it's polished like a replica."

"Whatever it is, I think it's the real thing," he said.

He leaned close to her, the dagger between them. The scent of jasmine was tempered now with sweat and booze. He felt her hair brush his cheek as she hopped off the counter.

"Anyway, that's cool, I like old stuff. You a collector?"

She went to the futon and brushed off the cards and ashtrays as she spoke. She threw a blanket across it and turned off the projector.

Ray ran his hand over his forehead. He felt feverish and his heart was thumping. He was at the end of a long bender and had assaulted his own mind to get away from what had been thrust upon him.

As he knelt to sheath the dagger, he caught a reflection again in its blade. It was Ada's instead of Lenora's this time. She looked pale and sleepless, skull showing through her skin. The girl's mouth was open in an "O" of agony. It was a warning that his reckoning was coming about, and if he thought he'd reached his worst and most degraded state, another cloud was opening to swallow him deeper.

"So lemme get your number before you go," said Lenora.

She was standing in front of him now, wearing a black kimono. How long had he stared into the dagger? He'd ripped his jeans forcing it back into his boot. As he stood, she handed him her phone, and he concentrated on tapping his number into it. He glimpsed the midmorning sun edging the dark curtains and didn't want to go out into it. *Like you do not want to read the headline of what you already know happened to Fenton.*

Lenora wrapped her arms around him, and squeezed him hard. "I'd say stay but we just met," she said.

Ray had no answer. *Yeah, it was a great time doing blow, drinking whiskey, and making smutty videos. Showing my dagger was a little much for the first date. Next time we'll go for ice-cream sodas.*

"Sure," he said. "If my car's good where it is, I'll call a cab."

"Where you staying?" she asked.

"Bushwick Inn," he said.

She chuckled. "Not as gross as they say."

"That's what I thought," he said.

"Come back to the club sometime. Like I said, you're not kicked out."

"Sure," he said.

Ray went to the door and stepped into the hallway. He heard her close it behind him and he didn't look back. When he made it down the stairs, he paused in the dingy lobby before stepping into the early spring sunlight. A cold, bright day awaited, and he could feel the first pulses of the excruciating pain that was about to assault his head.

When his phone buzzed in his pocket, he pulled it out and read the text:

come back

20

They couldn't stop kissing while they tore off their clothes. Falling across the futon and wrapping their legs around each other's necks, they stayed that way until clouds darkened the sun and wind blew rain against the windows.

She got up to close a crooked curtain and after that took him inside her. She stood facing the wall, arms spread, and they wrestled into each other. They tickled and bruised with pleasure and pain as they slammed their hips together.

The exertion cleared their minds, and the blow from the night before hung on just enough to quicken the pace. They enveloped each other with utter openness. They touched like they'd known each other a thousand years, yet still felt fresh as the flooding rain.

She turned around and pushed him back to the futon. "Get down," she said.

Ray fell back, heard the wooden frame crack as she pushed him again. She snatched the sheathed dagger from where it lay by his boot. A ringing sounded as she drew the blade and straddled him.

The steel flashed and her hand descended. He felt a hot sting as she slashed across his throat. The wound pulsed with his breath, and she slid down and began to ride him. She pushed the dagger into his hand and guided it upward as he cut along the top of her ribs.

After, she took another turn and stabbed him in the side.

The wounds they inflicted were potentially deadly, and yet instead of fading and feeling weaker, his body felt stronger and his mind clearer.

They gave each other more and shallower cuts as their rhythm slowed. They twisted gently in the slick of their arousal and put the dagger down on the pillow beside them. He glanced at its blade and saw their reflection had turned red. He kept his eyes on it as they writhed and swayed.

It was the only relief from the thoughts of his family and Ada and the eternity into which they had fallen.

***

It was dark when they finally passed out, and light again when he awoke. The rain had stopped and a cloud-blurred sun struggled through the cracks in the curtains. Ray stood and dressed.

He slid the dagger through his ripped jeans into his boot. Lenora lay naked on the sheets. Her lips moved in the nest of her long black hair, muttering something about bacon and eggs. He thought of waking her and wanted to, but knew he didn't have time. He spared them both even the lean-in for one last kiss.

"See you at *La Vela Roja*," he said, and left.

21

He drove north to Grand Street, rounded the block to the Bushwick Inn, and parked in the lot. The kid behind the desk was playing a console game on a big, loud TV. He considered reminding him about the car but decided it might just piss him off.

Instead, he headed up to his room, made coffee, and ran a shower. He felt rested and clear-minded, didn't even bother rummaging his duffle for any of Bonnie's leftover painkillers.

Back in their rookie year, Crespo used to joke that he drank himself sober. But Ray knew that bullshit was an excuse made by budding alcoholics, and really he was doing better because he and Lenora had slept all afternoon while the rain drummed hypnotically on the loft's roof. *And don't forget the dagger, the way it made you feel, how fast its wounds healed like you were getting even stronger.*

He banished the thoughts as he stepped into the shower and scrubbed his scarred skin. After, he made another cup of coffee and sat down with the folder and his phone.

"I know you're there," he said to Ada. He could feel her behind him as he sat at the desk. He didn't want to see what Heaven had done to her lately. Instead he spoke without looking up. "I'll find the demon," he said. "I'll make them let you go."

He wanted to get the headline from the same source as the article on Sadie Sparkle. It was an old tool he'd used in investigations, follow the same publication's articles, see when it looked like they'd gotten a better tip, then maybe pay them a visit.

Of course, when he ran the search for the *Brooklyn Crier*, it was all sensation: *Curtain Call: Aspiring Actor Found Mangled*. Whoever the P. Randall was in the byline definitely had an "in" to know Fenton Broadmore had his head torn off and thrown at a brick wall. And they were calling the killer the *Brooklyn Basher*, which was hip and had a ring to it. The press never failed to inspire psychopaths by handing out cool names.

Ray thought of the hunched man in *La Vela Roja*. Didn't look like it would be easy for him to swing a sledgehammer, but you could never tell a man's strength just by looking at him. And as far as the vape-sucking bouncers went, he doubted even those guys could rip a man's head off. Crush maybe, *but rip through flesh and bone and throw the damn thing?* That kind of strength was unnatural.

Still, he knew he would have to get a better look at the hunched man. As far as he knew, and after what he had seen back in Florida, the guy might have the body of a goddamn gorilla from the neck down. So he'd have to go back to the club at some point, though not too soon, as they'd be laying low after everything that went down.

Instead he lay back on the bed and searched more articles on his phone. He could head over to the precinct in the early a.m. when there was a chance it was quiet and see if any of the old crew were there to help him out.

As he read, the sighs of prostitutes sounded through the hotel walls. They sang above the generator from the Chinese place across the street and the frequent sirens on Grand as he slipped away.

***

He awoke to the groan of a crowbar and dashed to the window. He slid back the curtain and saw figures crowded around the Crown Vic. "Get off the car," he hollered as he opened the window and snatched the .40 cal from the desk.

He counted four when they looked up. The kid from the reception desk wasn't among them. There were two in hoodies, one in a do-rag, and one in a bandanna. He gave bandanna an A for originality, then shot him in the foot. The wounded man screamed while the two in the hoodies ran off.

Some kind of leader-type emerged from the corner of the lot. He was a pale-skinned, dark-haired dude with a goatee in a purple track suit. Ray sucked in a breath. Any gangster who came in person to a job this small had to be idiotic and dangerous.

Ray ran downstairs and out into the lot. He feinted right when Track Suit took his shot and missed like most fools with a handgun do.

Ray gripped the .40 cal in both hands and shot him the knee. Pale as shit, the motherfucker, yet somehow he remained standing. Ray closed the distance and kicked him where he shot him. This time Track Suit went down.

He followed up with a kick to his chin. *That oughta do it,* he thought.

"It's worth your fuckin' life?" asked Ray. He waved the pistol. "Get the fuck outta here!"

But Bandanna came at him anyway. He lunged, dragging his shot foot. "Rindete, pinche malo," he hissed, swinging at Ray's neck.

Ray dodged and spun, smacked him on the back of the neck with the butt of the pistol. He turned around just in time to face the muzzle of Track Suit's Glock-9.

He couldn't understand how the guy was back on his feet, but the time for second chances was way over. Ray shot a hole in the man's chest, point blank, knocking him back four feet and blowing a slop of lung and muscle clear to the sidewalk.

He spun again to finish off Bandanna, but before he could, the crowbar cracked his neck. Ray managed to feint just a little, boxer-style, tilt his head just enough to keep his face from being shattered. But the move gave Bandanna time to swing again, this time knocking the .40 cal out of his hand.

Fuckers aren't after the car, they're after me, he realized as he leaped back and dodged a third blow.

He'd thrown on the torn jeans, which made it easy to draw the dagger. He drew and struck in one motion, slashing across Bandanna Man's chest. As he let out a hollow scream and went down, Ray caught Track Suit's reflection in the car's side mirror. Despite his ghastly wound, he was sitting up and aiming the Glock again and wasn't going to miss this time.

Ray spun again and ducked. He felt the vibrations as the pistol exploded. He smelled gunpowder and felt the hot sting of something graze his cheek on the same side he'd been hit by the crowbar.

Before he swung the dagger, he grabbed the man's right wrist with his left hand. The bastard was too strong to shake the pistol free, but his next shot missed and blew a hole in the pavement.

Ray swung low, pushed the dagger up under the man's ribs, and gritted his teeth against another hollow scream. When they collapsed together over the car, he lay over the man's corpse for several minutes, dagger between them, bleeding and trying to catch his breath.

"Ray, Ray, hey Ray! You all right? Got here soon as we could. You all right, brother? Let me help you up."

Ray felt several sets of hands lifting him. He opened his eyes and looked through a blur of blood at a familiar face.

"Tolly, shit, what are you doing here?"

"Looking for you, man. Shoulda known I'd find you in a whorehouse." Crespo smiled into his handlebar mustache.

Ray was in no shape to laugh. "Seriously, what are you doing here? How the hell'd you know?"

"Got a call some old biker motherfucker was shooting up a bunch of gangbangers. Personally, I think you look more like a retired principal."

Ray frowned. What the fuck did he mean by we? What the fuck was he even doing there?

Ray let the paramedic bandage his neck. A half dozen

squad cars had arrived, accompanied by an ambulance. Crespo went over to talk to the sergeant, then came back when they loaded Ray in. "I'm coming with you, bud," he said.

Ray didn't answer. He closed his eyes against the red and blue lights as blood oozed in his reopened wounds.

22

Aside from the incident with the Ferrettos, he'd only ever shot and killed one perp in his entire career. He'd wounded plenty and had once beaten the right eye out of a rapist's skull. But he'd only shot and killed one.

It had been a bank robbery. The guy got his hands on a modified Kalashnikov and was either too impatient or too dimwitted to convert the thing back to full-auto. They had him trapped in an ATM vestibule, and Crespo kept him busy while Ray took him down with a single careful shot.

Turned out the guy was a hard-up divorcee more than a little behind on his child support. No criminal record and they chalked it up to suicide by cop. Ray never felt bad about it, but he didn't believe the report, either. He'd seen the guy's face. The look wasn't one of hopelessness. It was one of vengeance.

He glanced at his old partner now as he sat beside him in the ER at Wyckoff Hospital. Crespo was looking at his phone and his watch alternatively like one knew something the other didn't. It was one thing to follow him to Florida. It was another to follow him back to Brooklyn.

"How the fuck did those guys get up after I shot them?" Ray asked.

"Dunno, how do you get shot in the face and keep asking questions?"

"Grazed me," said Ray. And it wasn't the bullet that nearly

knocked him out, it was the crowbar. Hurt every time he drew a breath, and his throat was still swelling.

"Come on, let's get you comfortable so these people can to their jobs."

Crespo tried lifting the dagger from where Ray had it clutched to his chest. Ray didn't let go. Crespo grabbed it again, pulled. Ray kept his hold. He was about to speak when the doctor appeared. He had perfectly mixed salt-and-pepper hair that was feathered back like every strand had a number.

"Mr. Barrs is it? I'm Doctor Jasper. Looks like this is your lucky day, or at least so I've heard." He forced a tense smile. "Let's just do our due diligence and listen to your chest."

The doctor pried at the dagger, but instead of letting him have it, Ray set it on the steel table on the far end of the bed. From where he sat, Crespo would have to walk through the doctor to reach it. Jasper's smile turned to a frown as he glimpsed its bloody hilt.

"Family heirloom," Ray said.

Jasper nodded and turned his attention to his stethoscope. He listened to Ray's chest and nodded. "Let's have a look at that bruise," he said, patting Ray's neck with his cold fingers. Ray told him it was a crowbar and Jasper said, "Ouch!" as if it were a joke, then, "I understand you're a retired detective?" as if that explained why someone would hit you in the neck with a crowbar.

Before Ray could answer, a nurse appeared, and Jasper looked relieved to order blood work and prescribe prednisone. He punctuated it with the news that if the x-rays looked good he'd be out that afternoon. The smile was genuine on this point and Ray nodded. As soon as they were both through the curtain, he snatched the dagger back from the table.

"Hey, bud, I get it," said Crespo. "You've been through a lot."

"Yeah I have," said Ray.

Crespo went quiet and stayed that way for several minutes. Bad tie, beer belly, and weirdo mustache aside, he had to admit if there was anyone with a glimpse of understanding, it might be him.

"You know, when Carm left me, she didn't just take the kids, she got a restraining order," he said.

"For what?" Ray asked.

"Didn't lock my guns up," he said. "Her dickhead lawyer spun that into a threat. Ain't that the fuckin' irony? He turned an overworked cop's negligence into stalking. Like I was lying in wait for my own family."

Were you? They all said Carm got around. "That's awful," Ray said. "You hear from your son though, right? He joined the Navy?"

"Yeah. Tommy emails," said Crespo.

Crespo looked at him through the tinted shades. For him it must have been a detective thing. He remembered this fisherman in Florida who used to joke about how all the guys with the best rods and reels, best boats, best fitting shirts and shorts were the shittiest fishermen. It wasn't so much that Crespo had the best, but that even in his sloppiness he was going for that barfly, movie-detective look. Ray knew he was competent underneath, which made it that much more annoying that the guy tried so hard.

"Listen, Ray," he said, "I took care of the *Faustina* after you left. I went and checked on it in storage, paid the overdue bill. Some guys were asking if you wanna sell, I said no, but I could take care of that, too, just say the word."

"You didn't have to do that," said Ray.

"I wanted to," he said. "I wanted to just like I wanted to come up here and make sure you're okay. I also wanted to because I know something went down."

"It was family stuff," said Ray. He clutched the dagger so hard he almost cut through the johnny into his own stomach.

"I'm your friend," said Crespo.

"And this was family stuff," said Ray.

"Damn it, Ray, they found Bonnie. They know she OD'd, but they want to know how she got tucked into bed."

Ray shuddered. Tears stung his eyes as he saw past Crespo's shoulder. Ada stood among the ER's shadowy curtains. Her face was gray and her mouth cracked open so he could see her tiny teeth. She wore the robes of Heaven, but her teeth looked sharp. *We're eating you alive. Not Grandma and me. She's in Hell. The angels and me. Isn't it funny? You're trying to save me, and they're making me drive you crazy.*

"Bastards! You goddamn bastards," cried Ray. "I'll find you, I'll fuckin' find a way!" Ray threw his legs over the bed and stood. He ripped the I.V. out of his arm, and strode forward, dagger in hand.

"Whoa, whoa, easy! Whoa, Ray, stop, take it easy!"

Crespo leaped in front of him and stood between the bed and the curtains. Ray heard the nurses paging the doctor and calling the cops. He took a deep breath and made himself step back, then slid open the drawer on the dresser beside the bed and began to dress.

Doctor Jasper arrived and stepped in front of Crespo. He was holding a syringe and had two uniformed cops in tow.

"Mr. Barrs? Are you all right? Please return to your bed, Mr. Barrs. Please just calm down."

"I'm all right," said Ray. "I'm totally fine."

"We think you need a little more rest," said the doctor. "We need to get you x-rayed, remember?"

"It's just a little swelling," said Ray. He stood still to keep them from going for full-on restraint. Jasper lowered the syringe, and Ray put on his t-shirt calmly. "Really, I'm all right. It's just a misunderstanding. Listen Doc, I'm leaving. I appreciate your help, and I'll sign what I gotta sign. Just send me the bill."

If there was one thing about doctors he respected, it was their intelligence when it came to the bottom line. Jasper had been done with this mess the second it arrived. If all it took was a signed AMA waiver to get it out of his hair, he was more than happy to make it happen.

"Fine," he said. He put up his hands, palms forward, in that imaginary blocking gesture people used to avoid a physical confrontation. "I'll have the nurse bring the forms. You can get dressed. I'll still prescribe the prednisone."

23

Ray stood outside in the spring drizzle, waiting for the gypsy cab he'd taken from the airport. He could have Ubered it or taken a yellow cab, but he had the guy's card and liked that he had said nothing the entire ride.

Sirens and car horns echoed around him. and yet he still recognized Crespo's footsteps as they sloshed through the puddles in the lot's cratered pavement.

"Hey, wait," he said. He put his hand on Ray's shoulder. Ray turned and tried to keep from slugging him. "Look man, I'm sorry. I was just trying to help."

"Tolly, listen, I can't drag you into this. I gotta get this done on my own. You yourself told me you saw things you can't explain, things that shouldn't be."

"That's why I want to help."

"And you know they're gonna come after me about Bonnie."

"All the more reason to say I found you."

Ray went quiet and turned into the rain.

"Come on, Ray, I can help. You're goin' to the old precinct, right? Let me go with you. They're more likely to give us something if we go together."

Ray shook his head. He saw the black gypsy cab turn into the lot and plow down the flooded lane.

"No, listen, I gotta see about my car and get some rest."

"I already took care of your car. It's at *Fazio's*. In the

meantime, I know where you can get some rest. Just come with me, I know just the place."

They climbed into the cab, and Crespo gave an address Ray recognized as Windsor Terrace. With the Crown Vic taken care of and his gun already lost, there wasn't much back at the Bushwick Inn he needed besides the file on the murders. He figured they were headed to one of their old haunts south of Park Slope where cops and firefighters went to drink and watch sports.

By then, the prednisone was working its magic, and he admitted he could use a drink. The car seemed to float through the rain as they accelerated up the ramp onto the BQE and coasted back down the exit. He closed his eyes and imagined Lenora's apartment, the rain against the glass almost taking him back, if it weren't for the stench of cigarettes wafting off Crespo's suit.

"This is it," said Crespo as they turned south of Prospect Park and down a narrow lane called Fairport Street.

They climbed the slightly slanted but well-painted steps of a two-family townhouse. Electric candles shone in the windows, and a cardboard cut-out of a stuffed bunny hung on the door. Crespo rang the doorbell, and a small, tired-looking woman with frizzy black hair answered. She was beaming despite the premature lines on her face, and she kept back the yapping dog with her foot as she held a hiccupping baby in her arms.

"Tolly, I didn't think you'd make it," she said. She kissed his cheek in lieu of a hug.

"You know I wouldn't miss it," he said. "And you look great, still got the glow. Hey, I brought a friend along. Ray, this is Maribel, Maribel, Detective Ray Barrs. Well, former, I should say, like me."

"Hey what's the racket, who let *him* in?"

A red-haired man in a collar and loosened tie stepped into the hall. He hugged Crespo, then turned to Ray. "Brad Callaghan," he said. He was holding a beer in one hand and shook Ray's with the other.

"Ray Barrs," said Ray.

"Hey, you're Jimmy Barrs' son. You knew my old man."

"I did," said Ray.

"Well come on in, have a drink," said Callaghan. "And don't mind Tiny." He juggled his beer as he picked up the dog. It looked like the result of tragic cooperation between a chihuahua and a pit bull. The thing barked and showed its teeth as it squirmed in Callaghan's arms. *Maybe that's the goddamn demon,* he thought. *But no, just a spoiled puppy on Easter. How the hell did I forget it was Easter? Maybe I'm just jealous.*

Callaghan led them down the hall as Maribel took their coats. On their right, an arch opened into a living room where two kids, a boy and a girl, sat in front of some gun-thundering video game. The TV screen shined on their chocolate-smeared faces. Ray wondered how they could stuff themselves with candy and play games at the same time until he realized they were just watching someone else play online.

"I figure they waited 'til after church, so let 'em have at it," said Callaghan. "Beer?"

They moved into an eat-in kitchen where Maribel was adding two more settings to a table already set for six. An elderly woman in a wheelchair was seated at one end, next to a wooden high chair. She gave Ray a gummy smile, and he nodded back. The smell of ham, cloves, and roasting potatoes filled the air.

Callaghan put down the dog, handed them each a beer, then took a hard left through a narrow door onto a descending staircase.

"How about a quick meeting in my office," he said.

"By all means," Crespo answered.

The stairs led to a basement not quite carpeted wall-to-wall. A bar with four stools stood at one end and a dartboard hung on the wall between NASCAR posters. Callaghan caught Ray eyeing them and said, "Well, the wife ain't real keen on bikinis, so cars it is. How about a whiskey?"

Ray nodded as Callaghan pulled a dark green bottle from beneath the bar and lined up three glasses. "Ireland isn't known for single-malts, but this stuff actually is single-barrel."

"Long's it works," said Crespo. "To your health."

They all clinked glasses and drank. Crespo sipped, while Ray and their host swallowed theirs whole. Ray took a chaser from his beer while Callaghan poured another, and they drank again.

"Whoa," said Crespo. "Easy there, cowboy. You been takin' calls for domestics or what?"

"My whole goddamn life's a domestic," said Callaghan as he sipped his beer.

Crespo turned to Ray. "Brad's been a detective, what, three years now?"

"Four," said Callaghan. "Three at the 91st."

"He's the man on the scene in our old stomping grounds. No wonder it's gone to shit."

"You're an asshole, Tolly," said Callaghan.

"So you're workin' the *Brooklyn Basher*," said Ray.

"Van Meeks has that," said Callaghan. "He keeps me updated, but it's nothin' you can't read on the web."

"Come on, there's nothin' to that thing," said Crespo. "Some crackhead beats-down a hooker 'cause he couldn't pay. Or maybe 'cause she asked too many questions. They'll pick him up in midtown for vagrancy when his well runs dry. They'll get a DNA match and badda-bing."

You are an asshole, Tolly, thought Ray. He was about to ask again, mention the old woman who'd been among the victims, and Fenton, when he heard shouting erupt upstairs. Kids footsteps thumped across the floor and the dog's yapping reached new heights. The basement door swung open and Maribel hollered down the stairs.

"Could use a little help up here!"

"Could use a little help with the bills," Callaghan snapped back.

But it was the whiskey talking and his face reddened immediately as he excused himself and went up to help. The argument crescendoed, then stifled itself quickly. He was back down in ten minutes when Ray and Crespo were only on their second round of darts.

"Sorry, just givin' the wife a little backup."

"Nice to see you guys are still down for a quickie," said Crespo.

Callaghan glared at him, but took the darts and turned to the board.

"Oh come on, man," he went on. "We all got kids."

"S'all right," said Callaghan. He put two in the bull's and one on a triple twenty, then went back to the bar. "One more round for luck?"

"Fuckin' young guys," said Crespo, leaving the darts where they were and returning to the bar.

Callaghan poured and they all sipped this time. "Gotta be a game on," he said. He picked up a remote and turned on a small screen that hung in the corner above the bar.

"That'd be nice," said Crespo. "You know, I told you about Ray before, about him comin' up from Florida. He's the one goin' through some stuff like I told you."

Callaghan gave Crespo a look Ray had a hard time reading. He expected it to be a *So what? So I let him in my fuckin' house, what the fuck do you want?* But it was something else instead, something Ray thought almost looked like fear. He put on the baseball game but kept the volume low and his voice even lower as he spoke and sipped his drink and turned to Ray.

"Yeah, well, we're all goin' through stuff, right? Our goddamn tenants split while they were three-months behind on the rent. Two cars, a Brooklyn mortgage, and my old bills from Vegas got me payin' minimums on three different cards. Maribel needs a second car to cart around the kids and Christmas didn't fuckin' help."

"I hear you," said Ray.

"I lost my shit on some hipster kids blocking traffic on Bedford and told him I only make a hundred thousand and they started spewing shit about the one percent. Like half their daddies don't pay their bills."

"Hey, hey, come on now," said Crespo. "All I meant is you guys could relate. We don't need the laundry list."

As he spoke, Ray noticed his old partner's hand reach out and give Callaghan's elbow a quick nudge.

"Hey, I got an idea," said Crespo. "Let's take a walk after dinner. We'll take a walk down to *Frank's Place*, cut through the park. The fresh air will do us good. Whattaya say?"

"Don't think Mari would be too keen on that," said Callaghan.

"Really? I think she'd understand if you're catching up with a couple of brothers in blue."

"We'll catch up another time. Today's not good."

As they spoke, Crespo's and Callaghan's faces hardened. Ray detected a certain emphasis on the words *catch up*, a weight that he knew changed what they meant, though he couldn't be sure to what.

"Dinner's ready, boys," cried Maribel.

At this, the three of them headed back up to the kitchen. Ray took his place at the table, squeezed between Brad and his kids. Only when the ham was brought out did he realize how hungry he was, and how little he had eaten since he landed in New York.

24

"Are you a policeman, too?" asked the little blonde girl beside him.

"I used to be," said Ray.

"You don't look like one," she said. "You look like a pirate, or you know, one of the bad guys."

"That so?" Ray smiled and pulled the tip of his lengthening beard. *Beats a fuckin' high school principal.*

"Jenny, he's not a bad guy," said the older boy who might have been ten. "He's a narc. Narc's are good guys who look like bad guys."

"Hey, enough," said Maribel. "Eat your dinner."

"Aren't we gonna say grace?" asked the girl.

"We said grace in church. Eat before it gets cold."

Ray ate a hefty helping of ham and some greens but didn't ask for seconds. He breathed the rest of the feast, the aroma of butter, squash, and mint jelly. He smelled the kids' shampooed hair and Maribel's *Fendi* perfume and when she brought the pot of coffee, bit his tongue when he almost called her Bonnie.

It's the scent of family, the scent of home. He drank the coffee, then stood and poured himself a glass of water. *You're not fighting to get this back,* he thought. *You're fighting to know it ever meant anything at all.*

His standing up broke the spell and Callaghan came next, bussing his own plate and grabbing a beer from the fridge. "Go ahead," he said when the kids begged to be excused. "You go ahead, too," he said to Maribel. "Fellas'll clean up."

Ray gave him points for attempting some semblance of redemption, and by switching to beer, his own way of down-shifting. He took a few plates from the table and started loading the dishwasher. He'd felt Crespo's eyes on him the whole time they were eating, but now, after putting three helpings of everything into his crock-pot of a stomach, his old colleague pretended to check his phone while he avoided the chores.

"Where's your garbage?" asked Ray after he tied off a bag.

"Out front," said Callaghan.

Even better, thought Ray. He wanted to thank the guy and his wife for the Easter dinner, but that would guarantee he lost his chance. Instead he carried the garbage into the hallway. He looked around for his jacket, but it wasn't there. He peered through the arch into the living room where he saw Maribel stretched out on the couch and the kids sitting on the floor, watching a Disney movie now.

The boy and the girl sat on matching beanbags. Ada sat beside them in a nest made out of Ray's leather jacket.

She beamed up at him like he'd just given her permission to watch her favorite show. Her skin was all gray and silver outlines again, that image rendered in black and white. Dark patches spotted her face. A crescent of a bruise ran from her cheek to her chin. Her skin looked stretched, like she was a 90-year-old trapped inside a nine-year-old, and he realized that her sharpish teeth looked that way because they'd been cracked.

"I'm having fun," she said.

It took all he had not to turn away from the wreckage that was her smile. Instead he stepped toward her, reaching for his jacket.

"Patrick, quit it!" snapped the blonde girl at her brother.

The boy shoved his beanbag forward and elbowed his sister. "You're in the way," he said.

"Am not," she said.

"Are too," he said. "And you're a liar. You won't go to

Heaven. Father Prinzo said!"

"Will too!"

"Will not!"

Ray tried to get around the two of them as they started to wrestle. Ada slid the jacket just out of reach, and as he fumbled and danced, she leaned over and whispered something in the girl's ear.

The girl's face turned pale and she glared at her brother. "They beat kids in Heaven anyway," she said. "They beat them with golden sticks!"

"Jenny!" cried Maribel. Until then, their mother had tried to doze through the fight, something that probably happened a dozen times a day. But now the ante had been upped and she had to intervene. Ray took the opportunity to snatch his jacket while Ada beamed at the children, her work well done.

"Jenny, take a time out," said Maribel. "For God's sake, chill!"

"But Mom, it's true. I heard an angel whisper."

"Now you're scaring me, kid. Come here." Maribel crouched on the floor and took the child in her arms. "Even if there was a place like that, it wouldn't really be Heaven, would it?"

The girl shrugged. "I dunno," she said.

"Definitely not," said her mother.

At this, Ada crooked her head in the way she had in the car years before. The look on her face made Ray turn away. He slipped into the hall and headed for the front door. He turned to check the kitchen and saw Crespo talking on his phone. If he'd been keeping an eye on the hallway, he'd become distracted. Ray noticed the basement door was open too, no doubt so Callaghan could go down and resupply on the refreshments that made the broom sweep a little easier.

Ray took his chance and slid back the first in the door's column of deadbolts. A cool touch on his wrist made him turn. He expected to see Ada's awful, crooked-necked glare. Instead it was Maribel.

"Get a text from a lady friend?" she asked.

Ray let out a nervous chuckle. "Ah no, just takin' out the trash. Thanks for dinner, it was delicious. I just gotta go, but it was good, everything's good."

"How good?" Maribel retorted.

Ray was a little taken aback as Mrs. Callaghan's face flushed beneath her curly black hair. The freckles spread along her blouse's low neckline turned a shade redder. She leaned in, and he glimpsed how they plunged between her plump breasts.

She noticed him notice and laughed. "Quick, get outta here before they make you watch the game," she said.

Ray nodded, finished opening the locks, tossed the trash bag, and hustled down the steps. Without thinking, he glanced back and saw Ada next to Maribel. She had moved out onto the porch and stood beside her in a pummeled parody of a daughter and mother seeing their father off to work.

They beat them with golden sticks.

The words echoed in his head as his steps turned into a jog and then into a full-on run.

25

Ray strode north through Prospect Park, Prospect Heights, then on to Fort Greene. He moved up Vanderbilt along the Navy Yard with its gaunt buildings covered in frost-choked vines. Black windows stared out of crumbling bricks like empty eye sockets. A low wall separated the sidewalk from the old installation, and he quickened his pace again until he reached the newer section with its fenced-off gates and armed guards.

It's in one of those forgotten places, he thought, *hiding*.

As he continued north, he felt an invisible and unspoken pressure. He recalled the night they had taken Ada, the sky opening in the storm. He thought he could hear them now, the chariots with their spinning wheels. They would renege on their deal and send a soldier to crush him. He knew they were real, and all that was around him, all that human beings had constructed, was an infested hive where aberrations like the thing he had pulled from the moldy pool were concealed and waiting to be awoken.

When the rain started, he moved a block east to Park Avenue and walked beneath the BQE. The expressway curved over the city like an elevated concrete artery. Ray felt his own heart beating as the traffic rumbled above.

You lost the fucking car and the pistol, but you kept the dagger. He could feel it sheathed his boot as he strode north. Lenora had called it a seax, but he hadn't asked her how she knew.

What he did know was how good it felt when it cut him. The touch of its blade was like cold water quenching a deep thirst. It had helped him heal, and he could feel it. It was as if the weapon were attuned to him, the pain it inflicted was a balm to his flesh, and its wounds could bring strength as well as destruction.

He checked his phone and found two new messages. The first was from Fazio's saying he could pick up the Crown Vic. He wondered if it was worth the risk, and whether this was another way Crespo could keep track of him. *Sooner or later, I'm gonna have to confront him*, he thought. *Have a face to face and find out what he really came back for.*

But the second was from Lenora:

`where r u? call me`

His thumb moved to the screen, ready to tap the L, then hesitated. Lightning struck and the spring rain fell harder. A shadow moved ahead of him, a derelict who'd moved under the shelter of the overpass.

He caught up with her as she paused by one of the cement pylons. She wore a white thrift store dress and cowboy boots. She was soaked to the bone, a skeletal junkie with straw-like hair, yet with a smile like Maribel Callaghan's. It was as if she were feeding off his hollowness and hunger.

The smile cloyed at him as the shelter of the overpass curved away and he moved into the shivering rain. *Was he any different from her? A glutton for emptiness, a junkie to his distractions, literally derelict in his duty?* As he pressed on, he felt like both a groomsman and a sacrifice in a solitary procession across Brooklyn's concrete sepulcher.

He thumbed his response onto the phone's wet screen:

`not tonight`

26

He reached the *Bushwick Inn* by nine o'clock and found the kid at the counter playing video games with a cast on his right wrist.

The kid eyed him beneath his do-rag. "I watched your car, pendejo. Tried to stop those guys. Broke my wrist 'cause of that shit."

"I need a gun," said Ray.

"So it's always about what you fuckin' need?" the kid chuckled. "Vete a la chingada."

"I think there's shit we both need. I'll give you $500 as a deposit. That work?"

"Quizás. I'll call you," he said, already looking back at his game as he took the money.

Ray went up to his room and found his things more or less intact. The duffle had been rifled through for cash, and his files lay in a mess across the desk. But they'd left his clothes alone and didn't find where he'd hid the bag of what was left of Bonnie's pills.

He stripped down and showered and changed into dry clothes. The lightning was still flashing in the windows when he headed back out for a bottle of whiskey. He noticed the kid who was usually at the desk was gone, replaced by a girl in braids who looked about twelve years old. Hopefully it meant the deal on the gun was already going down.

He walked up to Grand, found the first liquor store he

passed was open, happy fucking Easter, and bought two fifths of *Evan Williams*. It was a good sign when he got back that the girl looked worried, and he headed upstairs.

The kid was waiting in the room with two other men, one in a suit, the other in a black, tactical-looking get up. It was the scene in the movie where the guys were supposed to open a suitcase and go over all the cool guns they had, and you were supposed to say, "I'll take 'em all."

Instead, the kid stepped up to him, holding a fat black pistol with an extra-long magazine. "Glock 18, asshole," he said. He pointed it at Ray with a shit-eating grin on his face.

Ray shook his head. "What the fuck is it with Glocks around here?" he asked.

He reached for the gun and waited while the kid enjoyed a few extra seconds of power over life and death. His Jesus-piece dangled inside his unzipped hoodie as he pointed the muzzle between Ray's eyes. But he knew that even more than not wanting police attention, a bloody mess would mean a delay in getting back to weed and video games. Ray took hold of the gun and the kid let go.

"Fifteen G's," he said.

"Deal," said Ray. "Ammo?"

"Two full mags."

Ray nodded. He gave the kid points for getting him a full-auto or at least knowing who to talk to. Pulling his roll from his pocket, he began counting out the hundreds.

"Did I say fifteen Gs?" the kid piped. "I meant fifteen-five-hundred."

"Shut up while he's countin'," said the guy in the suit.

The kid started at this but didn't answer.

Ray got to fifteen thousand, then paused. "What's your name again?" he asked the kid.

"You don't need his name," said the guy in the suit. His diamond earrings glinted over his razor-thin goatee. The man in the black tactical stood silently beside him, leaning over all three of them.

"Name's Eli," said the kid as the suit took the money.

"It's a pleasure doing business with you, Eli," said Ray.

The suit scowled at them as he recounted the cash, then handed Ray a plastic bag containing a leather holster. "You get the fuck out now," he said. "Don't come back to the hotel. Don't come near it."

"Wasn't planning to," said Ray.

"We know you're a cop and we know you're dirty," he said.

"What's your point?"

"We don't want your curse around here," he said. "El demonio te matará. Ya eres un fantasma."

Ray wasn't sure he fully understood but decided even if the suit knew something about the demon, he wasn't going to get much more out of him than an overpriced gun.

"Yeah, well, it's the second part that haunts me," said Ray.

The three of them waited while he packed up his duffle and stayed in the room as he headed downstairs and back into the storm.

27

Losing his base of operations, however ramshackle, put him on a necessary detour, especially without the car. He'd have headed up to Queens that night, risked Crespo waiting for him if he thought Fazio's would be open and he could get the Crown Vic. But he doubted he'd have the same luck with the garage he had with the liquor store, and instead headed south to Broadway, where he ducked into a Lysol-reeking dive for a whiskey.

He had walked all the way across Brooklyn in a downpour to try and shake anyone who was tailing him. Now, he needed to go on a mini-lam while he decided on his next move.

Lenora's place isn't far, he thought. He felt the dagger pressing against his leg again. Its blade had become slightly unsheathed as he had made his way south. It cut him a little and he could feel the blood oozing. When he closed his eyes and sipped the whiskey, he saw Lenora's hand on the scax, the flash of its blade as it sliced his neck. *Where are you? Call me.*

He made himself order another whiskey instead of pulling out his phone. He pressed his calf against the blade, deepening the cut. Blood soaked his jeans and dripped onto the floor. Anyplace but *Neptune's Lounge* would have had something to say about a man bleeding as he drank. But the old white-haired, piss-smelling bartender just tossed his rag over his shoulder and changed the channel from golf to *Jeopardy*.

Ray had to force himself to keep from dreaming awake.

Like the gargantuan storm raging against the Faustina when he'd gone out day after day to rescue Ada, the reality of his situation was pummeling his mind, bludgeoning him with the cold truth that he was not on the verge of success but collapse.

He left a twenty on the bar and headed back onto Broadway. It occurred to him he was further east than he had at first thought. Bedstuy was giving way to East New York. *Neptune's Lounge* had taken its name from dubious proximity to Coney Island, and the crack hotel looming on his left had a half-burnt-out neon sign that read *The Voyager.*

The letters glowed an anemic aqua over a sickly white shape that might have been intended to be a wave. The brick façade and paint-slopped window frames slanted like the whole building was about to cave-in.

When Ray strode up to the door with the steel grill, a large man in a puffy jacket stepped out of the shadows. He asked if Ray knew Tommy. Ray said no.

"What are you looking for?" he asked.

"Just a room," said Ray.

"For what?"

"Sleep."

The man laughed. "Go ahead," he said.

Ray went through the cigarette-stinking vestibule and bought a two-night stay for three hundred bucks. The guy in the grimy nook that served as reception seemed incredulous that Ray wanted a room for more than a few hours.

The room was on the second floor and larger than he expected. A corroded mirror hung on one wall, and a crumbling brick fireplace tilted into the bare plaster on the other. Cigarette burns speckled the carpet like a swarm of dead beetles.

The TV ran a blurrier stream of porn than at the *Bushwick Inn.* If there was a light switch, he didn't see it. Instead, the streetlights combined with the TV's glow as they shined through the crooked window. He only needed to see long enough to open his whiskey, down a third of the bottle, and tuck the dagger under the filthy pillow. He was asleep in an instant as if he were running late for the first of three dreams.

28

In the first dream, his father appeared. He climbed up the basement stairs and limped into the yard of their old townhouse in Sunset Park. He had a black eye the size of a fried egg and a bottle of *Cutty Sark*. "You can't have any," said James Barrs. "You're drunk enough, and you also pissed me off."

"What else is new?" Ray asked.

"Your mistakes. You want a list? I don't have time for that. We're gonna look at the highlights." His father walked across the yard, his shirt untucked and his thinning brown hair unkempt and patchy like the grass. "You comin'?" he asked Ray.

"Do I have to?"

His father shook his head as he opened the gate in the fence. "Come on, Ray. I gotta show you somethin'."

"Who the fuck are you, the *Ghost of Christmas Past*?"

"I'm the guy who puts coal in your stocking," said James Barrs. "Now hurry up before we run out of time."

He couldn't tell what train they were on as they made their way into the city. It seemed to move fast, but the gray circle on the front contained no letter. "I was proud of you when you joined the force," said his father. "No offense, but I never thought you were gonna amount to much."

"None taken," said Ray as his father took a gulp of the *Cutty Sark*. *Do I look that bad when I drink?* he wondered.

"I woulda got you into the Port Authority if I knew you had

it in you. But then you just went to the Academy on your own, made detective early. My son, a goddamn detective. I thought your fearlessness was courage. Now I know you're just a damn fool."

"You're sayin' *I'm* the fool?" said Ray as he looked into his father's black eye.

"What? Johnny Ferretto gave me this himself. I wear it for eternity now. Everything I did for you and you gotta go and hit a gangster's son. I had us set up, Ray. Then you gotta go and bring it all down."

"Why's it all about you? I did what I had to do for me."

"Hey, I said I was proud you became cop. You coulda gone far with that if you'd a' listened."

"Listened to who? Maybe I was good where I was at."

"See that's your problem, Ray. You can't make up your goddamn mind. Are you in, or are you out? Is it Ferretto, or the NYPD?"

"Neither," said Ray.

His father shook his head and pulled on his bad whiskey. "Oh look, we're here."

They stood by a subway entrance in Alphabet City. Still no letter in the gray circle on the sign. They walked further east along Tompkins Square Park. It was evening, a Thursday or a Friday, judging by the crowds on Avenue A. You could smell the weed in the summer air. It must have been years ago because it didn't have the vape pens' touch of perfume.

Hucksters sat on the sidewalk next to blankets spread with purses, rings, and CDs. Crusty homeless kids huddled in doorways with their dogs, and cliques of happy drunks stumbled out of dive bars. They passed the neon sign of one of these, a white, red, and yellow rooster belied by the arc of letters above it spelling *Chickenhead*.

"Dad, I don't get it, what the fuck are we—"

That's when he saw himself walk out of the bar with one of the cliques of drunks. It was his younger self, maybe thirty years old. He wore a snug t-shirt and jeans and was tapping a number into a screenless cell phone with plastic buttons. *I'm calling Bonnie*, he thought.

The scene was from the hard time they had a few years after Beth was born. Money was tight, motherhood had strung Bonnie out too much to work much at the bar, and overtime was wearing Ray out, too. "Stay home a few years," he had told her, "I can handle it." She had glared at him then, the way a prisoner glares when you close the door of the cell, and said, "Yeah, but I don't know if I can."

The stress had almost split them up. And even worse, he didn't just stay out of the house for work. He was hanging out to get drunk and high when he was off duty, deleting his body from their home and his brain from his head.

As the dream carried him drunkenly down the street with his friends, he realized he had merged into the self that had stepped out of the bar. His father had vanished, and yet he still felt the man's presence somehow, like a face in the distant, darkening clouds, a face frowning judgment as they moved further east.

The term "friends" was a loose one. He had just met the girl April (was that really her name or was it just the dream?) and a couple that was hanging out with her, Laney and Bo. April was blonde and Laney brunette. One was from Montana, the other from South Dakota. Bo looked like a prettier and darker-skinned Bob Marley in his dreads and olive-drab jacket. They weren't the "cop bar crowd" by a longshot, and that night, that was how he wanted it.

"Do you really teach criminology?" April had asked over kamikaze shots.

"Yes," said Ray. It was only half a lie.

One more shot and a trip to the bathroom for a bump later, Bo said, "Let's go. We can stop by my friend's place."

By the time they made Avenue C, Ray and April had already stopped twice to kiss. Bo ducked into the brownstone squat that was his friend's place and picked up a couple more foil-wrapped grams of blow. A kid in a leather jacket followed him out. He had scruffy sideburns like the kids on the blankets with the dogs, but he wasn't crusty and didn't smell.

"Yeah I got a Jeep," he said. "If ya'll wanna go for a ride."

He was looking at Laney. She had large, dark eyes and a wide smile. She wasn't tall, but otherwise movie star beautiful, with a silky semi-see-through top that simultaneously mocked and celebrated glamour. Sideburns kept staring at her after he spoke and Bo stepped closer to her and wove his fingers through hers.

"Come on, let's go," Laney said, ignoring Sideburns and continuing east.

***

They did a few more bumps in her bathroom then spread throughout Laney's railroad apartment, sipping sugary wine and talking across rooms. They had broken off into couples so they could hang out but also have a little privacy, and Ray lay with April across a row of mismatched couch cushions in the middle room.

The apartment smelled damp and April's perfume mixed with the scents of wine and sweat. He kissed her neck, and she caressed his shoulders. He moved to her hair as her fingers played over his wrist. When he swigged from the bottle, some of the liquid leaked.

"Don't spill," she said.

"I'll try not to," he said.

They laughed as desire rose between them like a mist-blurred moon. Its glow was a little too sweet like the wine, but it was still very drinkable, and they were both ready to swallow it for as long as it would last.

"If you're gonna fuckin' ignore me, you gotta pay me first."

It was Sideburns, shouting from the bedroom.

"You're drunk, dog. Just get outta here," said Bo.

"If you ain't got money, she can pay me in the bathroom," said Sideburns.

"What the fuck did you just say?" said Bo, louder this time.

"Damn, we gotta help," said April.

Ray followed as she slipped off the cushions and rushed into the bedroom. There Bo and Laney lay semi-clothed on the bed. Her mascara was smeared and it looked like they hadn't cared Sideburns was there at first but now saw the asshole wasn't capable of a graceful exit.

"This motherfucker's gotta go," said Bo. He was skinny, but his muscles were lean and taut as he hopped out of bed and confronted Sideburns.

But the man just chuckled into his red whiskers. "I'm a Ferretto. No shit, I could call Joey Ferretto right now."

"Get the fuck outta here, you ain't no fuckin' gangster."

"The fuck you think a gangster is? Motherfucker with a forties hat and cigar, playin' dice games? We sell coke, asshole. Now you gotta pay."

"Fuck you," said Bo as his right-hook flew up and hit Sideburns in the chin. His jaw made a popping sound, but he kept laughing and said, "Now you done it, you dumb motherfucker!"

He pulled a .45 from inside his leather jacket and held it in Bo's face. The gun was massive but cast a weak shadow in the room's low light. "Now she's *gotta* come with me. Understand? Now she's *gotta* come, all 'cause you wouldn't fork over fifty bucks."

"I'll get the money," said Bo. "You gotta let me go to an ATM."

Sideburns turned to Laney. "Your man don't listen, do 'e? He's cheap and he's deaf. Now go on, get in the bathroom." He made a quick wave with the pistol then held it back on Bo. "Now I'm gonna be a little while, so don't try no shit. Don't any a' you fuckers call the cops. Remember she's in there with me and she's in there with this." He waved the pistol once more as he put his hand on Laney's shoulder.

"Babe wait, you don't gotta go," said Bo.

"No, it's better this way," she said, voice shaky. "It's better and we'll be all right."

Ray admired how she steeled herself as she fought panic.

Sideburns kept laughing as they pushed past April toward the bathroom. "Don't you go nowhere, neither," he told her. "You'll get your own turn."

Bo was already pulling a hunting knife from under the pillow and getting ready to go after them when Ray put his fingers to his lips.

"Shhhh," he said.

"The fuck you mean shhhh?" Bo started

"I'm a cop," Ray whispered.

***

The dream jumped to the bathroom. Manhattan's smoggy sunlight shined through the window onto Laney where she sat in the empty tub. She was wrapped in a pink towel and had her elbows on her knees and her fingers in her ears.

Still she shrieked each time Ray smashed Sideburns' forehead against the sink.

"Stop! Gah! Gaahhd damn," he cried as the sink gonged with the impact of his skull. "You gotta stop, I know J-J-Joey f-fuckin' F-Ferretto!"

"I don't care if you know Prince Motherfuckin' Charles," said Ray. "You're under arrest."

"Bullshit, you ain't a cop! Where's your g-goddamn handcuffs?"

"In my dresser drawer with my badge," said Ray.

He pulled Sideburns' bloody face from the sink once more and smashed it with a right hook. The man went quiet then aside from his slow, gurgling breaths. Ray held him by the collar and dragged him to the door.

He caught his reflection in the mirror. Sweat drenched his hair and his t-shirt. Veins bulged around his muscles and he had a red line down his forearm from where a round from the .45 had grazed him. He looked like some kind of beast of the wood, a bear dragging his prey. He moved on, pulling Sideburns' body across the warped hardwood floor and into the hallway.

A sharp knock sounded on the door. He hadn't called Tolly yet, was going to drag the bastard outside and do it there, maybe grab coffee from the deli while he waited. *Yeah, my pal's had a few too many*, he was going to joke while the dudes filled his cup and stared. *Gonna call 9-1-1.*

But instead he opened the door and faced Joey Ferretto. He still had the gelled hair, but had traded the track suit for sharp, gray *Armani*, like he was going to Sunday service at the Stock Exchange.

"Ray Barrs?" he said. But the surprise lasted less than a second before he drew his Sig-Sauer.

Ray had already dropped Sideburns' torpid body and pulled the .45.

"You're under arrest," said Ray.

Ferretto shook his head and gritted his teeth. "What the fuck are you doin'?" he cried. "Why do you gotta be so stupid? I thought I was done with your ass! You run straight into the goddamn fire! What, your father need another black eye? You need me to cut it out of his skull?"

"Put down the weapon and get on the floor."

"You gotta be—"

The pistols went off simultaneously. The flash seared Ray's hand as he grabbed the Sig's muzzle and shot Ferretto in the knee with the .45.

Two weeks later, when he went to Ferretto's compound, he would find Joey lying on a hospital bed, leg amputated, and waiting for a prosthetic. The don's eldest son would echo the words from the day he was shot: "Now you're dead! You're dead for-fuckin-ever! You run to the fire, you burn forever!"

29

In the second dream he saw his mother.

She sat at the kitchen table in his and Bonnie's old condo, eating a plate of cold spaghetti mixed with tomato sauce and sour cream. It dripped off her spoon as she shoveled it in her mouth. Her eyes met his knowingly. *You want me to watch your kid and now you want me to help with your new problem, and I'll do it. But there's one thing you can't have, and that's for me to stop dripping sauce on your table.*

"I know your father's whore never cooked for him," she said. In the dream the mound of pasta swelled on her plate. With every bite it increased instead of diminished. The sauce leaked into a pink river that ran off the table onto the floor. "It proves he is a fool. I let him have his affair, so why run off?"

"Ma, they're still out there." He was a thirty-year-old man, but his voice was a child's. He went to the condo's front window and pulled back the curtain.

The black BMW was parked across the street along the southern edge of Prospect Park. He recognized the big bald guy as Alexey Rinkov, a former Russian enforcer who worked for Ferretto. Beside him sat Pietro "Pitts" D'Antona, a hairy little rat boy of a gangster barely old enough to buy a beer.

The kid was itching to prove himself, and Ray knew that he would put a bullet in his baby daughter's skull without a moment's hesitation. The way he wriggled in the beamer's front seat and fondled the tie of his bad suit was like foreplay for sadism.

Ray looked back to the kitchen. His mother was listening to opera and drinking cold coffee. The sour cream had turned rancid on her plate. Fermented chunks floated in the tomato sauce and its stench filled the air.

"You think that whore took care of him?" she asked. "She took care of selling the house while he died alone."

"Ma, they're still out there. They're waiting for me to leave."

His mother found a nugget of sour cream so rancid it resembled feta cheese. She scooped it up with some sauce and put it in her mouth. When she smacked her lips, her teeth looked bloody with tomato juice.

"Ma, goddamnit, pay attention!"

Ray would have shouted at her in Italian, but she had never taught him to speak. He rarely even heard her speak the language aside from pop-Brooklyn profanity, like now, when she cried "*ah fongool*" as tomato sauce dripped on her dress. He knew that her mother had been from Milan and her father from Naples and that was all. His father talked about her background like it was exotic, in that slightly bigoted two-beers-in-the- belly middle-aged guy way—*I married a Mediterranean mermaid with black hair and green eyes.*

"Maybe you oughta pay attention," she said.

"I am, I'm tellin' you those guys are waiting. The second I leave they're comin' in."

"So what, you want me to make 'em a plate? Tell 'em, *you look skinny, you gotta eat?* What the hell's wrong with you, Raymond?"

"What's wrong with me? I'm tellin' you what's happening! I'm telling you what they're gonna do to all of us!"

"You know Raymond, your father said I never worked a day in my life. Your father said I have a problem, what would I do without him? Your father said I never made anything, I can't make anything. But I made something, I made the only thing. I made a *family.* Your father, he let these men and their whores destroy him. He let them break up our family and break up his life. Now you say they come for us. And now you say you're worried about me—now you say it! And now you're worried about your wife, and your little girl and how's it gonna feel to get shot in the face? And so here's what I say—" Her voice had become stern and real blood ran between her teeth. "What are you gonna do? What are you gonna do, Raymond? *What are you gonna do!*"

***

He was halfway across Parkside Ave when Pitts reached for his piece. He counted on the rat-boy jumping the gun like the kid's girlfriend counted on premature ejaculation.

It was Rinkov he worried about. He saw the man's eyes widen when he realized how the board was set up and the kid's imminent mistake.

He had to make the split-second decision whether to shoot or drive, but Ray knew Ferretto didn't want just him dead. He knew the man had ordered them to do his entire family and wouldn't settle for anything less. The thing had gone from deflated basketball to men shooting children in the face. That's what it looked like, but underneath it was something else, too.

It was Ferretto's rage at a deeper offense—*the failure to do what you're told.* He despised Ray's middle finger to the natural order, the gall that he might checkmate the checkmater, a baby god castrating a titan.

"Son of beech!" cried Rinkov. He decided to reach for his own gun, but Pitts was ahead of him.

That was all Ray needed. He let off three rounds from the .40 cal. The first shot off Pitts's nose, the second obliterated his face, and the third blew a hole in Rinkov's hand.

Ray opened the car's door and pushed into the passenger seat. "Keep your mouth shut and drive," he said. "We're going to see Johnny." Rinkov put his one functioning hand on the wheel and pulled into the lane as Ray shoved the kid's bloody corpse into the backseat.

"I lose the blood," said Rinkov. "It make me dizzy."

"Keep driving," said Ray, though he yanked off the kid's tie and knotted it around the wounded man's hand.

Cops and gangsters called Ferretto's ugly yellow brick buildings set back from Brighton Beach "the compound," but Ray knew the old man called it his *villa*. Either way it was a shitty parody at best. He'd gutted three old apartment buildings and made their interiors luxurious. But the exteriors he'd sloppily covered in grapevines and trellises in an abomination of an attempt to live up to the image of an old-fashioned don.

When they arrived, he saw the old man's shadow move away from the barred windows. Ferretto somehow knew he was coming, but Ray didn't care. He made Rinkov get him the shotgun from the trunk and hand over his .44 before he shot the man in the head. He let him lie on the sidewalk as he blew the lock off the gate and went inside.

But it wasn't the rush of fear from his kamikaze attack that nearly caused him to wake in a shivering sweat. Nor was it knowing that it ended with the massacre of the don's entire family by his own hands.

Instead, it was the appearance of Tolly Crespo. His friend had appeared behind Rinkov's BMW, running down the BQE at a speed bestowed by the dream. He was running with his badge dangling, wearing his untucked shirt and wide tie and ugly brown shades.

"Don't do it, Ray," he cried. "For the love of God, stop! You're gonna run right to the fire! Why you always gotta run to the fire?"

30

He was alone at first in the third dream. He was steering the *Faustina* south into the open sea. The sky was clear, but the waves were rough, hard-hitting whitecaps that tumbled and churned. An island appeared on the horizon, and he jumped forward and anchored in clear shallows where the sun shone on white sand sprinkled with sand dollars. He walked ashore with his pants rolled up and noticed he wore slacks and a collared shirt like he was headed to some type of business meeting.

Hoping it wasn't so, he looked around for something he wanted to see, maybe even Lenora waiting and wanting to be with him. *Not your kind a' scene,* he'd say, *but hey, I brought the dagger.* He smiled like a salesman and didn't check to see if he really had the blade.

Instead, he saw someone else walking along the edge of the palms. A girl in cutoffs and bikini top, her skin scarred and tattooed. He quickened his pace as the wind intensified. It grew stronger and colder as he tried to keep up with the girl who wouldn't turn and show her face.

When he finally reached her, she'd already stepped into the grass behind the dunes. Trash littered the ground around the thickets, and he followed her onto a rickety wooden bridge. The place felt more like Coney Island now, or further east toward Jones Beach. The girl's cutoffs were shredded and stained and her skin patched with bruises. Ray put his hand on her shoulder, said, "Hey!"

"Are you coming?" she asked. It was Beth. She pointed down a path that stretched beyond the bridge into the palms. Toward the end, he glimpsed a clearing and a ranch house standing within it.

"It's our house," he said. "Is your mother there?"

"Why, were you expecting her?"

"I've seen everyone else," he said.

"No, it's only me. She's done. She's somewhere else."

"Where is she?" he asked.

Before she could answer, lightning struck and obliterated the scene. Somehow he knew it was the most important of the dreams, and yet he couldn't remain. He awoke with a mid-drunk hangover and thirst only more whiskey and painkillers would quench. He rolled out of bed naked and rummaged through the duffle. In a side pocket, he found some of Bonnie's old pills and swallowed two.

With the medicine downed, he took a few more pulls from the bottle and lay back across the bed. He knew he had lost the luxury of simple dreams in the same way he had lost the knowledge that death was any kind of relief. His one purpose waited somewhere in the city's labyrinth, and yet he needed to see Beth again. *She wants to show me something*, he thought. *Something ahead in the clearing, something inside the house.*

He closed his eyes as the booze and pills mixed like a riptide in his veins. The pain diminished, and though the dreams didn't return, he managed to sleep. When he woke again, the weather was warmer, and he smelled a hint of the sea through the cracked windows. He showered and dressed and found the shoulder-holster fit well under his jacket. It wouldn't hide the pistol if he was patted down, but it was otherwise inconspicuous.

He headed downstairs and out of the hotel, made his way back to *Neptune's Lounge* where he called a car to take him to *Fazio's*. $2,800 in cash and the Crown Vic was ready to roll. Fazio usually had to come out and try to sell you ten more unnecessary repairs between repetitions of *you-and-me-we-got-a-lot-in-common.*

But Ray made sure to roll out before the old man made his appearance.

First, he went to his bank in Manhattan. Up until now, he hadn't assessed how much damage he'd done to the cashed annuity he was using to finance this trip. He and Bonnie had socked away a decent nest egg, over four hundred thousand. He still had a lot left after accepting all penalties and liquidating the funds back in Pensacola.

Now he frowned at the balance printed on his withdrawal receipt. One week in New York and he'd spent over thirty G's. *And when you've brought Ada back, when you've brought her someplace safe, what will you do?* Presumably, he would try to find Beth again. But the girl's mother had intentionally disappeared and visited him only in dreams. *Because she has known about them all along, the demons, the angels. She has known and done her best to inform her father on an as-needed basis.*

Ray crumpled the receipt and headed back to the car. Either way, whatever was left would go to his girls—if there were anything left at all.

31

The night was young with the first real taste of spring in the air. He drove back into Brooklyn over the Manhattan bridge, hooked up to the BQE, and exited in Williamsburg. He kept north, staying on Metropolitan as he made his way east toward Bushwick. At some point, he had to stop at the 91st precinct and see what he could get beyond the flimsy documents in the angel's file. But first, he needed a look at the club from another angle.

He maneuvered through the blocks he'd always thought of as Old Maspeth. It was an odd-looking neighborhood with squat brick townhouses built in the nineteen-fifties. They were the types of homes mom and pop who worked at the shop could still afford in the nineteen-seventies. They stood in the shadows of the Greenpoint gas tanks, a pair of round towers painted with red and white checks along the top that kids would joke were dogfood factories.

Nowadays the gas tanks were gone and half the townhouses were abandoned. Their windows had gone dark, and their empty frames leaked silent secrets into the night. What families remained were surrounded by hipstervilles, decaying warehouses, and the dank waters of the Newtown Creek.

A sliver of affordability like this in a city like New York would normally attract the huddled masses á la the words on the Statue of Liberty. But the lady colossus didn't shine her lamp on this particular pocket of ruin. There were other places of refuge, and this no-man's-land between Brooklyn and Queens was left like an empty place on an old map filled with drawings of monsters.

He turned south then east again on Maspeth Ave. He needed to find a block just north of *La Vela Roja* where he could see who was going in and out of the club without being seen.

The sign on his right read Slater Ave, a street that ran diagonally back the way he came. He drove halfway down and parked on its north side. He could see the club's glow and the fenced-off lot behind it. The back door was obscured by a pair of vacant townhouses, bent trees, and trash-strewn bushes along the fence. But it was only by a few feet, and if anyone stepped out, he'd have a clear view of who it was.

He checked his phone. It was just after midnight, prime time for the dancers. He saw another text from Lenora and wanted to answer, felt the sting from the blade in his boot pushing him to do it. Instead, he turned off the phone, killed the headlights, and let his eyes adjust to the night.

The streetlights cast their glow over the puddled pavement. He picked out Grand Street on the other side of the club, the downward-sloping hill that brought foot traffic from Williamsburg. To his right, he could see the gas station's lights, and along with them the HIDs on the container trucks parked in its lot.

Steady traffic rolled on and off Vanders, in and out of the lot. He settled down in his seat and kept his eyes on the club's back door. The night was dry but had turned cold, and a breeze shook the trash along the fence.

It wasn't long before both bouncers came out for a smoke. A dancer joined them, wearing a winter coat and little else. She laughed between puffs, shared out a few of her tips, then went back inside. The boys shook their heads like damn this was how they liked it, the night was ramping up, they could feel the energy in the air.

They were still smoking when he heard voices behind him

and to his left. At first, it was confusing, like the dancer who had been smoking had thrown her voice. But the dancer was gone, and the girl behind him wasn't laughing. She had a husky voice and her words slurred.

"No, where are we going?" she asked. "Let's just get a car."

"We just got out of the car," he said. "We're goin' to the club remember?"

"The what?"

"The topless place, remember? You said you wanted to do shots."

"Lesss go home and do shots. Lesss get a car."

"We just got out of the car. You said you wanted to go to the club, you said you wanted to do this."

They were moving south down Slater Ave, about a block away. The clustered townhouses and sunken pavement created an artificial valley that made their voices echo. Ray looked back at the club just in time to see the bouncers go inside.

He pulled the dagger from his boot and lay it across the dash, then drew the Glock. He kept it ready in his right hand as he alternately watched the club through the windshield and the street in his rearview mirror.

The drunken couple was closer now. He watched as they stumbled down the crooked sidewalk. The girl wore a crop top, leather jacket, and jeans, and was falling against the skinny dude in a hoodie and cowboy boots. He couldn't make out their faces, only that she had a mop of dark hair, and he seemed to be wearing thick-framed glasses.

"Really, this place is chill," he said. "I like, hungout with the bouncers one night, this guy Louie is so cool, he'll totally get us shots."

"Let's go home and get shots," she said. "Come on, Lee, lessss get a car."

"No, it'll be all right, ah, damn, take it easy."

The girl started to collapse, then caught herself and crouched on her heels. Ray thought she was going to heave, but then no, she was up again and walking. He checked the windshield again and saw there was another dancer behind the club, Lenora's friend Bobbie in a skirt and jean-jacket. She shivered as she smoked and checked her phone.

The traffic on Grand lightened a little, and the shadows cast by the withered trees deepened. He thought he saw something move up and to the left, along the club's rear roof. This was a shadow inside a shadow, barely discernable, legs skittering along the edge, and something else he couldn't make out.

Turn on the headlights, Ray thought. But if he did, he'd reveal his position. *Better to get out.* He reached for the door latch. The mirror showed the couple had reached the trash-strewn fence. The girl was walking a little better, a few dozen yards and they'd be on him.

As they neared one of the dilapidated townhouses, the hedges in the yard began to shake. Ray lowered the window and leaned out just as an immense red hand tore through the fence. Somehow it had not appeared in the rearview mirror, but when he looked back, he saw the washed-out red flesh he'd seen in the club.

Its fist alone was the size of a wrecking ball. The girl didn't have time to scream as it bashed a bloody hole in her back and rammed through her chest.

Her shoulder blades collapsed inward and her broken spine stabbed through her hip. Her ribs flew apart like splintered twigs and her organs flung out in a gristled clump. In lieu of a scream, her lungs deflated in a wheezy, whistling rush.

"Sadie!" Lee cried.

The fist opened and grabbed onto his shoulders. It spidered its fingers around his chest and crushed his torso in a meaty pinch. Its thumb pushed upward and popped off his head while the girl's body was still wrapped around its wrist.

Ray moved as if in a dream. He knocked open the door and raised the Glock 18. He fired a burst into the ball of the thing's thumb, opening a bloody wound. For a second, the whole hand turned to him, fingers rearing like red serpents. The next second, it was gone, withdrawn into the old townhouse's yard.

Ray sprinted up the sidewalk, then spun as pain exploded across his left thigh. When he turned, he faced the man he'd seen in the club with the long leather jacket and hunched back.

Except he didn't wear a jacket anymore.

Instead, strips of leathery flesh spread out from the hump on his back. They began to flap and raised him off the ground. He was holding a sword which he'd just used to cut Ray's leg. He lowered his head and flew at him again, rasping and hacking through sharp, gray teeth.

The Glock grew hot in Ray's hand as he squeezed off two more bursts. The gunfire flashed orange and lit up the flying man's body. His chest and arms looked like bones and sinews sloppily knotted together, as if he had grown out of his own flesh.

"Hell hungers," he rasped.

Ray fired again and sent his attacker spinning. The bullets stunned him, but he recovered and charged back, slashing with the sword. The Glock's mag was almost empty, and even worse, the dagger was out of reach. *If I can blow off his wing,* Ray thought, *get him on the ground.*

But there was no time to try because he could hear the red beast closing in behind him, cracking the pavement with its thunderous strides. His assailants had him boxed in, leaving only one option.

Ray fired the last of the mag, popped open the car's door, and jumped into the driver's seat. The final burst blew the flying man back over the hood, sent him screaming and spraying gray saliva and black blood as he slashed through the windshield.

Ray felt a shard of glass bite into his face as he started the car, put it in reverse, and stepped on the gas. The sudden momentum sent Leather-wings rolling off the hood. He felt the back-end slam into something solid as a stone abutment, and he heard the rear fender crunch. But he didn't look back as he shifted into drive and spun left onto Slater Ave.

Cold air rushed through the empty windshield, blew more broken shards against his face. Ray narrowed his eyes and barreled around the corner onto Grand, then cut left again onto Elmstead.

He flew past the railyard heading south, zig-zagging through Bushwick, then slowing down when he reached Broadway. He considered his bleeding thigh as he rolled past the brown fortress that was Woodhull Hospital.

But even at Woodhull, they might ask questions about the wounds and the wrecked car. Instead, he kept moving east until he reached *Neptune's Lounge*.

32

Piss-smelling old man didn't ask questions other than "What'll it be?" Ray decided the answer was *Wild Turkey*. Old pisser had only the 101, which worked just fine.

He downed two glasses then had to run out for bandages. All the big pharmacies were closed, but the bodega off Halsey had a first-aid kit, which was good enough. When he came back, he had a fresh whiskey poured. Ray shot it, then picked up the bottle and headed to the bathroom. The door wouldn't close, but that didn't matter because old pisser only cared about TV and money.

"Another drink?" he asked, eyes still on the golf.

"I'll take the bottle to go," said Ray. He finished bandaging his leg and left eighty bucks on the bar on the way out.

He stopped at the Crown Vic where it was parked on the corner, took his duffle from the trunk, and walked the half-mile further east to *The Voyager*. The wound in his thigh reopened on the way, and he had to bind it again in the hotel bathroom before crashing.

His head swam with the pain of his wounds and even more with the pain of his mistake. He should have gone to the precinct before he tried to ambush the demon. Every detective knew more than half the hunt was preparation. It was an act of impatience to think he could get lucky and off the bastard in the lot just because he'd seen him once in the club.

Ray popped two more oxies and checked his phone. Lenora had stopped calling, and he didn't blame her. He hoped he'd see her in his dreams and found himself cradling the dagger as he fell asleep.

The wound in his leg was leaking again, but the wounds Lenora had given him on her futon had healed well. He traced their scars with the blade as darkness descended.

But he didn't see Lenora in his dreams. Instead, he saw the brush-covered island, the wooden footbridge, and Beth leading him down its planks. The ranch house was waiting for them in a clearing among the trees.

"Come on," she said. "I have to show you something."

"What do you see in the sky?" he asked.

"Don't be sarcastic," she said. "If you want to have a chance, you have to come with me."

"Where are you staying?" he asked. "I can help you if you'd only come back."

His daughter stopped on the bridge. Her face was clear, but her tattoos blurred in the dream-sun's wan light. "Now who wants to play house, huh? I'm trying to help you, I'm trying to save you."

"I'll save Ada," he said. "I promise. I know now, I know what she saw in the sky."

"Please, come with me," she said, extending her hand.

"I will," he said. "I'll be there soon. I'll come as soon as I can."

He turned away from her

***

and woke to the room's shadows.

He'd slept clear through the day into the early evening. The pain killers had done their job and he hadn't had that much whiskey. He pulled a fresh pair of jeans from the duffle, re-sheathed the dagger, loaded one of his two remaining mags in the Glock, and holstered it.

He looked in the cracked mirror above the fireplace and noticed a few tears and bits of broken glass in the leather jacket. There was also a clotted cut on his forehead, but after an attack like that, he considered it more than all right and headed out to the car.

The first stop was *Fazio's*, where, with the Crown Vic in the shape it was in, there was no avoiding the proprietor. He parked in the main bay and gave as much information as he could to the mechanic before the little man emerged from the office.

"Raaaaay Barrs, I heard you was back in town." Pete Fazio stood smoking amid the disassembled cars. By the number of mechanics who were also smoking around the gas fumes, he had to at least give the guy credit for not being a hypocrite. Ray was hoping he had arrived late enough that there was a chance that Fazio was already out at one of his upscale Queens versions of *Neptune's Lounge*, but there was no such luck.

The man's cheap sport coat hung over his shoulders, though his arms weren't through the sleeves. He'd say the guy was going for gangster wanna-be, except that the jacket was beige with faint plaid stripes. "Holy shit, whachya do ta this baby? You was just in here with this thing! Goddamn back-end looks like you was reamed by a bulldozah!"

Fazio stood grinning. The gray curls on his head matched the ones sticking out of his open shirt, half the latter choked off by three gold chains. "Shit, you got a scar, too. You got into some shit already?"

"It's just the windshield and the back-end," said Ray. "Doesn't need to look pretty."

"Listen, Ray, what are you doin' back up here? You a narc again?"

"I'm retired."

"It's okay, man, shit, you can tell me."

"Not working, really, just up here on a personal matter."

"It's the Basher, isn't it? They want you to help with that

guy who's been bashin' the shit outta the kids and the dancuhs."

"Pete, I'm retired. I appreciate the help with the car."

"You ask me, let 'im bash a few more. Most a' these entitled little shits got it comin', know what I mean?"

"He killed a grandmother in Williamsburg and father of two who worked in a bakery."

"Oh, so you is workin' the case! Holy-o-shit, wait'll I tell the boys!"

Ray stepped close to Fazio. He didn't touch him, but because of the man's small stature, the fist he held clenched at his side was inches from his face. "You won't say a fuckin' thing to anybody," he whispered.

Fazio's smile vanished. "Jesus, Ray, all right, settle down."

The little man looked around nervously to see if his crew had heard, but they carried on with their work and their smoking.

"I need another car," said Ray. "Hook me up, and we'll leave it alone."

At this, Fazio regained half his smile. He nodded and took Ray into the back lot where they looked over a five-year-old Charger (he already had one cop car), a Cooper Mini (snazzy if you're on the way to the golf course), and finally settled on an ancient Plymouth Acclaim, which ran like a tank and had no chance of being stolen.

"Fuhgettabout it," Fazio said when Ray tried to pay him. He was trying to make good after his previous obnoxiousness, but Ray knew it would be on the bill when he came back to pick up the Vic.

33

With the duffle in the trunk of the Plymouth, he headed south on the BQE. It was time to pay a visit to the 91st. He should have done it on his first day in town and realized now that he'd been putting it off. *How many years had it been?*

They'd chained him to the desk while the lawyers sorted out the mess with Ferretto's family. Six months he lasted before they arranged his transfer and threw him the going away party for Pensacola.

He felt like goddamn Macbeth when they cut the cherry-drizzled red velvet cake that was a not-so-subtle reference to what he'd done to Ferretto, his crew, and, as it went down in the mythological version, his entire family. Nevermind Johnny held up his grandson as a human shield, and Barbara, the college-age niece, held him off with a long rifle from behind the balcony doors, and he only found out who'd had him pinned down after he shot her.

In the end, he was just lucky rat-boy Pitts D'Antona drew his pistol first. The coterie of lawyers was looking for something to work with, and that was the seed. His reputation also stayed solid with the older cops and on the street. But walking into the precinct now was another matter.

After pulling off the expressway onto Metropolitan, he took a right onto Union Ave and rolled down the last three blocks. A newer, hipper version of *Checkers Diner* was still there, but the old brownstones and warehouses were gone. In their place stood high rise condos, trendy vegan and sushi restaurants, and even a hotel.

The building that housed the bar across from the station still stood, but now it was a pet supply store. He remembered the poker games in the back room where the owner Mikey would set off a siren when someone took a big pot. The dealer would howl "*9-1-1 in the 9-1!*" He couldn't remember the girl's name, it had been damn near twenty years, and he was worried no one at the station would remember his name, either.

I could ask for Van Meeks, he thought, as he parked the grandma car and did the last half-block on foot. It was possible Captain Dooley was still there, too. But he didn't want to talk to Callaghan. If he saw any sign of the kid and his old pal Crespo, he'd cut out quick.

He walked up the ramp to the precinct's glass doors. Like most police stations, anyone from the public could just walk in. The fact that was becoming increasingly surprising spoke to the progressing insanity of the times.

He didn't recognize either of the officers at the desk. One was a young guy who vanished the second he came in. The other was a muscular woman who neither smiled nor frowned, but raised her eyebrows skeptically as she asked, "Can I help you?"

"Yes, my name's Ray Barrs," he said. "I'm here to see Detective Charles Van Meeks?"

"Is he expecting you?" she asked.

"No, but I'm an old associate of his."

Ray hoped she wouldn't recognize his name, but Van Meeks would. Instead, she said, "Detective Van Meeks isn't here right now. Would you like me to give him a message?"

She gave a Ray another once over, her eyes stopping where the holster hung under his jacket and again where the dagger's sheath pressed against his jeans. She was one-hundred percent on top of his bullshit and kept her hands low in case she needed her weapon. She already had the attention of the two uniformed cops in the office behind her.

Ray couldn't blame her. Anyone who thought the front desk of a police station was a cushy job was a fool. From idiots who turned in bombs by tossing them into the lobby to nutcases who walked in pointing at bumps on their bare dicks because they thought it was the ER, it was a gig that nurtured a life-saving sense of paranoia.

It was also a great place to make arrests, particularly when somebody came to bail out their cousin and forgot they had a warrant. Ray knew they took him for one of these cases. But it was better than being recognized by the whole crew over Ferretto. He was running short on the ability to stall when he saw a guy with an untucked shirt stand up behind a desk.

"Hey, Tisch, is that you?" Ray asked.

Benny Tischer's eyes widened and his stubble-crusted jaw dropped. Ray had never seen the mountainous man move so quickly as he pushed past clustered desks and around into the lobby.

"Ray! Jesus man, what's goin' on! You look awesome, dude! Love the hair!"

Ray noticed the desk attendant was still staring, but the two beat cops had lost interest and moved back into the office.

"Thanks, man. I was just dropping in to see Charlie," he said.

"Ah, Charlie's not here now, man. You know, with all the stuff that's been goin' on."

Tischer's head snaked forward and nodded as he spoke. He stank of cigarettes, coffee, and fast food.

"Hey, you hungry?" asked Ray. "I was thinkin' of trying that Thai place up on Metropolitan. Wanna come with?"

Tischer blinked and his jaw dropped again. His stubbly moon of a face was beaming. "Are you serious? I mean, yeah, let's grab dinner." He shook his head and tried to compose himself.

"Cool," said Ray. "Let's go."

"Right," said Tischer. He cast a glance back to the officer at the desk. "Hey, uh, Deena, I'm gonna get some dinner. You know, with my old colleague, Ray. You know him, right?"

Deena kept her poker face and said nothing. Ray admired the fact she still kept her hands low and ready and was accepting no bullshit until he came up with a better reason to be there or left.

"Anyway, I'm gonna knock off a little early," he said, and without giving her time to answer, followed Ray out. "Ya know, I've actually been to this place before," he went on. "Fucking awesome panang chicken, dude. Whoa, Ray, dude, fucking awesome to see you!"

Ray nodded as they made their way north on Union Ave. The big man's belly bounced and jiggled. It might have been forty-two degrees without the wind chill, but Tisch wore no jacket. Just an old t-shirt and his gaudy gold, bottom of the line Rolex.

Ray noticed the t-shirt he originally thought was just sweat-stained and dirty actually had a faint black and white image of a shirtless Arnold Schwarzenegger holding a sword. Something from an old *Conan* movie, Ray gathered. The caption was faded to illegibility, said something about seeing enemies driven before you and hearing the lamentations of women. *You can say that again*, thought Ray, as Tischer let out a pre-dinner belch.

"Holy deep cover Batman, is this your ride? This thing takes the cake."

Ray nodded as he climbed into the Acclaim and reached across to unlock the passenger door. "Hop in," he said.

34

They drove north past *Checkers Diner*, then turned right onto Metropolitan. Two more blocks east and they parked in front of *Curry & Qi.*

If Tuesday was supposed to be a quiet night, you'd never know. The little restaurant tucked into the windowy first floor of an old townhouse was bustling. Clutches of mostly twenty and thirty-somethings crowded around small square tables sipping cucumber martinis. Steam rolled off hot bowls of curry, and water trickled through a fountain at the base of a pagoda. It stood against a wall where mom's old flower-patterned wallpaper peeked out of the edges of the paint job like the ghost of spaghetti dinners past.

Tischer studied the menu while they waited for a table. It was the first time he closed his mouth since they left the precinct. Ray remembered Tisch when he first started as a sprightly civilian IT guy at the 91st back in the early aughts. There had been a little Renaissance for nerds during the Internet's youth where it was okay to wear a band t-shirt or carry a skateboard to work if you could code, network, or even format.

Most cops didn't give a shit as long as their laptops booted and their reports printed. Ray had always been congenial with the techs. It could pay dividends to be on their good side, as long as you managed to keep the right professional distance.

He spotted Tischer early as a nerdy, holster-sniffing street expert who was mostly harmless. But that was the thing about those types, they always came off that way at first.

There was the young hottie version, the type who just kept appearing by coincidence until you succumbed to an illicit tryst. They usually just wanted to ruin your marriage, spend your overtime, and if they hit the jackpot, get on your benefits, and touch your gun.

There were male and female varieties, gay and straight, and no cop was immune. There was Henrietta Parker, a detective from Staten Island who'd lost her husband and custody of her kids because she'd fallen for a nineteen-year-old weed-dealing informant. She was a friend of Crespo's, and Ray remembered sitting with her when she had her head down on the bar the day after her suspension. All she said was, "Good God could he screw."

He also knew a beat cop who befriended a knockout of a bartender who "just needed a ride home one night." Two weeks later, he was busted for holding her cocaine. Ray never found out if the kid did time, but he never saw him wearing blue again, either.

But the starry-eyed, true crime fans like Tischer, the LEO wannabe street experts, they were another variety altogether. They were pretty much always male and spent a lot of time on the Internet and watching movies and TV. The smarter ones read a lot, too. Often they lived in their moms' basements, but not always. For some, it was a more complex obsession. A sure shibboleth you'd come across one was the mention of serial killers early in the acquaintance. The mechanic who asked you if you were working such and such a case, who said, "Ya know, he did her in just like the Green River Killer." That was a good sign you had this type of holster-dog on your hands. And the other problem was that, like hypochondriacs, they weren't always wrong. It was a 'cry wolf" effect, mostly bullshit, except when there really was a wolf.

Benny Tischer had a lot of this type in him. Ray learned through office gossip that he'd grown up in Ridgewood, Queens, not far from the no-man's-land portion of east Maspeth where the demon was doing his damage. His father was a criminal lawyer whose practice never got off the ground. He kept their house perpetually mortgaged until he died of a heart attack, then his mother finished off their funds.

He let it be known that she died not long after, so Benny moved to Brooklyn to make a career in IT during the dot-com bubble. He managed to get himself the proverbial "real job" and presumably an apartment. But over the years, Ray watched him stagnate, never really getting any of his sometimes-mentioned web businesses up and running. He liked to ask Ray about the rules concerning when he was allowed to use his weapon and was nearly ecstatic that he'd been in the precinct the day Ray had to fire a shot during the bank heist.

It wasn't long after that he'd had a water-cooler conversation with Tischer where he put the brakes on his escalation toward the inappropriate.

"Hey, I was talking with this dude on my blog," said Tisch. "He was saying we used excessive force, and the perp was unstable and shit, so I'm gonna feature a whole entry on why it was necessary to take him down."

"Don't mention anything about what happened on your blog," Ray said. "Never talk about the precinct or anything related. You'll lose your job. At best."

He had to hand it to Tischer—after that, he shut up. What's more, he started doing better work for Ray. He had his computer humming and showed him new ways to format and search documents.

The guy obviously wanted to keep himself in cheeseburgers and rent money. But there was also something else, something Ray detected in his intelligence that was unnerving but also dangerously useful. Tischer was competitive. Half lost in fantasy as he was, he was more than a stopped clock right twice a day or the boy who cried wolf. He was the Cyrano de Bergerac of true crime, a skilled and poetic mess who could make things happen.

"Of course, the DA has a hardon for the *Basher*," said

Tischer. "But the precinct's pushing him away like some stalker ex-boyfriend." He stopped to swallow a fried spring roll whole, then continued: "The chief carries on like it's business as usual, meets with the Hassidim about hate crimes, reminds people to lock their cars, brings in the leaders of the Latin community to talk about building codes and school safety. Most of the men, most of the community leaders, they don't want to talk about a killer on the loose at meetings. They wait and go off behind closed doors about what they're gonna do to the bastard. They got guns, legal or not, and this and that. It's the moms who bring it up at the meetings, call shit out, and come at us on the web."

Ray smiled and sipped his soup. *Sure thing, Tisch. Us.* "Who's in charge of the investigation?"

"You know, Van Meeks."

"Who else is on it?"

"Mostly just you and Crespo, consulting."

So Crespo had been there and told him some bullshit. He had Callaghan helping him out. But what exactly were they up to?

Tischer paused, confused why he would ask.

"It's all right," said Ray. "I'm not surprised Crespo let you in. Just, it's technically confidential. I had to make sure you knew."

Tischer gave a thrilled smile. He nodded and winked, then stuffed three heaping spoonfuls of panang chicken in his mouth.

"That's why I'm glad I ran into you," Ray went on. "I was there looking for Charlie, but I think you can help just as well."

"That's what I'm here for," said Tischer.

"So I have some documents, mostly photos and stuff from media contacts," said Ray. He held up the folder the angel had given him, flashed it without opening it. "I'm not sure who's ahead right now, I just thought I'd reach out to Charlie and see what he's got. You know, in light of recent events."

"Yeah, dude can you believe that shit? Fucking gruesome, he tore that chick up on the street in front of the dude, like, ritualistic man, except right out in the open, then ripped off the damn dude's head!" Tischer let his inner fanboy out again. That was part of the fun, except with him that was also part of a more twisted game, and possibly another profession altogether.

"So first I need the actual police reports for the murders," said Ray. "If we can swing back by the precinct and get a look at those, that's a good start. Then we can meet again tomorrow and go over them. You can tell me if you've heard of anything they mighta left out."

Tischer looked at him askance. Something was wrong. "I don't know if that'll help," he said. "Van Meeks redacted the shit out of those. I mean you know that, right? I mean, I assumed you guys did, you and Crespo. He shredded the hardcopies and wouldn't let me touch the PDFs. Kinda pissed me off." Tischer looked to the side, eyebrows raised as if his pride had been wounded. "He made me walk him through the redactions and then the security settings, over and over. He triple-checked that the blacked-out text was irrecoverable, *nada, fini*. I mean come on man, you want that guarantee, you should let the expert do it himself!"

That requires trusting said expert, thought Ray. But Charles Van Meeks, for all his aloofness, was too smart for that. Ray didn't know the man well, but it was a running joke at the 91st how far west the guy lived in Jersey and how he was like an alien in Brooklyn. As a detective, he was almost more lawyer than cop, by the book and methodical. Rumor had it he was an expert shot and had seen action in the military. But above all, the DA trusted him, and that was why he was the go-to man in the unfolding catastrophe.

"Really, you want something done right, know it well enough not to need a walk-through," said Tischer. "That's rookie stuff, right?"

"Sure," said Ray. "Just wondering where that leaves us with the reports."

Tischer was done gorging himself, and now sipped his jasmine tea and stared blankly into space. He had him. He had forgotten to wonder why Ray wouldn't know this or that, had gone beyond into a place related to his pride, a challenge, and most importantly, curiosity.

"I don't know, man," said Tischer. "I don't think I can get the unredacted reports. I mean, if he actually did it right, that text is *gone*." He stared again, sadly this time, as if he'd spoken of drowned children. Then his eyes flicked back. "I can get you something else, though."

Ray stopped the waitress as she passed the table. "Could I get the check?" he asked. He turned back to Tischer and said, "Go ahead."

"You gotta come over to my place," said Tischer. "It's over in Bushwick, by Woodhull Hospital. I can't talk about it here." As he spoke, his eyes flicked back and forth in case the denim-clad hipsters at the next table were agents in disguise. He leaned in close and whispered, "I have some stuff on my hard drive you should see."

35

They drove out Metropolitan, hooked a right on Leonard, then took a left on Broadway. Woodhull Hospital rose in front of them, a cruel stone structure the color of rusted iron. It looked more like a factory than a hospital, a relic that survived the collapse of industry in the late Twentieth Century. Now it stood like a vengeful golem sandwiched between gentrification and rot, awaiting the call to some obscure and darker purpose.

"Hang a right here," said Tischer.

Ray turned right on Park, drove a few blocks south, then parked in front of a low brick building with boarded-over windows.

"You live here?" he asked.

"Yeah," said Tisch. "Kinda raw, but it's cheap."

As they approached the stairs that led down to Tischer's door, Ray noticed Hebrew letters stenciled on the sidewalk, spread intermittently along the western side of the street. On the eastern side, kids in hoodies huddled around the stoops of old brownstones.

A Hassidic rabbi and his family walked by, wrapped in black. Ray noticed they made a wide berth of Tischer and his building, and neither they nor the hip-hop kids looked his way. It appeared the sprightly IT kid from the dot-com days had gained a certain type of notoriety.

As they drew closer to the stairs, they were approached by

a woman in a torn winter jacket. She turned abruptly when she realized Tischer was with Ray. Her jeans looked worn as well, and with her matted curly hair and bare chest showing through her unbuttoned shirt, she had all the trappings of a prostitute.

She turned and went back across the street and crouched by the gate of an abandoned building. That's when Ray noticed someone else, a slender Hassid in a wide-brimmed hat standing on the far corner. He was staring at them as they walked, and didn't look away when Ray looked back.

"Come on," said Tischer as he headed down the stairs.

Ray followed him down the crumbling steps. He looked back once more for the Hassid, but the man was gone.

The word *antiloft* popped into Ray's head as they entered the musty basement apartment. The place consisted of one large open room with steel support beams, exposed brick, and a damp cement floor. There were a few mold-spattered sheetrock partitions that rose not quite to the ceiling. He saw the bottom of a toilet behind a pair of curtains. There was an electric stove plugged into the wall and presumably a shower somewhere.

But the raw space was offset by jumbled passages of new-looking computer towers, monitors, TV screens, and circuit boards in various states of assembly. The labyrinth culminated in a desk set with three screens, two keyboards, and rack-mounted gadgets that looked like sound and video editing gear. It stood opposite a king-size bed with a four-poster canopy, like a sacrificial altar to the god of silicon.

"Have a seat," said Tischer, rolling him a swivel chair. He slid up a leather hassock for himself. "Would you like some rock-cocaine?" He held up a chunk of crack pinched between his thumb and forefinger. Ray shook his head. Tischer shrugged, pulled out a glass pipe, and lit it up.

The fumes assaulted Ray's nose, an awful blend of burnt plastic and sizzling hair. He'd detected the smell when he first came in (though only barely, somewhere beneath the socks, armpits, and pizza grease), and now it was confirmed. "So what did you want to show me?"

Tischer took a smooth drag from the pipe and then accepted the bottle of *Evan Williams* Ray offered. He pulled on the whiskey, then touched one of the monitors.

"First I'll show you the reports," said Tischer.

"I thought you didn't have the reports," said Ray.

"Not the police reports from the 91st. These are from the CRU, half a dozen batches over the last ten years."

"*Ten years?* You're telling me the Conviction Review Unit's looking at stuff they think's related from ten years ago?"

"Yeah, they came and gave it to Van Meeks, told him to have a look. Except Charlie couldn't have a look because he couldn't get the damn data vault open. So guess who he calls?"

"Grandmaster Tisch?"

"The one and only!" Tisch smiled into his puffy stubble. The gnarled hair still contained some curry. "He calls me and I crack that thing open like a soft-boiled egg. Coulda called the DA's office for the password, but for some reason, he wanted to avoid those guys at all costs. Well, the cost was copying the contents to my back up drive. A few hundred unredacted PDFs for old Tisch. Come to papa."

Tischer puffed his pipe and pulled on the whiskey again. He was opening folders by touching the screen, lining up PDFs and video files, but not opening them yet.

"So they locked up a guy named Jimmy Wilson for murder," he went on. "He was a petty dealer in Jansen Projects. Only Wilson swore he was innocent with like, biblical proportions. He went on about how he'd pay his soul's debt, he'd go down, that's fine, but he wouldn't make a deal, wouldn't plead guilty, because he didn't commit the murders, *no man did.*"

Ray took the bottle back and had his own pull on the whiskey. The trip to Tischer's sulfurous apartment was beginning to pay off just a little, like uncovering the first coin symbol on a cheap scratch off.

"Anyway, these pro bono bleeding hearts and community groups all show up wanting to get him off. They get detectives involved, nobody from the 91st, Jansen is too far east. But the cops start knocking on doors around the projects. Of course, nobody wants to talk to them, that's a given. But this time they're downright aggressive about it. One lady got a hold of a cop's cell phone and just blew it up with these weird texts, saying he was cursed, and he brought Hell with him, there was fire where he walked. She said he was a dead man and all this shit about the roaches and flies of Abaddon. She said she had protections on her apartment. She said if he came around again, he would stay cursed forever."

At this Ray looked past the canopied bed and into the basement's shadows. He saw Ada staring back at him from under her mussed hair. She mouthed A-bad-don and held his eyes until he looked away.

"So they go back to Wilson and he tells them about an old customer of his, a fuck-up lawyer named Edwin Lobe. He said Lobe used to come around with another dealer, a guy named Chrissy Blood who wanted PCP. He said he hung out and partied with them and found out how nasty Lobe really was."

Tischer paused and put down the pipe, but snatched another pull of the whiskey. "See now, my dad was a lawyer, too, a *failed* lawyer. He mortgaged himself through law school and never made back the money. He was a crumb-snatcher and he was impotent with my mother. If I didn't have his nose, I'd think my real pops was the mailman. Our place over in Ridgewood was a grimy parody of *All in the Family*, only at least Archie Bunker had balls. But Lobe, he was another breed of asshole altogether. He worked Wall Street gigs making over five-hundred G's his first year out of law school. Bond offerings and shit like that. He was in line to be one of the youngest partners at his white-shoe firm.'

"Only he was a greedy little fucker and he liked to party. He made off-color jokes at the office and was mean to the assistants. Some women at the firm complained about him, and when they brought him into human resources he said, 'Why would I harass anyone here when I can just pay for it?'

"But it wasn't the bigotry that brought him down. He had a buddy who happened to work IT at an I-bank. They put together a scam where IT-guy leaked tips on IPO's, Lobe bought up the stock, and they split the cash when it went up and he sold. It was in the papers for a hot minute back in the aughts. Sad when one of your own does something like that. I take it personally when a colleague brings shame on the profession."

Tischer gave him another curry-fabulous grin. Not only was he an IT and law enforcement professional, but a wizard of irony.

"So they got busted and turned on each other. IT-guy got sentenced to ten years but died before he served any time. He fell off a roof while he was out on bail. They called it a suicide, but we know better. Anyway, Lobe avoided prison, but they cleaned him out. He lost all of his assets and got disbarred. Lobe's family was broke to begin with, he was a self-made kid from out west who'd come to the big city, so he had no help there. Instead, he found himself a shithole in Queens and began living bottle to bottle. On the surface, he freelanced as a proofreader to pay his rent and buy his booze and other treats. But Lobe still had his brain and despite the habits began to rack up cash. Some say he figured out a blackjack scam, bussed out to Jersey casinos, moved it around so he kept under the radar. Others said he did some kind of 'under the table' legal advising for the Russian mob.

"That was about when he started hanging out with Chrissy Blood and this other guy. The reports say the other guy was some kind of cop, not a beat-cop or even a detective, but some kind of brass with a double-life. He was the only one the CRU didn't name in the reports they gave Van Meeks.

"Enter the *Basher*. According to Wilson, it was the three of them who were behind the murders in the projects. He didn't say they actually did it, ya see. He said they *summoned a murderous spirit*. The three of them, the failed lawyer, the crooked cop, and the petty dealer. Sounds like a joke. But Wilson said they had like, a *mini-cult*. He said they worshipped the Devil, that they needed sacrifices to appease the Devil's minions. He said the princes of Hell rewarded them with money and strength in exchange for souls. Do you believe this shit?"

Ray considered pointing at the dead girl watching them from the corner of the room. He considered pointing at her and telling him that she had more than one body, that the image was the reflection of a child laboring in the cold clouds of Heaven.

Instead, he said, "Not sure. Go on."

Tischer nodded. He didn't give the grin this time as he touched the screen and brought up one of the CRU reports. "This is where Wilson talks about the cult. But there's something else in it. Further down they mention "Officer X" and the name comes up a lot. But it's not about the murders around the projects they pinned on Wilson. It's about the Sligo Beach murders."

For the first time since they'd arrived in the basement, Ray felt cold. The Sligo Beach murders had stumped the NYPD for more than a decade. They were named after a little strip of shore on Long Island called Sligo Beach. A dozen bodies and parts of bodies had been found there among the brackish dunes. Most of the victims were Internet prostitutes. More disturbing than what they found were the number of missing persons considered to be possible victims.

"They always thought a cop might be involved," said Tischer. "They were looking closely at Officer-X, and seeing a connection with the Jansen case. But like, the real connection is the way the victims were killed. I don't have the autopsy reports, but they talk about the autopsies in these. See, the bodies had slash wounds on their fronts, on their faces, and on their torsos. One girl living in a loft off Throop was eviscerated in one stroke. That's why they pinned it on Wilson, said he used his Bowie knife.

"But the cuts weren't what killed them. It was massive trauma from being either ripped apart or crushed.

"Wilson was only convicted of one murder," said Ray. "A drug dealer, a beef over turf."

"That's what they got him on, but they let the investigations on the college kid and the prostitute go cold. They insinuated it was Wilson even though they didn't have the evidence. They told the families they had their man. But they were still looking into the cult, and they still are. When they were first looking into Officer-X, they questioned Lobe. But guess what? Lobe could afford an attorney by then. Lobe had purchased an off-the-beaten track gentlemen's club called *La Vela Roja*. Heard of it?"

The grin was back, though now it was a madman's grin, the kind a cannibal made to his last remaining comrade on a lifeboat.

"Yeah, I've heard of it," said Ray.

"Lobe's lawyer gave the detectives an expensive version of 'don't come around my apartment no more,' just like the residents of Jansen Projects. He wouldn't talk to them and didn't have to. But they weren't giving up because they had footage. They had a little archive of surveillance video they'd cobbled together from security cameras on businesses around the neighborhood, even a body cam from a cop who responded to a call and almost caught the perps in the act.

"One of the videos had a guy in a ski mask they think was Lobe, and get this, he was swinging a four-foot sword. It was the college girl's murder, Sandra Minnowski. A furniture store camera caught it from across the street. A dude stepped up in this leather duster, mask on his head, and cut her belly to chin. She took one staggering step, and that's when it hit her from behind."

"What hit her?"

"Nothing. That's just it. Nothing hit her!" Tischer laughed giddily. He was all out of food, drugs, and booze, and now leeched off his own mania. "Her spine snapped like something plowed into her from behind. But on the video, there's nothing there!"

Ray watched as Tischer opened a folder full of videos, found the one he was looking for, and played it. The store's camera was poor quality and the screen filled with fuzzy images.

He saw a girl moving up the sidewalk of a street he didn't recognize. By the elevated train track ahead of her, it looked like she was headed north toward Broadway. A tall, slender figure walked opposite, head down so the ski mask looked like a knit cap.

When they got closer, the figure stepped to the side and blocked her path. The girl stopped and spoke. Her mouth moved but the video had no sound.

When the figure didn't react, she slid her backpack off her shoulder like she would drop it and run. The figure looked about the right size to be Lobe, and Ray noted that his back wasn't hunched. *Because he didn't have the fucking wings yet.*

Lobe's jacket opened. Ray recognized the sword with the lugs and the wide crossbar. The blade slashed up and across the girl's jacket. She reeled back, mouth open in a silent scream.

It was still open when her spine was knocked inward, and her body bent in half. Her knees hit the pavement first, then her chest and her face.

For a second, she was still. Then her head rose from the ground and floated upward, serpent-like, bringing her torso up with it despite her broken back. Blood gushed from her neck when it was ripped free.

Now it really did float above the sidewalk, gibbering and bleeding. After a few seconds its jaw stopped moving and it fell to the ground as if it were dropped.

"See, nothing," said Tischer.

"It was something," said Ray. "We just didn't see it."

A rap on the window interrupted them. Ray looked up and saw the woman in the tattered jacket peering through the narrow sliver of glass. She pointed at Tischer's bed and smiled.

"Looks like Odette's in the mood for a smoke," said Tischer. He waved at the window and said, "I'm busy, come back later."

The woman grimaced but didn't move.

"I said later!" Tischer hollered, and the girl scowled and trudged off.

Great, sex with drug addicts, thought Ray. He wondered if it was a fetish for Tisch, or just a convenience.

"So what do you think?" Tischer asked.

"I think it's foul and kinda mean," said Ray.

Tischer looked confused then chuckled. "Not the crack-lady, the video. What do you think hit her?"

Ray could have told him about the red hand that reached from the filthy hedges. He could have described how it broke the drunk girl's back and clawed through her boyfriend. He could have said the MO was a perfect match and made Tischer feel like he was in a TV show.

But the longer he stayed with the aging IT troll, the more disgusted he became. He had good information, but he needed to see more of the videos. He wanted to understand why the demon didn't show up on the recording and also why it hadn't appeared in his rearview mirror. Before he could hunt it, he had to figure out how to see it.

"Tisch, this is perfect," said Ray. "Can we look at a few others? Or, um, if you're gonna be occupied, maybe just make me a copy?"

Tischer gave him a quizzical look. He was sizing him up, knowing Ray was playing him, but wondering how much.

"Look," said Ray. "You really helped me out, but I gotta keep it on the DL. I can't bring you in on the investigation, not officially. But if I can go over this, we can talk again."

Tischer looked up at the grimy little window, then back at the computer screen. "Well," he said, "you know I wanna help, but that was really the only video that has the whole attack. The rest are bits and pieces."

"Bits and pieces build an investigation," said Ray.

But Tischer was looking at him askance. "I think that's really all I got. Don't know why the killer doesn't show. Military stealth fabric seems farfetched, but maybe because one of the unsubs could be police, maybe they could get their hands on something. But they're also interested in this other interview with Wilson where he totally goes off."

"What interview is that?"

Tischer fingered through the folders on the screen, drilled down to a zip file that needed a password to open. "This here," he said, pointing at a PDF titled *Son of Magog*. He opened it and read from the interview—"When asked what he meant by 'crazy stuff' Wilson said, 'the crazy stuff they said when they got high. They said they summoned the *Son of Magog*. They said the demon strikes from behind, he breaks the souls of men by breaking their spines. No man sees the *Son of Magog* but as a flash in the corner of his eye. He is a reflection of the Devil himself. To resist him is to look in a mirror and see damnation. To summon him is certain death for any man who yet harbors even the faintest doubt in his love for destruction. But he will reward his true appeasers. He will let them suckle the teats of infernal power in exchange for the chance to murder the sons and daughters of men and drag their souls to Hell.'"

Tischer finished, pulled a tissue from the box on the desk, and finally wiped the curry from his chin. He closed the folders containing the CRU's files, pulled out the hard drive, and put it on the desk between himself and Ray.

"All right," said Ray. "I got it." He opened his wallet and counted out ten hundred-dollar bills. "A thousand is my first and final offer."

Tischer nodded and took the money. Ray took the hard drive.

"Let me know if you ever wanna get dinner again," said Tischer. He was following Ray as he made his way up the basement stairs. When they reached the street, Odette was waiting for them. "See you round," said Tischer as he took her by the hand and led her back down the basement steps.

36

He kept the radio off as he drove back to *The Voyager*. He'd left the bottle of Evan at Tischer's, but he didn't feel like stopping at *Neptune's Lounge*. Instead, he just pulled over to one of the cloudy-windowed liquor stores and bought a couple of fifths of bourbon. The late afternoon sun brushed its warmth against the brownstones like a clumsy passer-by. By the time he reached the Plymouth, the icy breeze was blowing again.

A few more miles east and he was back at the hotel. He put the duffle at the foot of the bed, but didn't pull out the laptop. Instead, he lay back on the mattress and drank whiskey. Tischer had taken a lot out of him, a lot more than he wanted to admit. He gulped down half a fifth of bourbon, found a baseball game on the fuzzy TV, and let himself drift.

He became aware he was clawing at sand as the waves pushed him on. They kept hammering at him as he fought to bring himself up, fought just to breathe.

He saw the dunes and the grass ahead of him, and the bridge through the brackish swamp. As he began walking toward it, he heard a motor from the direction of the waves. When he turned, he saw Crespo on the *Faustina*. His partner just tilted his head, as if to say, "Come on." Ray turned around and waded back out to the boat.

Once onboard, the island vanished. They'd moved out to sea and trolled for sailfish. Ray hooked something, something long that rolled among the whitecaps. He saw fins and spines, but they weren't the majestic blue-gray he expected. They were a muddy brown, translucent and oily. The fin-thing rolled, and he yanked at the rod and cranked the reel.

"You're horsing it," barked Crespo.

He was grinning into his handlebar mustache as he sipped a beer. His Hawaiian shirt was unbuttoned, showing gold hair on his tanned chest.

"Goddamnit," Ray hissed.

He pulled at the rolling fish. It made a little leap, sad and crooked. Its nose was not the sleek, sword-like spike of a sailfish, but a set of long, serrated mandibles. Its fins looked barbed and insect-like, and its side tore open and he saw Ada's half-jellied corpse in its gut.

"Goddamn it!" Ray hollered. He cranked the reel harder, hauled back on the rod.

"Come on now," said Crespo, "You're horsing it. Take it easy, have a beer."

His friend was poking his elbow with a freezing can. Ray lost his grip on the rod, regained it, then lost it again. "Damnit, damnit, damnit…"

He awoke to a snowy newscast on the TV. He made out police cars and yellow tape and a reporter talking mutely into a mic. He turned the thing off, searched the duffle for the last of Beth's oxies, and swallowed all three.

Telling himself he was recharging, he stayed down through another wave of light and darkness. He needed to figure out how to flush out Lobe and the demon and take them both down at once. Tischer had given him something useful in revealing the thing's tactics. *But if it always attacks from behind, and casts no reflection, how are you going to see it?*

On the second afternoon, he woke up to empty bottles and went on another liquor store run. He came back and parked on the side street as usual, and when he came around onto Broadway, he saw Lenora standing in front of the hotel. She was smoking with the desk guy, chatting in Spanish beneath the entry's dingy green canopy.

"You never answer me," she said.

"Only saw one text," he replied.

Her black hoodie obscured her face so she looked like just another neighborhood kid hanging on the sidewalk. The desk clerk finished his cigarette and went inside. Lenora lowered her hood, setting free her long black hair. He tasted smoke as they kissed and their cold hands touched, fingers caressing each other's wrists.

"So this is where you're staying?" she asked.

"Yeah," he said. "We can go to your place."

She shook her head and led him inside.

***

The shadows in his room blended with the gray carpet and walls. Bars of sunlight barely penetrated the window. They knelt on the bed and resumed their kissing. He moved to her neck and felt her pulse against his lips. When she kissed his wrist, she bit at his flesh, stopping just before she pierced his skin.

"Pull it out," she said.

Ray nodded and reached down. He drew the dagger and thrust it at the same time, stopping millimeters from her face.

Lenora leaned in and licked the edge. Her reflection blurred in the blade, and a line of blood appeared on her tongue. They kissed again so they could taste it as it flowed.

She took off her leather jacket and undid her blouse. Her dark nipples winked behind the locks of her hair. She took the dagger out of his hand and sat back, caressing her ribs and stomach with it while he undressed.

When he was fully naked, she leaned against the headboard and let him kiss her breasts and stomach. As he worked his way down, she traced the blade across his back, cross-hatching the old scars with new cuts.

"Can you feel it?" she whispered.

She was talking about the pain, but something else, too.

Something that was making him feel clearer and stronger. Like a fever that brought energy instead of fatigue. He let the blood run down his back and kissed her lips again.

"Fuck yes," she said, and the blade bit deeper.

Ray felt his muscles tense as he returned to her nipples, breasts, ribs, and stomach. He could still taste the blood on his tongue as it mixed with her sweat. She worked the dagger deeper into his back, stabbing him slowly. She cut through muscles and veins, nearing organs.

He moved lower and lower, beneath her pelvis and into her unzipped jeans. She wriggled backwards and stabbed deeper. They hesitated, their bodies slow explosions of sweat and blood and their hearts lit fuses.

Their eyes turned all a blur as the room filled with darkness. They began to moan and sigh and screech and snarl, and their voices echoed in their bones, and their blood rushed like rivers colliding, filling every void and crushing every inward dam. The world fell away beneath the immense current of pain that was also strength, clarity, and scintillating assurance.

37

They awoke in a pool of blood. A pair of speed junkies were fighting in the next room, screaming and thumping and crying.

Lenora lit a cigarette. "So where'd you get that thing again?"

"A friend gave it to me," he said.

"What friend?" she asked.

"What's it matter?" he asked back.

She shrugged. "It's valuable," she said. "You ride around Brooklyn, a retired cop blowing money and getting high. What'd you do? Walk out on your wife? Get diagnosed with cancer? That would make sense. But an antique dagger? For what, good luck? That's kinda weird."

"No weirder than you knowing what it is," he said.

Lenora shrugged again and dragged on her smoke. The night was clear and the moon shone on her hair. He saw her phone light up and her thumb move across the screen.

Ray rolled out of bed and went to his duffle. He pulled out the first aid kit and a bottle of spring water. He downed the water in a gulp and began a preliminary wrap with the bandages, just to stop the bleeding. But the wounds in his back had already clotted well. He opened another bottle of water and used a t-shirt to swab the hole where the dagger had entered. Adding some peroxide from the first-aid kit, he then began to wrap it in gauze.

Lenora took her phone in the bathroom, made a call with

the door closed, then turned on the shower. Ray went to the cracked mirror and took in his reflection. The bandage showed red stains where some blood oozed, but it should have been much worse. The scars that crosshatched his body and throat looked more like old war wounds than slashes taken within the last week.

Ada appeared behind him. She wore a white robe, its hood pulled over her face so he could only see a few locks of blonde hair and her frowning mouth. She reached with her small fingers and traced his scars. The caresses were a parody of comfort. She did not speak, but he felt her suffering.

He made the mistake of closing his eyes, avoided seeing her physical form only to see her as if in a dream, her body fastened to a chariot's wheel. A laughing angel stepped into the golden car and lashed a pair of white horses with glowing blue eyes.

They leaped into a gallop and pulled the chariot across a white marble pavilion. Charging down a street lined with alabaster columns, they joined a line of chariots advancing on a pillar of clouds. The thunder of the stallions mixed with the whir of wheels as they spun with the souls of screaming children.

What'd you walk out on your wife? Get diagnosed with cancer? Lenora's words were like a final jab punctuating the vision of Ada. Bonnie had once asked if he'd ever reached out to one of the police psychologists about OCD. He'd said compulsive maybe, but he didn't know about obsessive. He'd joked that's why he was less about foreplay, but always spontaneous.

Except he knew now what it really was. It was a burden that haunted every detective—the need to be thorough versus the race against time.

It was a race he was currently losing. He felt it every time he saw Ada's ghost. When he had first begun to see her, when she had been dragged again and again into the waves, it was as if her soul was still fresh. The newly dead still had some life in them, screamed the way the living screamed, clung to the world like a it was a familiar place, a place that was still their anchor.

Over time, they began to change. They became creatures

of another place. Their torments distorted, their souls stretched, and what was left took on a kind of insanity.

Ada was losing what she had been, and the seed of her life was blossoming into an aberration, a small black hole that was erasing her brief existence on Earth and replacing it with eternal pain.

"I gotta see your boss," said Ray as Lenora emerged from the bathroom.

She walked naked across the room, sat on the bed, and put on her panties and jeans.

"Why, you wanna gig as a bouncer?"

"No, I gotta ask him something."

She turned to him, wearing only her jeans and boots, her naked torso almost boyish. "Can I borrow a t-shirt?" she asked.

Ray nodded and handed her a black t-shirt from the duffle. "Maybe I can meet him at the club. Does he have an office, maybe in the back?"

Lenora shook her head. "He won't talk to you. The bouncers know who you are now."

"Maybe you can tell him I want to apologize. I just have to see him."

"You wanna kill him, right?"

Ray didn't answer. He left her on the bed, picked up the first-aid kit, and went for a shower. He told himself what he felt for Ada was all he had left to feel. She was the crown that stood-in for the kingdom that had been his family. He told himself there was no room for anything else. But really, if Lenora couldn't get him in a room with Lobe, he hoped she'd take off, be gone when he came out. Not because he didn't want her, but because he wanted her too much.

He took his time removing the bandage, scrubbing down his scarred body, toweling off and re-wrapping his wound. Already it had stopped oozing and left no stain on the fresh gauze.

He went back in the room and found Lenora holding his gun.

"What is it with Glocks around here?" she asked.

In his black t-shirt and her jeans and boots, holding the automatic pistol, she looked like some kind of urban prepper. She aimed the weapon at Ray's head. Ray looked from the barrel to the open bottle of bourbon on the night table.

"When you pick up a gun, you should assume it's loaded."

"Oh really?" she chuckled. "It wasn't, but it is now."

"And never aim at anything you don't intend to shoot."

"You shouldn't stab people, either," she said. "And I hear coke's illegal."

Ray gave half a nod and went to his duffle. He put away the first-aid kit and began to dress. He heard the click of the pistol's spring and felt a tap on his shoulder.

"Feel better?" Lenora asked as she handed him the magazine.

"Thanks," he said. "So are you a cop?"

"Are you crazy?"

"Military?"

"No way," she said.

"Where'd you learn to shoot?"

"My mother taught me. We used to camp in the Sierra Madres. Gotta watch out for wolves."

Ray nodded. There was something off about her, the way there was something off about Crespo. Somehow, they were telling the same kinds of lies, the kind where what you actually said wasn't untrue, but you omitted what really mattered.

She almost showed a little of her hand when she asked about the dagger. *And it was your own weakness not to ask her more, because you're afraid she won't use it on you again, and you know you need her to, you know it's your only way you forget, more potent than the booze and the cocaine, in her hands the blade is your obsession and your compulsion.*

"Here," he said. "Put this on and see if it doesn't show under your jacket."

Ray handed her his shoulder holster and gave her back the magazine. Lenora strapped it on and let it hang on her left side.

The problem was not that it bulged, but that it dangled loose. He tightened the strap as much as it would go, then handed her the other spare mag.

"There are only two," he said. "Remember that."

"What are we gonna do?" she asked. She gave him the same look as the night she showed him the bloody penguins.

"Like you said, we're gonna kill Edwin Lobe."

"All right," she said, putting the extra mag in her inside pocket. "But we can't do it in the club. I told you, he won't let you near him. He has guards, you know. I'm not just talking about the bouncers. He has, like, allies."

"It's the allies I'm interested in," said Ray.

"Then let's do it," she said. The fact she wasn't fazed by the last line was another slip. *She identified the dagger, and she also knows something about the demon.*

"So when was the last time you were at *La Vela Roja?*" he asked.

"Last night," she said. "I work every night except tonight. Tuesdays are slow as shit anyway. Bobbie bartends, doesn't bother dancing."

"You saying the club's still open? Even after what happened?"

"You mean the shit in the parking lot? Shit always goes down in strip club parking lots. Besides, the cops are off it after the shootout over in Greenpoint."

"What shootout?"

"Where you been? Some petty gangster went nuts. Some old guy, washed up. He made a stand in his basement and shot up a bunch of cops."

Ray recalled the neighborhoods at the north end of Williamsburg. Unlike the no-man's-land further east, they had been places where the older Italian mob nested. They had a heyday in the 1970's and 80's. Now the successful families had moved to Jersey and Long Island. They still did business in the city, but left a lot to the Russians, Mexicans, and Dominicans. Most who stayed behind were either in decline or crazy. Ferretto had been the latter, it had been a matter of extreme pride for him. But for some of the others, the Verenas and the DeLisis, it was feast or starve on the last crumbs they could snatch.

Either way, the distraction spelled a little luck for Ray. He could spend the whole night going through the videos, or he could go on the one lead he had while the 91st was overwhelmed. He could take the offensive before Lobe found out how much he knew. *The demon strikes from behind, breaks the souls of men by breaking their spines.* That tip alone was enough to put together a trap. He had Lenora on board *(as on board as anyone could be—how she knew what the dagger was, he'd sort it out after, and by then it wouldn't matter, when he'd freed Ada. After that, he'd just as soon let her cut him to ribbons)*.

"You ever hang out at the club on your night off?"

Lenora shrugged. "Sometimes. But like I said, we can't just walk in shooting." Here she grinned like she was reconsidering the merits of such a plan after all.

"No, that's not the way," he said. "I had something else in mind."

38

They climbed in the Plymouth and drove north. "Second he sees me he'll call the bouncers," said Ray. "I'll say I'm looking for you, which he'll ignore, but it'll piss him off."

"This thing's sweet," said Lenora. She pointed the Glock out the passenger window as they made their way up Graham in the shadow of Woodhull Hospital. Bushwick Houses sprawled on their right like a brick labyrinth.

"Careful with that," he said.

"Whatever," she said, releasing the mag and testing the action, click-click-click.

"You can set up on the south side of the street. There's an old bakery there. The boards on the windows are rotten and you can break in and sit like a sniper in one of those. When they throw me out of the bar, I'll cross in front of you on the north side of Grand."

"Why not come right by the window?"

"Because the demon will be watching. If we're too close, it might see you first."

"What's wrong with that?"

"I need you to take it down when it comes at me from behind. I've never seen all of it. From what I did see, it's a big fucker, and if the plan works, you can broadside it, shoot across the street on full-automatic. According to the angel, bullets won't kill it, but they'll take it down. So we're gonna ambush an ambush. You'll wound the bastard, and I'll finish the job with the dagger."

Lenora slid the magazine back in the Glock and holstered it. "Did you say *the angel?*" she asked. She gave him a sphinx of a smile, both knowing and mocking. *At least she looks alive*, he thought, *not crooked necked, not ethereal and mechanical like all the damn devils and ghosts he'd been driving around.*

Ray took a right on Graham, then hooked another right on Elmstead. He drove past where he'd parked that first day, twice as far into the old railyard, finally stopping by a filthy crater of a pond, a gravel pit that drained off the Newtown Creek.

"Here's the spare car key," he said. "You can head back here as soon as the thing's down. I'll try to meet you. If we get separated, or if you can't make it back to the car—"

"Just fuckin' run?"

"Yeah, just fuckin' run."

There was no mockery in her words this time, and the plan felt solid. They walked back to Grand Street, and the club's music grew louder as they got closer. The Reggae-tone was drum-heavy but sounded like a bootleg of a DJ spinning with live bass and guitar players. The guitar was even a little rock'n'roll in the lead line. It reminded him of his narc days backing up the guys in the 77th and the 75th. He wanted to take it as a good omen.

They stopped before they reached the corner of Grand and stepped into the shadow of the abandoned bakery. The old cinderblock building stood diagonally across from the club.

Lenora found a first-floor window covered by a rotten plank. "This one," she said, and Ray drew the dagger and pried the screws out of the frame. He began working his way upward, but she stopped him. "That's enough," she said. "I can fit."

"Okay," he said. "Once you get me in the club, you'll slip out and come back here. Say you're gonna smoke or something."

"Don't worry about it," she said. Hopping up onto the frame, she tested to make sure she could get in and out. "Okay, we're good," she said, hopping back down. "Let's go."

They crossed Grand to the club's entrance. The blonde lug

only nodded as they entered the bar. He seemed a little too lax, Ray thought, though Lenora did work there. Maybe he assumed she was dragging Ray back for some kind of apology.

They took a pair of stools close to the door and Bobbie waved to them from the other end where she was pouring drinks. The kid Kev was there in his denim vest. He looked baggy-eyed and sullen as he clutched his drink. He was likely still traumatized by what happened to Fenton, and Ray wondered what brought him back so soon.

La Vela Roja was otherwise emptier than the first night he'd been there. A lone dancer glided around a pole. Bobbie wore a tank top and jeans and had her hair tied back. A few truckers were drinking *Modellos*, but nobody was pressing for lap dances. Ray would have called it relaxed, but there was something else lurking beneath the off-night chill.

He scanned the room's back wall and noticed none of the lights were on in the hallway. Where there had once been track lighting, the tin ceiling trailed off into shadows. *If Lobe was there watching, he wouldn't know.*

To make matters worse, he saw two men he recognized sitting at the bar, ogling Bobbie's tank top as she mixed them margaritas.

"Ray, where the hell ya been?" asked Crespo. "I had to hit up Benny Tischer just to find where you were at."

His voice was loud from the drinks he'd already had, and in the club took on a vaguely hip-hop accent. His buggy shades, handlebar mustache, and brown leather jacket remained in full effect as he moved down the bar.

Callaghan followed behind. The younger man's mouth was straight and his eyes sober. The look belied his partner's drunkenness and told Ray they meant business.

"Where you been hiding *this* place?" Crespo asked with a laugh. He put his hand on Ray's shoulder and hollered to Bobbie, "Hey let's get some shots down here!"

"I'm not hidin' anything," said Ray.

"You sure about that? I haven't met your friend."

Crespo nodded at Lenora, whose face was lit up by the glow of her phone. Ray felt a pang of jealousy as he saw her sharp features and black hair the way Crespo was seeing them for the first time, the way he was reading the crescent of her physique beneath the jeans and leather. And noticing the fucking holster.

Bobbie arrived with the margaritas and said she'd be back with shots. "Hey, how'd you do with the bouncer?" Crespo asked.

"What do you mean?" Ray asked back.

"I mean, he didn't try to take your piece, right? Or are you not packin'?"

"What's it to you?"

"Hey man, no big deal," he said. Crespo put up his hands like he was making a big *Excuse me!* then went on, "I just thought, you know, that knife in your boot, that's like a collector-thing, right? You don't want 'em holding that in the coat check."

"No coat check here, Tolly."

Crespo squinted behind his shades. The shots arrived, but nobody touched them. Callaghan stood with his hands at his sides and Lenora looked up from her phone. Ray forced himself to stay in his seat. It had gotten a little hot, and he had to remain inconspicuous if he wanted to flush out Lobe.

"Hey, Lenora, what's going on?" asked Bobbie. "Everybody okay? Hey, Kev's here, ya know. He's kind of a mess still, you should come cheer him up." She sounded her bubbly self, but the way she looked at them it was clear she knew something was fucked.

Before Ray could answer, another voice spoke: "Just leave us."

Ray turned and saw Lobe step off the wall. His face was bone-white and he held the sword beneath his long leather jacket. Instead of being hunched, his shoulders looked high and pointed. Though his body was still distorted, it had become more angular, *aerodynamic*.

"Oh, so you *are* a regular around here," Crespo said to Ray. He picked up the tequila with his left hand and shot it, while his right moved toward his belt. Callaghan didn't move at all. They were aware of who Lobe was somehow, maybe even had some kind of agreement with him, yet were still wary.

Ray saw the plan was in jeopardy but wasn't ready to give it up. *"You're horsing it! You're horsing it! Here, have a beer!"* the Crespo of his dreams had cried. The man who was still fifty-one percent his friend wasn't all wrong. *It may be going to shit, but stay cool.*

"Fuck this," said Lenora. She stood up and turned to Ray. "Is there anybody you don't have a beef with? You got somethin' to prove every place we go? Fuck this, I gotta smoke." She pulled a pack of cigarettes from her jacket and headed for the door.

Good move, Ray thought, *but they're not gonna let me off that easy.*

"Listen, Tolly, I need to talk to you," said Ray. He stood up and took Crespo by the elbow. He made it casual, turned his friend around like he wanted to lean in and whisper, and in the process put him between himself and Lobe.

"You do not understand," said Lobe. He pushed past Crespo, seized Ray's jacket by the shoulder, and pulled him down the bar. "You were a fool to return, but it will be your last mistake."

Lobe was stronger than he looked, supernaturally so, and kept a firm hold on Ray's jacket. As he shoved him along, the bald bouncer emerged from the darkened back hallway and joined him. Ray knew if he didn't make his move, he'd be too far inside to get back to the front door.

"Hey, hey, take it easy," said Ray. "Why don't we just do a shot?"

Lobe didn't have time to answer before Ray snatched a tequila from the bar, flung it in his eyes, and smashed the glass on his forehead. He sprang forward before Bald Man could hit him and rammed Callaghan, knocking him against Crespo.

The opening was there, and he dashed down the stairs and out the front entrance.

39

Ray made a quick left on Grand before the second bouncer realized he was there. He peeled across Slater Ave, heard a horn blare as a livery cab almost slammed into him. Continuing east under the streetlight's glow, he moved along the torn fences and low walls of the run-down townhouses.

That's when he noticed it in his periphery. The thing was twice the size of a linebacker, yet skittered nimbly across the rooftops. Its red, naked flesh rippled with muscle, and its arms and legs were impossibly long.

He looked for its head but saw none. It was only when it leaped down to the street that he realized the immense hand he'd seen tear apart the couple on Vanders *was* its head. With a massive fist atop a huge human-like body, it was a walking red assault. It came after him with heaving strides, casting its distorted shadow over the street.

There was no need to signal Lenora. If she was in the window, she saw it. He flipped himself around and drew the dagger. The thing's neck-arm craned above him, the fist opened, and its calloused palm dripped steaming sweat. Its fingers spread like the legs of a giant spider ready to wrap around him and squeeze.

The crackle of gunfire sounded in the bakery's window as the Glock let out three consecutive bursts. Black blood exploded from the thing's neck-arm and mixed with the sweat that rained from its palm.

Ray aborted his attack to dodge the thing's fingers. It seemed to dance back into his periphery, keep itself in the corner of his eye while its hand hovered above the melee, grabbing at him.

He scuttled back along the rusty fence and the demon stomped after him. Its legs cracked the pavement as it moved down the street. Ray pulled himself forward with the help of the chain-links. The demon tried to clench him, but Ray spun away, stumbling again and working to catch his breath.

In a rage, the demon made a fist and bashed Ray's shoulder.

He took the blow to keep hold of the dagger and cried out in pain as his clavicle splintered and his chin snapped. Blood gushed from his nose and filled his throat and mouth. Yet he also realized that the blow should have pulped his shoulder and chest entirely. *Because of what you and Lenora did with the dagger, the wounds you inflicted, they have made you stronger.*

He made a sudden stop, turned, and reared back with the blade. For a split-second, he had the demon in front of him. He swung at its bleeding palm, then leaped into the street. Flinging out his arm, he slashed once more, lower this time. The blow connected, opening a wound between its steely stomach and the hairless bulge of its cock.

The monstrosity's entire body shivered from the foot-long cut. A second cavity opened in its chest and let out a sonorous, unearthly scream. Though it had already scuttled around behind him again, he had glimpsed the hideous hole and seen ribs that were not ribs, but teeth. The thing's hand was its head, *but its entire chest was its mouth.*

Ray felt its hot breath behind him as he sprinted east on Grand Street. The Glock let out another burst, but they were already on the second block and the bullets tore into a boarded-up townhouse.

Tires squealed behind them. Ray glanced back and saw a pair of cars pull onto Grand. One was coming around Vanders Ave from the club, the other turning off Elmstead from the old railyard.

The sedans slammed into each other, taking up both lanes. Grand Street was momentarily devoid of other traffic, and they bashed into each other again, vying to take the lead.

Ray reached the Metropolitan Bridge and crossed, moving south where the avenue split off Grand. He was sweating and bleeding and swimming with pain. He zig-zagged, slowing the creature down by making it work to keep in his periphery. His heart was slamming in his chest, and he was running out of breath. Soon he would collapse on the pavement where it would cage him in its fingers, splinter his bones, and tear off his head.

When he tried to turn and slash low again, the demon danced to the side and craned its neck for a final assault. Instead, Ray rolled over and shoved the blade upward in a desperate last attack.

That's when he saw the Plymouth roaring down Metropolitan. Something had hit its front end, partially crushing it. Only one headlight still worked, but he made out Kev at the wheel and Lenora in the backseat.

She fired through the broken window.

The demon's chest let out another unearthly roar as bullets splintered its rib-teeth. It was too stunned to turn when Ray stood and stabbed once, twice, three times under its shoulder. He struck above its gaping mouth, just under its armpit. The thing was massive, but the blade was long. Ray threw all he had into it, urging the tip deeper, grinding inward to pierce its heart.

He felt his hip crunch as its fist bashed him again. Forcing himself up on one leg, he staggered to the Plymouth's open door. He caught the demon in his periphery, its body shredded by the gunfire.

Its open chest heaved, flaps of skin covered in black blood suctioned in and out. Its organs pulsed as the cavity coughed and spit. Intestines protruded from between its red muscles. It strode toward them, a shambling wound, head-hand open wide to seize the entire car.

"Fuckin' get in!" Kev cried.

Lenora waited until the last second, just as they were

peeling away. The hand was descending, cutting a shadow across the streetlight as she emptied the last of the mag into its palm.

Kev swung the car back into the lane and floored it down Metropolitan. The half-smashed little car cranked up to seventy, blue smoke rolling out of its hood. Ray caught sight of a black Suburban in the rearview mirror. It was gaining on them fast, straddling the center lane. After midnight, traffic was light, mostly cabs. Their horns screamed as they swerved out of the way. Ray knew it would be a matter of seconds before a half-dozen or more police cruisers were on them.

The Suburban sped up and came in close to their rear fender. Ray's body hurt all over, but he kept the dagger clutched in his right hand. Lenora dropped the Glock, pulled a .357 magnum from her jeans, and aimed through the rear passenger window.

"Where the hell'd you get that?" Ray asked.

"Mine," she said. She fired two rounds at the SUV, putting holes in the driver's side windshield. The vehicle swerved but kept coming. The passenger window opened and a figure flew out and spread its leathery wings. Its bones looked dark beneath its pale flesh and it held a four-foot sword.

Fucking Lobe, thought Ray as he pivoted and leaned out the window. The winged man flew at them like a bolt from a crossbow, blade thrust forward.

Ray kept the dagger tucked, ready to dodge and slash back. If he could trap the sword under his arm and slash Lobe's shoulder, he could bring him down and knock him under the Suburban's wheels.

But even as he turned, he glimpsed the demon among the warehouses and abandoned brick buildings. It scurried from roof to roof again, flung itself from awnings and broken windows. It picked up momentum, its red-black bleeding mass looming larger with every leap.

Sirens wailed as Lobe crashed into the Plymouth's right side. Instead of attacking Ray with his sword, he smashed its entire length against the car's front windshield. Shattered glass exploded over the front seat, Kev screamed, and Ray shoved the dagger into Lobe's neck. Instead of retreating, he struck again, the hood of the car this time, and with his left hand, seized Ray by the neck.

Ray gritted his teeth and met the glare of Lobe's crazed white eyes. Cloudy and choked with mucous, they seethed with rage. Ray had seen it before and knew it well. You didn't need to be a goddamn mutated warlock to be pissed off when someone fucked up your scam. Nothing got to a gangster like random interference, someone without business or a beef sticking his nose in their operations.

But by the same token, this was his business. That's how it went, they saw you as an interloper, but really you were doing what you had to do for your own. *Take it up with the angels, or the devils, or whoever you bitch to*, Ray thought as he clamped his own hand onto Lobe's neck.

They strangled each other as the Plymouth roared on. Kev's face was all cut up, but he clung to the wheel and kept his foot on the gas. Ray could hear sirens ahead of them and behind them now.

It wouldn't be long before the squad cars forced them off the road. If the demon attacked then, Ray would still take a chance to make the kill. Whatever happened after that, at least it would be on Riel to hold up his end of the bargain.

They were emerging out of Bushwick and into Middle Village. Metropolitan Ave eased out of bruised industrial buildings into a spatter of cheap chicken joints, furniture outlets, and convenience stores. He glimpsed a few more cars enter the avenue and slam on their brakes as their caravan of blood and smoke careened east toward *All Faiths Cemetery*.

Lobe was still squeezing Ray's neck as the demon leaped over the cemetery's low steel fence and flung itself from headstone to headstone. It had come even with the car and was striving to get ahead, cut them off on the narrow strip where the cemetery's fence trapped them in on both sides of the road.

Kev swerved as lights from an oncoming police cruiser washed over the broken windshield. Lobe slashed his chest with his sword, and he screamed into the freezing wind.

"Move, fucking move," Lenora hollered. Ray kept his grip on Lobe's neck as he threw his head forward and down. The pistol thundered above him, and when he looked up again, half of Lobe's skull was missing. Ray thrust the dagger into his throat, then let his flailing body fall to the street.

Kev hauled on the steering wheel, first to the right, then hard to the left. Ray ducked down as they smashed head-on into the cemetery's steel gate. The Plymouth broke through the lock, but the impact demolished the rest of its front end.

Blue smoke turned to flames, and the car filled with the odor of burnt flesh mixed with singed hair and gasoline. Kev tried his door, but it was stuck. He grunted and pulled himself through the smashed windshield, dove across the scalding hood, and landed sprawling on the cemetery's lawn.

Ray shouldered open the passenger door and spun around with the dagger. He saw the police cruiser across the street where it had crashed through the cemetery's fence on the south side. Lenora's pistol thundered again, and black blood rained down as her bullet pierced the demon's shoulder.

The thing had leaped clear across the street and over their crashed car. It straddled Kev where he lay writhing in the grass. Ray feinted a thrust at the thing's stomach, then flipped the dagger and plunged it into the demon's knee. He sank the seax's blade so deep its tip stuck out the other side.

The demon's ribcage of a mouth emitted another sonorous moan. Its body crashed down beside Kev's and thumped against the ground like a felled tree.

Ray noticed that while the holes from the gunshots had already begun to close up, the wound from the dagger gushed blood and widened. It ate at the thing's leg like it had been splashed with acid.

Ray dashed over to Kev and closed in on the demon's throat. If he put himself in Lenora's sights, it was a chance he had to take.

As he came within striking distance, he made out a rat's nest of pulsing arteries. The web of veins pumped and pumped, and the ribcage-mouth in its chest moaned and spat. Ray flipped the dagger around again and swung in an arc aimed to cut through a dozen veins in one slash.

But before he could connect, the demon's massive hand took hold of Kev's legs and swung his body like a club. Ray felt the screaming man's skull knock against his own, and he fell back on the cemetery's paved road. The demon stood and strode toward him despite its wounded leg.

Ray rolled to the side, tried to scramble away, but the thing managed to keep behind him in his periphery. He caught only a flash of the thing holding Kev's body in its smaller hands while its giant fingers pinched and plucked off his head. Ray dove behind the burning Plymouth, but the demon threw Kev's severed head at him, cracking their skulls once more.

Nearly knocked unconscious, Ray staggered away from the burning car. He heard the demon close behind, its quaking footfalls, its squelching wounds. It was still feeling the bite of the dagger's blade, and Ray took the chance to force himself to run. He fled deeper into the cemetery, first down the paved road, then peeling to the left, over the grass and inward among the graves.

40

Ray checked his periphery as he ran among the tombstones. He saw the demon lumbering after him, its body covered in bleeding wounds as it leaned on the old crypts and slanted headstones to keep on its feet.

Dragging Kev's body in its left hand, it trailed blood across the tufted grass. Its moans took on a strange sound, like breathless laughter, like what it had done was heartily funny, and it was a sadistic child proud to have slain a rodent.

The thing was gaining on him with every step. Ray slipped through a grove of twisted oaks and entered a glade of poorly tended graves. Their stones tilted like rows of rotten teeth, and he stumbled among their dank and soggy weeds.

A rain-worn sculpture of a nun clutching two young children stood among them. She held their eroded faces protectively against her hips and seemed to point the way to a malformed oak where he might take cover.

Ray pressed on, as wounded as his enemy, and on the brink of collapse. His calves throbbed, and his vision blurred. His broken clavicle screamed with pain and seemed to float at the top of a river of wounds.

In his periphery, he saw the demon kept one hand on a tombstone and with the other swung Kev's body in circles like some grotesque tribal weapon. Ray ducked just as he hurled the headless man past him, sent him sprawling across a row of flat, mostly grown-over monuments.

The body is headless, just like the demon, Ray thought. *The Son of Magog makes his victims in his own image.*

Ray slipped around the malformed oak, its trunk bulbous with tumorous growths. He put his back against the tree so the demon would have to attack him head-on. *I'll make it fight face to face, even if it has no face. How does the damn thing see? Echo-fucking-location?*

But when he turned back to the glade, it wasn't the demon who staggered toward him. It was Kev's headless body.

"What the hell?" he rasped as the dead man came on. But even then, he realized he had seen it before. Those thugs who attacked him at the hotel, they had stitches on their throats. They kept coming at him, though they had been shot. They were dead men, just like Kev was, corruptions in service of a greater corruption.

When it was within ten feet, the corpse charged. Its neck tilted forward, severed esophagus hanging out like a single hollow eye. Ray kicked the corpse in the stomach, causing its throat to belch blood. When the demon's giant hand reached around the tree, he swung the dagger and slashed across its fingers.

The hand withdrew, but the thing's smaller arms clawed at his wounded shoulders. Taking hold of Ray, they pulled him toward the cavity in its torso.

The corpse recovered from the kick and grabbed Ray's arm. It pried at the dagger while the demon pulled him closer. The gibbering mass of ribs and muscles that served as its jaws opened wider. He gagged at the stench as it drew him inside.

Ray strained to free his arm from the corpse's grip, but it had hold of him with both hands, and it was all he could do to hang on to the dagger.

He was about to give a final shove when he heard the boom of the .357 in the nearby cluster of oaks. "Fuckin' run," cried Lenora. It exploded again, and Kev's corpse flew backward. Three more shots slammed into the demon's back, shocking it enough to lose its grip on Ray.

But with his arms free, he did not run. Instead, he gripped the dagger in both hands and cut at the pulsing veins in the thing's neck. It was a sure kill, but with his own wounded shoulder, he couldn't bring the weapon down fast enough.

The demon struck first and bashed him once more in the head. Before he lost consciousness, he saw his slash had gone low. The thing moaned and staggered, but it was not dead.

And beneath its suffering, he heard a fainter sound, Ada's sighs of pain in Heaven's distant clouds.

41

"What is Grace?" he asked Beth.

His daughter sat across from him at the diner where he'd found her that day with Ada. Except the Reverend wasn't there now, and she wasn't dressed like the women from his cult. She was in a tank top that showed off her tattoos. The fat demon was laughing, and the Florida sun shone through the window on her face.

"Grace is the settling of accounts," she said.

"So breakfast is on me," he said.

She sipped her coffee. "Sure," she said. "But that's not the bill you have to pay."

"What is it then? What do I owe?"

"Come out to the house. I'll show you."

Ray left cash on the table and followed her out the diner's door. It led to the path through the marsh. Except it wasn't Florida this time. It was Sligo Beach, Long Island.

A grove of pines stood ahead of them. Bones lay among the sand and needles, old rotted bones and partial skeletons. Half a mother clutched a whole child. The infant's skull tilted back, wondering where the rest of her had gone.

"This way," she said, pointing at their house. The remodeled ranch looked awkward among a row of abandoned seaside bungalows. Black mold streaked their doors, and shards of broken glass lined their window frames.

"Dad, come on," said Beth. "Dad, where are you going? Come on, come on…"

"…Ray, come on, come on, pal, come on."

It was Crespo's voice. He stood over Ray, his silhouette cut out of the moonlight. He was shaking his wounded shoulder, slapping his face. They were still in the cemetery. Police radios crackled in the distance. He made out Callaghan's shadowy figure standing in the background.

The demon was gone.

"Tolly, damn man, I'm banged up. The thing banged me up," said Ray.

Crespo slipped his arm around Ray, lifted his shoulders, and sat him against the oak's twisted trunk. He pulled off the boot with the sheath on it and shook it out.

"Where'd it go?" he asked.

"I dunno, it ran off, I stabbed it in the neck. It's wounded real bad."

"I mean the dagger," said Crespo.

He was holding a flashlight in Ray's face now. He put up his hand and squinted. "I dunno, it's here somewhere." He pawed the grass between a fallen tombstone and the oak. "Did you call an ambulance? I don't know if I can walk."

Ray tried to make out Crespo's face behind the light. "Hey pal, I need you to listen," said Crespo. "What'd you do with the dagger? Did you leave it inside the fucker? Did you stick it in and leave it?"

"He don't have it," said Callaghan before Ray could answer. The younger man was grimacing. "I think he lost it." He nudged Crespo as he spoke, like it would make him hear better, and kept looking over his shoulder.

But Crespo ignored him. "Okay pal, I need you to listen. Are you listening?"

"What—"

Crespo smacked him across the face with his boot.

"What the—"

He brought his hand back and clubbed him again, harder

this time.

"What the fuck, Tolly?"

"You listenin' yet, bud? Tell me where that fuckin' dagger is, or I'll let you bleed out here." Crespo lowered the flashlight and looked at Ray through the sunglasses he still wore in the night. Between the round eyes and the angular mustache, he looked bug-like in the darkness.

Ray gritted his teeth and slid his back higher against the tree. His wounds stung and gnawed, but he could at least feel his limbs. Maybe he could walk, and if he *could* walk, he might be able to run.

"Look, Tolly, I know there's some shit going on with us, but I don't got a lot of time. You mentioned Bonnie. Does this have somethin' to do with Bonnie? Did you two have a thing, and now you're pissed?"

At this, Crespo gave a hint of his old smile. "You're one ignorant fuck, Ray. You know that?" He clutched the boot with the heel dangling like the weighted end of a sap. "There's nothin' left for you."

"What's that supposed to mean?" asked Ray.

"Means I wasn't gonna let you see me. Now gimme your hands." Crespo dropped the boot and pulled out a pair of day-glow green plastic handcuffs.

Callaghan stood over them with his .40 cal held low by his thigh. He kept looking over his shoulder, watching for the rest of the cops who would inevitably make their way deeper into the cemetery. Whatever these two were trying to do, they wanted to keep it on the down-low.

Ray pulled his wrists back as Crespo tried to put on the handcuffs. "Ow, watchit," he hissed. "The hell you doin?"

But the old detective just pulled his arm under his elbow and kept him in a hold while he wrapped the plastic band around his wrist.

"Hold still. You're only gonna make it worse." Crespo was all business as he tightened the band until it cut into Ray's wrist. "You know, I was gonna watch him take you down," said Crespo.

"See, once the angels had your grandkid, see then you were already all done. You know that? You were already all done."

"Then what the fuck are you doin' here?"

"I need that dagger, Ray. We didn't count on that little rhinestone cowboy of an angel to give you a real weapon. It's worth somethin', that dagger. And you caused enough goddamn trouble with it."

"Just take it then."

"Where the hell is it?"

Ray leaned forward and stretched out his arms. With his wrists bound, it was harder to search the grass. The blade had to be nearby. *Unless you stuck it in the damn demon.* But no, he'd kept hold of the grip on his last attack. *Maybe the damn thing took it when you were knocked out.* Ray felt his muscles seize up. He didn't want Crespo to get the weapon, but it was even worse if the demon had taken it. He'd never see Ada again. They would be condemned, each to their own tormented eternities, her in Heaven and him in Hell. Such would be their fates. *Fini.*

"The demon twisted when I cut him," said Ray. "I couldn't hang on. I musta lost the blade. I think it landed over there." He nodded at a trio of slanted tombstones. Their shadows crisscrossed, and Crespo took the bait and stepped toward them.

Ray hopped up and rammed his shoulder into Callaghan's gut. The little bastard was fast, landed an elbow in Ray's back, just right of his spine. Hurt worse than his busted clavicle, but he ran anyway.

He sprinted for another grove of trees to the north. This one was larger and denser, oaks and evergreens edging an already narrow path. He felt his hands and knees go all pins and needles as he forced himself on.

"The fuck you doin'!" he heard Crespo shout.

He knew what was coming next. He ducked even though the bullet hit high and to the right, shattering a dead branch.

Ha, Callaghan didn't want to kill him anyway, or he would have used the pistol before when Ray lunged at him. That shred of hope gave him enough power to make a final sprint and come out on the other side of the grove. The cemetery's fence was less than a hundred yards off.

He charged and vaulted, cleared the gate, then faded left into an alley behind a Chinese-Mexican restaurant. A gray-haired woman in jeans and a greasy apron dropped her garbage bag when she saw the bleeding, handcuffed ghoul of a man standing beside the dumpster.

But two Ben Franklins dug from his pocket turned her shock into a satisfied nod. She waved him into the restaurant's kitchen, where she swung a cleaver the size of a tennis racket. The cuffs were gone in a single stroke.

42

By the time he reached Broadway, he felt utterly torn and broken. His blood had clotted, but the wounds reopened and seeped as he trudged through the three-a.m. drizzle. Assuming Crespo knew where he was staying, he considered hiding in one of the derelict brownstones and casing the place before he went inside.

He had cash in the duffle, as well as his clothes, his files, the laptop, and a survival knife. If Crespo got to the hotel first, he was screwed. At least he had his wallet and his phone.

"Fuck it," he said aloud. He looked down an alley, through a bodega's half-closed roll-down gate, expecting to see Ada staring at him, crazed by now, nearly gone. But there was no more, "*Over here! I'm over here!*" No more tossing sea. There were only the city's empty windows waiting to swallow him into an eternal pit of rust and nails—if he was lucky.

Fuck it. He staggered into *Neptune's Lounge* where the best way to wait was with whiskey. It wouldn't be a half-bad way to die. If only he could expect the comfort of oblivion, he would seek out Crespo deliberately. Instead, he would drink an hour, then check *The Voyager.* If it was clear, he'd get the duffle. If there was any evidence of his old friend, he'd find an ATM and resupply.

And if you couldn't kill the demon when you had the weapon the angel gave you, what will you do now?

He didn't answer himself. Instead he watched the old man

fill his glass with bourbon and nodded when the whiskey neared the rim. "Leave the bottle," he said, putting three twenties on the bar.

The old man left the bottle. Ray counted the cash left in his pocket and noted he was down to $320. One of the fifties was covered in blood. He added it to the twenties on the bar.

Where was Lenora? Had it gotten her? Or maybe the police had. Taking a deep breath, he finished off the bourbon and poured another. The bar reeked of Lysol, piss, and mildew. He caught his reflection in the mirror on the far wall, a pale face floating in tacky, box-store glass set into once beautiful woodwork. *Just like your soul since you started seeing ghosts.*

"Just like your soul when you started seeing ghosts," said Ada.

Ray looked at her reflection as it appeared beside his. Her eyes had gotten bluer somehow, cobalt and unnatural.

But when he turned to where she sat beside him on the stool, her hair covered her face. She wore a filthy white smock, a medieval-looking cassock. She had bruises and cuts on her arms that he could see through the tears in the sleeves. *That's how she looked when they put her in the cramped cell in that wall-prison.* When she stood, it pained her to move, as if her joints were an agony.

"Come with me," she said, taking his hand. "It's time."

Ada led him to the door. Instead of opening onto Broadway, they stepped through a panel of bright white light, his dream letting death and satire mock one another.

"Show him," Ada rasped.

She let go of his hand as Beth appeared and beckoned him forward.

"I want you, Momma," said Ada.

"You gotta hang on," said Beth.

The girl lowered the hand that was still extended and tried to nod. Her neck crackled and her muscles twitched, and as she fell to her knees, her body began to heave.

Ray wanted to run back to her, but before he could, the bar disappeared.

They were standing on a beach beneath an overcast sky.

"She won't last much longer," said Beth. She walked ahead of him, barefoot in jeans and a tank-top. "If we don't bring her back soon, there will be nothing left of her. She will be a system of suffering. Pain with consciousness. That's what they will do to all of us."

Ray hustled to catch up with her. She was only walking, but somehow she was moving very fast. "Who will do that to us?"

"Heaven's officers, and Hell's. They were once soldiers in the same army. They want to do with all of us what they're doing with Ada. They hurt us, mostly. And like some beaten mother when someone calls the cops, we defend them, mostly. We pretend one set's better than the other. It's a natural reaction in our condition. Stockholm Syndrome."

"That's pretty bleak," he said. They were nearing some grassy dunes cut with brackish streams.

"Maybe. But if you have time for philosophy, the next question's why they bother. There must be something they want here, with us, with Earth. That means it's worth fighting for. You might be a selfish, compulsive asshole, but you taught us that much."

"How do you know?"

Beth gave the slightest smile. "Like you always said, Detective Barrs—look for the motive. What do we have? We have the Earth, and we have our bodies, and the angels, the devils, what do they have? They have power, and what do they do with it? They use it to emulate us, to dominate us, which means, in a way, they want to be us."

Ray looked at his daughter and her Mona Lisa-grin. For all of her messing around with religious cults and biker gangs, there was thought beneath the wandering.

"Maybe you coulda been a professor," he said.

Beth laughed. "Maybe you coulda sent me to school."

"I woulda, if you'd been interested."

She laughed again. "I guess that's why mom hoarded her pills. The moment you wised-up and decided to invest in your kids, a lot of that nest-egg would have gotten spent. After that, what's a junkie to do?"

"Don't talk about your mother like that," he said.

"What? Her being a junkie? An addict, and a skank, too? Oh, but I'm getting ahead of myself."

"Damnit, Beth, I—"

"No, you don't, you don't damn anything. Others have taken care of that. Like I said, you're the only one in your messed up way who's trying to do something about it. Think about it, Dad, did Mom lament how your job got in the way of some Broadway career? Cry about how rearing children stopped her from going to school?"

"No, she wasn't like that. But I would have encouraged her."

A belly-laugh replaced the Mona Lisa-grin. "So you still choose to play the fool? I knew long before my dreams showed me more. Even in her *Buca's Bar & Grill* days, she was sampling the goods. I was drinking eighty-proof breastmilk. And she didn't start the pills at the end. She just didn't hide them by then. No, she was a dutiful little stay-at-home junkie. The more overtime you worked, the better."

"If that's true, I never knew. Maybe I saw some, but not all."

"You sound like a fortune cookie," said Beth. "Now come with me. As Ada said, it's time."

As they reached a bridge over one of the streams, she pointed to the pathway he had seen before. Slowing her pace, she took his hand as they moved down its sandy planks. He couldn't tell if he was in Pensacola or Long Island. The house standing in the pines up ahead was their house in Florida. But the grass that surrounded them, the clouds of flies, and the bodies in different states of decomposition were from Sligo Beach.

"Chain lightning," she said. "Problems handed down from your father to us."

"If you're talking about what happened with old Jim and Brooklyn, I took care of that. It's no concern of yours."

"But it is, it got handed down to us, ricocheted like chain lightning."

"What's that got to do with Ada?"

"Dad, if you're gonna fight, you need to know this." They reached the end of the path and entered the clearing. The devil tattoo on her arm seemed to nod as she moved. It mouthed words, and the dream read its lips. *Did you know apocalypse is Greek for revelation?*

"Hurry up," said Beth. She stood in the doorway, beckoning.

The scene changed as Ray moved toward her. They were in Florida on a hot, humid night, and he could see the glow of the nightlight in Ada's bedroom window. Criss-crossing gusts of wind ruffled the lawn, warning of a storm. They'd left the kitchen light on, and he saw shadows moving through it. They stepped through the front door like ghosts, and as they entered the carpeted hallway, he heard voices speaking in harsh whispers.

"He'll be home any minute. You should go."

"Don't worry, doll. Just gonna finish my drink."

When they reached the kitchen, Beth stepped back and stood beside him in silence. By the stove's low light, he saw Tolly Crespo at his kitchen table, sipping bourbon. Bonnie stood against the counter, wearing her bathrobe. The tie was loose, and the top hung open, revealing her bare breasts.

"You should go. He'll be back from the marina any minute."

"Bartender texted me. We're good. He's watching the game."

"What if Ada wakes up? I'm tired, I gotta go to bed."

Bonnie stumbled off the counter as she spoke. She was drunk, and if what Beth had said was right, probably on Oxy, too. Her bathrobe fell the rest of the way open. Crespo chuckled and planted a kiss low on her stomach, just above the bush of hair.

She pushed him away. "Stop, just go home."

"Gonna finish my drink," he said.

Bonnie shook her head clumsily. "No, I'm not going to bed until you leave."

"You know, you coulda been a dancer when you were young."

Crespo was already wearing his shades and grinning into his mustache. There were fewer gray hairs, but the seventies look, complete with the badly patterned short-sleeve dress shirt, had already made him a creepy old spider of a man. His hands were all over Bonnie's thighs as he kissed her again, lower this time. She didn't push him away and instead took a step closer.

"Come to the bedroom then," she said. "Let him catch us. It'll be done."

Crespo pulled his head back and took his hands off her thighs. "I'd love to, doll, but you're a little tired. Why don't you go on?"

"I'm not leaving you alone in here."

"Why not? Just gonna finish my drink. I'll let myself out the back door." He chuckled at his joke.

"Ada said you came to her door last time."

"I was just saying hello," said Crespo. "Ain't she the cutest little kid?"

"She said you said you had something to show her."

Crespo chuckled. "I got her some candy."

"Jesus Christ, Tolly, that's not funny! Do what you want to Ray, to fucking me, but leave that kid alone!"

"Shhh, be quiet," said Crespo as he stood. "You'll wake her up." He leaned in and wrapped his arm around the small of Bonnie's back. "You think I'm a pedophile? You think that's what I am?" His body tensed, and his sinewy forearms flexed beside his paunchy gut.

Ray stepped forward. He wasn't going to let the bastard hit his wife, but Beth held him back.

"You can't touch them here. You have to watch."

Tears formed in Ray's eyes as he moved back to the wall.

Crespo relaxed a little, though the tension remained in his stance. "Why don't you just go to bed, doll? Let Uncle Tolly finish his drink. In fact, why don't you just have yourself a nightcap?"

Bonnie had one hand against the stove, was blinking her

eyes against her drunkenness. She looked up just as Crespo grabbed a fistful of her hair and yanked her forward.

She made a short, sharp shriek, but the bottle's neck quieted her. Crespo shoved the bourbon in her mouth while he pulled her hair from behind. When she tried to spit the whiskey up, he yanked again on her hair. Finally, she swallowed a few big gulps and slid down to the floor.

When he turned to put the bottle on the table, his movements sped up, like he was in a video on fast-forward. The stove's clock added minutes as if they were seconds. He went down the hall to the bedroom and came back with a pillow. Putting it behind Bonnie, he propped her up.

He took one more swallow of whiskey for himself, returned the bottle to the cabinet, and put on the tea kettle. He drew two packets of hot chocolate from the cabinet, put them in mugs, and poured in hot water and milk.

While the mugs cooled, he slid a small gym bag from under the table. He took out a miniature cooler, the size of a lunch box, set it on the table, then brought over the mugs of hot chocolate and a fork and a saucer from the cupboard.

Jesus Christ on a fucking swizzle stick, thought Ray. This was seven years ago, the night he came home and found Ada awake while Bonnie slept on the kitchen floor. *Grandma was sad tonight*, Ada had said. *She misses my mom.*

Crespo left the kitchen again. Ray heard knocking in the distance and low voices he couldn't make out. *He's gone to Ada's room*, he thought. When he came back, the girl was with him. They sat down at the kitchen table, and when he slid her the mug of hot chocolate, time slowed down again.

"We're just gonna have a snack while your grandma takes a rest," said Crespo.

"But why are you here?" asked Ada.

"I brought you something," said Crespo. He opened the cooler and reached inside with the fork.

Ray gasped at what he brought out.

It was an insect slathered in something that looked like

amber, except the pitch was still liquid.

Mandibles extended from its jaw, and its body had a half-dozen, ant-like lobes. Its head and legs reeled and wiggled in the thick liquid, and Ray knew he had seen the thing before, a thousand times larger, on his boat, with Ada inside it.

"I dipped it in something sweet," said Crespo. "Like honey."

"What is that thing? It's gross," said Ada.

"Have another sip of hot chocolate," he said. "Then swallow it. You don't have to chew. It'll make its way down."

"Get it away," she cried. She slid back her chair and stood. At five years old, she was barely taller than the table.

"You have to swallow it," said Crespo. "It's like medicine. You've taken medicine before, right?"

"That's not medicine," she cried. "Where's my Grampa? I want Grampa!"

"Grampa's not here," said Crespo. He reached in the gym bag, drew out a .38 revolver, and put it on the table. The bug twitched on the saucer beside it, too heavy with the liquid to crawl off. "Here, take the fork," he said. "Just stick it in and pick it up like a hotdog. You do it, or I'm going to do something very bad to your grandma."

But Ada glared back at him. "You better leave. My Grampa will hurt you."

Crespo chuckled. "I don't think you understand, little girl. It's more like it's your grampa who will hurt you."

"I don't believe you," she said. "He knows what to do. He's a detective. He hurt all those bad guys in New York, and now you're a bad guy, Uncle Tolly."

"Funny you should mention that, kid. Do you know who those bad guys were, back in New York? Did you ever hear him talk about that?"

"Maybe," she said, her voice less sure.

"And do you know why he moved way down here to Florida with your grandma and your mom?"

"Kinda," she said.

"Kinda? You *kinda* know? Well, let Uncle Tolly *kinda* tell you something. Your grandfather killed a man named John Ferretto. But he didn't just kill *him*. He killed Johnny's wife, his brother, his daughter, son, and even his *granddaughter*."

Crespo leaned forward and slid the saucer with the squirming insect toward Ada.

"So this is what we're going to do. First, you're going to swallow down your snack. It'll be real easy, and you know what? You won't even die. Once you do that, Uncle Tolly's gonna leave. Then you're gonna stay here, drink your hot chocolate and keep an eye on your grandma. When your grampa gets home, you know what you're gonna say? You're gonna say, *Grandma was sad tonight. She misses my mom.* You got that?"

Ada began whimpering as Crespo slid the saucer closer. The insect was wiggling its legs and spattering honey on the table. It clicked its mandibles, belying anything Crespo said about it going down easily.

"But why are you being a bad guy, Uncle Tolly?" Ada sobbed.

"Well kid, let's put it like this. You know why they call me Tolly? It's short for *Bartolomeo*, my middle name. See, my dad's name was Francis Crespo, but you know what my mom's name was before they got married? My mom's name was Donnatella Ferretto, and her brothers were Bartolomeo and Giacomo. Giacomo changed his name to John, John Ferretto, and that's the man your grampa killed. And that's whose whole family he killed, everyone except my mother. He woulda killed her too, except he didn't know. And now you will eat this cursed creature like the priest said, and you will swallow it, and on your family will be visited the second death, and if you do not do as I say exactly, your sentence will be carried out immediately and you will be delivered that death not next year, not tomorrow, but tonight!"

Crespo grabbed the back of Ada's head as he had her grandmother's and picked up the wiggling insect with the fork. When she opened her mouth to scream, he shoved the thing inside and clamped her mouth closed. The girl began to gag, and she would have choked, but the creature moved too fast. Her esophagus bulged and her skin reddened as it made its way down.

And then it was inside her.

She sat coughing and sobbing at the table as the thunder boomed, the clouds burst, and rain flooded the windows.

43

The smell of piss and Lysol woke him. The bartender stood over him, holding the empty bottle.

"You want another one? Maybe a pillow?"

Ray closed his eyes against the mind-shattering pain. Bonnie had a pillow behind her head the night he found her lying against the wall. He'd just been out with the boys, *haha*, watching the football game, *haha*, retirement was sweet.

He opened his eyes. "Glass of water," he said. "How long was I out?"

"A while," said the old man. "It's eight o'clock."

"In the morning? Do you guys ever close?"

The old man stiffened his lips. "I don't give a fuck. I live upstairs. Go to bed at ten. The day girl comes in at noon. You want a pillow?"

"No, just the water, thanks."

The old man nodded and poured him a glass. Ray saw the money was gone, including the bloody fifty. He guessed a hundred and ten bucks bought him one bottle of whiskey and some sleep. But everyone's patience ran out eventually, even when they smelled like piss.

"Thanks," said Ray, putting one more twenty on the bar.

He made his way out onto Broadway. The sun shone warm, but the breeze was cool. The brick and brownstone buildings crowded the intersection, dark windows watching. His wounds had closed, but his head was a sphere of bright, blasting pain. He wondered if he was already in Hell as he staggered east toward *The Voyager.*

The hotel was quiet. No arguments sounding from the windows, no one hanging around the entrance. When he glanced down the side street toward Bushwick Avenue, he noticed a newish, black Jeep parked by the corner.

So Crespo might be here, he thought. *If he was, fuck him.* Ray was up against the ropes. The crushing blows from the thing in the cemetery, the gut-wrenching truth of the dream, they had worn him down, and the knockout was coming.

And the worst of it was that he had lost the dagger. He stepped into the hotel's scratched-to-shit hallway and crossed its stinking gray carpet. *You think you're smart, Tolly? You hit me with something worse than death, and I still found a way to hit back. I keep hitting back because I know nothing else. Even in the face of eternity, I do not go gently into that effed-up night.*

But he needed the dagger. It had wounded the demon, and it had gotten him close to saving his family. *And it was a better drug than you've ever tasted, in her hands, in your flesh, in each other's blood.*

He made it to his room without being ambushed. The duffle was by the bed where he left it, but the TV had somehow been broken. He went through the bag and found the only thing missing was two bubble-wrapped oxies from a package he didn't know he had. They even left the hunting knife.

He checked the closet and under the bed, but the room was empty. Seemed if it was Crespo's Jeep, the man would have waited there to finish it. He went into the bathroom, stripped off his clothes, and assessed his wounds in the mirror.

His clavicle had healed but hadn't set. It stuck out ghoulishly by his neck, surrounded by blood and bruises. Tangled lacerations coated his flesh head to toe. Clotted scabs covered him like red-brown continents. He was a walking map of pain, and he wondered again if he was already damned.

"Am I in Hell?" he asked the mirror aloud.

"This place is too shitty to be Hell."

Lenora's reflection appeared beside his.

He turned. She was there, standing in the room, framed by the doorway. Ray came out of the bathroom, crossed to the bed, and sat down. She stepped closer, and their eyes met.

Her black hair hung over her studded leather jacket, and her steel-toed work boots made her look taller. When she leaned to kiss him, the mirror reflected the pistol stuck in the back of her jeans.

"Thought I'd say goodbye," she said.

"Do you have the dagger?" he asked.

She shrugged. "Sold it," she said.

"You what?"

"Anyway, I have to go to Berlin. Probably won't see you again."

"What are you, a fuckin' diplomat? Where's the blade?"

"I have to go," she said. "I came to say goodbye."

"You sell my fuckin' dagger, then you buy a plane ticket?"

"Don't be stupid," she said. "I helped you out. Did what I could. You know, maybe you should get outta here, too. Leave the city."

"Tried that," said Ray. "Didn't work."

Lenora nodded. When she folded her arms, her triceps creased the leather jacket. He tried not to think of their bare bodies and that same arm holding the seax between them.

"So all right," she said. "I mean, it was fun and all, but I gotta go. You should really get outta here, too. Your wounds… they won't heal as quick now."

"I'll keep that in mind," he said.

He stood and stepped in front of her so that they were face to face. For a second, Lenora turned to the window, then looked back at him. She sucked in a breath and kissed him again.

They moved away from the bed, still kissing. He was naked, and she was not. She pushed off his hand when he tried to lift her t-shirt. She reached low, gave him a rough squeeze, then raked her nails over his stomach. When they paused to catch their breath, she put her hand against his chest. "It'll be the last time," she said.

She took off her jacket and draped it over the broken TV. She chuckled as she gripped the bottom of her t-shirt and lifted it off, baring her small breasts. She unbuttoned her jeans but didn't pull them down. Instead, they slid with the swing of her hips as she moved back to him. He caught the reflection of the pistol in the wall mirror, barrel exposed where the small of her back met the crease underneath.

They kissed harder, and he caught the gun before it fell.

"You should be more careful," he said, setting it on the bed.

Lenora laughed and pulled him to the floor.

Their hands moved between her thighs with their fingers intertwined. She began to moan and buck her hips, and just as he thought maybe this was all she wanted, she laughed again and kicked away her crumpled jeans and boots.

He looked up as she wrapped her legs around his back and enveloped him slowly. Their reflection was an excitement and a parody. They lay across the crack hotel's burnt carpet, stomach to stomach, like 1950's newlyweds in a missionary position.

But her teeth and nails said otherwise as she bit his lips and clawed at his scars. Her nails gave a strange sensation like he was wearing a jacket of his own flesh. When they found one of the few stretches of skin left without the wounds, he cried out.

"It's different without the dagger," she whispered.

Her stomach was strong, and she twisted him wherever she liked. Her hands tore at his back, and she moved her mouth lower and bit his jutting clavicle. She hinted with her rhythm that she could go harder, and he wished they had the blade. She knew what he was wishing and did go harder and harder again.

It'll be the last time, he thought as they rode with mounting speed and sleek, wet warmth. Clouds covered the sun in the window, and rain began to whip against the glass. A flood of fire coursed through them, and they clung together as it burned.

Their eyes met once more as their insides turned to ashes, and when it was over, they tore themselves apart.

44

"Sell me your gun?" he asked as he pulled on his jeans.

"Sure," she said. "I'll take it out of your cut."

She had just emerged from the bathroom and was already dressed. She handed him the .357 revolver, then dug into her pocket, pulled out a roll of bills, and counted out $5,400 in fifties. "Here, makes six-thousand with the gun."

"It's money from selling the dagger," he said.

"Yeah," she said.

"I need it back," he said.

"Sorry dude, it's gone," she said. She gave his hand a cursory squeeze and kissed him lightly on the lips. Her hair smelled refreshed with a hint of argan oil. He reached for her hand again, but it jumped to her phone. She stepped back and turned away.

"We're going backward," he said.

"No such thing," she said, then laughed. "Hey, check out this link, it's hilarious. This kid with rabies says goodbye to his mom, like he pushes away water and shit."

Ray felt his phone buzz and instinctively thumbed the screen and opened the link. The kid was as pale as the sheets he lay on. He shook and coughed thick white drool. "Love you too, mama, love you too, I gotta go swimming... gotta go now..." She offered the water. He pushed it away.

"Jesus fuckin' Christ Lenora, you gotta be fuckin'—"

But when he looked up, she was gone.

45

Ray took a gypsy cab to Queens, picked up chicken and plantains from *El Sabor*, then crossed the street to *Fazio's Auto World*.

"Ya shouldn't have," said Fazio as he snatched the bag and dug into the plantains.

"So the car's ready?"

"Good as new! Ready to rock-and-roll!" Fazio waved at his boys as they brought up the Crown Vic, purring and polished, and handed Ray the keys. The old man smiled, plantains already stuffed between his teeth. Ray hoped the takeout would catch him a break on the bill, but Fazio already had it written out.

"You're lookin' a little rugged there," said Fazio.

Ray glared at him. "Yeah, well, like you said, I'm workin' a tough case."

"Hey, I didn't mean nothin' bad by it. Some honeys like that look, ya know?" A chuckle laced his gravelly voice. "Hey, you wanna come out with me tonight? I know a dancuh, over at this club, she got these," here he cupped hands over his chest, "great, big, blue eyes!" The old man's chuckle rose to laughter. "And ya can't beat the price at this place, just a few blocks south."

"*La Vela Roja?*" asked Ray.

"What? No way, that place is a dump, and it's all shot to shit. You didn't hear?"

"No, I didn't hear," said Ray. "They shut it down?"

Fazio gasped. "You could say it shut itself down. Shooting

spree, except not gangbangers, some old guy, they're sayin'. Disgruntled customer. You know how it is now, a shooting a day in the U-S-A. They got that place locked up, crawlin' with cops. Hey, you're pullin' my leg, aren't ya? You know all about it! Hey, you know, they say it's related to what happened to Verena a while back, when the Feds took down Chaz Verena. That true?"

Ray looked at the bill. "How about I give you two G's," he said.

"What? Whattaya talkin' about?"

"I'm gonna give you two G's for the repairs. Enjoy your dinner, I'll see you 'round."

Ray got in the Crown Vic and closed the door. Fazio trotted up to the window, gray curls blowing in the cold spring breeze. "Hey Ray, whachya doin'? It's another eight-hundred, Ray! Hey now, wait!"

Ray raised the window and peeled out of the lot. In the rearview, he glimpsed Fazio, jacket fallen off his shoulders, gold chains swinging as he ran. "Hey, come on, I'll take ya to the club."

Two lefts and Ray was on Queens Boulevard. He hooked up to the BQE and headed south. The old man's voice echoed in his ears as he drove. *Some old guy, they say. Disgruntled customer.* His head pain mocked him as he crossed back into Brooklyn. *You hunted the demon down and made your move. But you didn't kill it. What's worse, Crespo made his move, and now you know the truth.*

Beth had tried to warn him. Beth and Bonnie knew all along while the NYPD and the reporters made a big deal about the cop who finished his business, the man who took on the mob. Shit, before they moved to Florida, some kid from NYU called him about a screenplay, the next big shoot 'em up where he takes down the Ferrettos in the climactic scene.

Except Beth and Bonnie knew. His wife knew what her husband had really done and what the consequences were. His daughter knew what her daddy's mistake was and had been fighting to survive it all her life. And now Ada was paying the highest price of all, a soul whose only purpose was pain and servitude, an eternal flame of vengeance.

They were all the consequences of his so-called success. Such success was always cast in the best possible light by those who admired it and wanted it to be possible. But when you stripped it all down, the circumstances were always mitigated. The ones who made it to the moon or cured the disease or won the case, they relied on those who'd patiently held back the flood to keep them from drowning, and usually, even after the deeds were done, they still held back the flood, God knows why.

Ray checked his accounts on his phone. One of them had been frozen somehow, and the other was running low. He was down to $22,000, plus the cash Lenora had given him for the dagger. Crespo had finally sold his boat but hadn't deposited the funds. *Because hey, after damning your entire family to eternal suffering, I thought stealing your boat would be a nice fuckin' garnish.*

He was up against the ropes and running out of time. There was no getting around what Lenora had done. The dagger was gone, and whoever the hell she really was, he knew her well enough not to bother pleading with her again.

At this point, he had two choices, head to Callaghan's or head to Tischer's. He'd seen indecision in Callaghan when they attacked him. He wasn't related to Ferretto and was only there because Crespo had likely threatened him, had given him a choice like, *help me out, and I'll pay you, fuck it up, and I'll bury your wife and kids.* Ray might be able to use that.

Then there was Tischer. If he forked over a little of the money he had left, Tisch might be a resource. If anybody had a chance to track down the dagger or a weapon like it, it was him. And if anybody was going to believe what was really going down with the demon, his granddaughter's soul, and the insanity of a place called Heaven, it was a curry-slurping dude on speed in a *Conan* t-shirt.

46

Ray pulled off the BQE at Vanderbilt and crept back north under the shadow of the overpass. He passed an empty school with shattered windows, a string of warehouses, and the occasional brownstone. As he crossed into Bushwick, Jansen Projects loomed on his right and Woodhull Hospital on his left. Behind it, the sun was setting over Manhattan's skyline.

When he reached Tischer's block, he parked the car, checked the pistol's ammo, and waited. Hassidim were closing roll-gates on the warehouses, breaking off in groups of two and three, and heading west toward Williamsburg. The wind got colder as the dusk drew on, and the kids in the hoodies left their stoops and corners, ducked through the worn security doors, and vanished into the halls of Jansen's colossal apartment blocks. The Crown Vic didn't stick out, just another cop.

He wondered for a minute if he might be able to score some pain killers from a corner dealer, though he knew that wasn't the main commodity around here. Strangely, his pain had subsided on its own. It was as if his ability to heal hadn't wholly worn off. The dagger's power had closed his wounds, and its residual effects left his mind a little clearer and gave just enough of a spark to his muscles to make one more bid.

Ray looked over his shoulder as he got out of the car and saw a man standing on the corner of Throop. It was the youngish Hassid he'd seen the last time he'd come to Tischer's. He looked slender and trim in his dark jacket. His reddish beard was long, and his curls framed dark eyes that met Ray's for a split-second before he vanished around the corner.

Ray considered following him, but he had to get his business with Tischer done first. He checked the .357 once, then headed down the stairs to the basement apartment. The door had been left ajar, and a weak light shone in the shadows beyond. As he drew closer, he detected a new odor mixed with the stale fast food, armpits, and crack fumes.

The stench of blood.

"Hey Tisch, you there? It's Ray."

He stepped inside, checked behind the door, then moved slowly into the room. The bed was empty, and so was the chair at the desk. His eyes took time to adjust to the low light cast only from the computer and a faded lava lamp.

He made his way further into the maze of old motherboards, box towers, and tangled wires. The gaming books and papers had been swept off their shelves, and several of the replica weapons had been knocked off the walls. A splintered bed-post lay across the floor, and the mattress had been yanked off and flipped. It had not been a struggle. It had been a rampage.

"Rrraaayyyyy... ovvverrrrr heeeere..."

Ray looked again at the desk. A dark lump covered in whiskers and blood-clotted hair opened one eye.

It was Tischer's head.

"Rrrayy," it rasped. "Watch out!"

Ray twisted and ducked. Tischer's body sprung out of a pile of trash bags stuffed under the stairs, swinging its fists like clubs. It wore only boxer shorts, yellowed in the front, stained brown in the back. Blood caked the corpse's jiggling stomach, and a hole had been bashed into its ribs. An intestine hung out like red sausage and flopped around as the thing swung its fists.

Ray fired two shots with the .357. The first blew a new hole in the thing's ribcage, and the second obliterated a chunk of its chest. He could see its heart beating erratically, stopping and starting and belching blood. But the thing kept on attacking, and

Ray couldn't fend off the second round of blows. He fired the pistol and missed just as the gun was knocked out of his hand.

"Rrrayyy, the aaaxx," rasped Tischer's head.

Ray scrambled through the mess of circuit boards and wires. He leaped across the mattress as the thing stomped after him. The corpse picked up the whole king-sized mass of it in one hand and flung it against the far wall. It took hold of his belt and reared back its fist.

Ray looked around on the floor beside the bedframe for the ax, saw only a sleek green dildo and a book titled *The Dungeon Master's Guide*. He tried to twist free, but the corpse's grip was too strong.

Just before its fist came down, he glimpsed the handle of one of the replica weapons and grabbed it. He was already swinging it when he saw it was the double-bladed battle-ax. He gave it all the force his right shoulder could give and chopped into the center of the corpse's neck.

The blow sliced through its already torn body, cutting it nearly in half. Ray swung again, this time slicing through the thing's stomach, down through its stained boxers, and out between its legs.

Its halved body fell to either side, giving a clear view of Tischer's severed head watching from the chair.

"Critical hit," it rasped. A parody of the old Tischer smile spread into the head's swollen jowls.

Ray dropped the ax and ran to the desk. Tischer's eyes rolled up in their sockets. "Thanks, Ray," he said. He smiled again in grotesque admiration. "Pick me up," he said.

"What the hell?"

"Pick me up and hold me in front of the screen. Click on the folder that says Taxes. Let it scan my retina and you're in."

"In what?"

"You'll s-see," said Tischer. "I'll be g-gone... I'm runnin' out fast, Ray... h-h-hurry up..."

Ray turned to the computer, an oversized tablet turned on end. He touched the Taxes folder, and when the prompt appeared, he clamped onto Tischer's bloody mop of hair and turned his face to the scanner.

"Therrrre, you'rrre in..."

Ray put his head back on the chair. *Now what? Hang in there? You're gonna be all right? I'll get you to a hospital?* "What can I do?" he asked.

"Nothing for me," said Tischer. "Look in the f-folder, it'll h-h-help." The head gave a hollow cough. "Rrrayy, tell my f-family I d-died in the line of d-duty."

"All right, where are they?"

"Nowhere. Hell maybe. N-nevermind, they'rrre g-gone, m-momma's g-gone, I'm g-g-g..."

The head stopped moving.

47

He played the videos first. They were motion-triggered security cameras. Like the trail cams his father used when he hunted years ago on Long Island. He wondered if these were the "bits and pieces" he had paid for but neglected. Perhaps he knew intuitively that Tischer had ripped him off and kept the good stuff, and yet now, in his death, was making up for that debt.

The first video showed Haldor Street, a trashcan falling over and dumping its rotten contents as if a strange wind struck it down. Nothing. That's just it. *Nothing hit her,* Tischer had said. *Her spine snapped like something plowed into her from behind. But on the video, there's nothing there!* And there was nothing there now, either. Just the tipped trash, the splashes of the puddles on the steps, and a door banging against its frame.

The second video followed, the sensors streaming each clip that had captured something. It began with an eyeful of the short-haired prostitute astride Tischer's girth on the bed. She looked flexible and bored. A dusk-colored rash spread from her shoulders to the small of her back. It was sprinkled with blisters, cuts, and callouses. Yet the fact she spent all of her money on crack cocaine made her lithe and slender. She had the proverbial "ripped" stomach and thighs, and Tischer looked transfixed by the love he had purchased.

His eyes widened with ecstasy when the demon bashed his head so hard it nearly flew off. Instead, it dangled from his broken neck by a few torn scraps of muscle. Ray caught sight of the thing in the body length mirror beside the bed. Its flesh might have been immune to being captured on video, and it might have cast no natural reflection in his rearview mirror, *but the camera and the mirror together captured its form in full.*

It hovered over the bed with its head curled in a fist. Its legs were like pillars, and its red flesh even more fiendish and distorted in reflection.

The head-fist bashed Tischer again, this time knocking his skull across the room. It landed by the desk, and though it drew no breath, managed an unnatural, hollow moan.

The prostitute leaped off the bed and bounded up the stairs like a doe fleeing a wolf. Ray saw the flash of Tischer's watch in one hand and her jacket in the other. The thing opened its hand and ran after her.

It wanted to seize her, but Ray noticed something else, something he hadn't even seen when it attacked him in the cemetery. He paused the video, zoomed in to verify, and saw that it was true. The demon had slitted eyes on its fingertips, just under its nails. They looked like little slashes, cuts in puffy callouses. But now there was no mistaking a black pupil against pinkish sclera, shifting and searching.

So it didn't just attack from behind for the element of surprise—it didn't see well. It had a problem with depth perception, maybe when its fingers were extended. And when it made a fist, it was temporarily blind.

If only he had known when he had hunted it that night with Lenora, he might have set a different trap. *Might have, you compulsive old fuck? What about what you did with her all the nights before? Was that about the "power" of the dagger, or were sex and high-octane cocaine just the greatest getaways?*

Ray closed the videos and began opening PDFs. They were unredacted police interviews with Chrissy Blood. Van Meeks had been onto Lobe, and apparently, Blood was willing to make a deal and sell him out. Van Meeks wanted to know if Lobe was acting alone:

Blood: I told you he ain't alone, he done sold his soul, he got a fuckin' demon, man! He summoned a goddamn demon!

Van Meeks: Okay, a henchman, this henchman, can you describe—

Blood: Not a henchman, motherfucker! A goddamn demon! Something wrong with your ears? A demon from Hell! He got him and he's comin', you gotta help me, I need that witness protection shit, I need that—

Van Meeks: If you want us to help, you need to calm down. Now this henchman...

Ray closed the interviews and went on to Van Meeks' personal notes. During February, several entries theorized they had another base of operations where Lobe's accomplice was hiding bodies.

He thought the accomplice was somehow "under the radar," a foreign national, or even an out-of-stater who'd lived off the books for decades. By March, he was convinced the gentlemen's club was only a hunting ground. He said they were working out of another building somewhere in Brooklyn or Queens. It might be abandoned, and they were operating without the owner's knowledge.

He had begun to lookup missing-persons cases. They were doing something with some of the bodies, putting them somewhere. There were definitely more victims than had been found.

Van Meeks wanted more interviews with Chrissy Blood,

but the man had gone missing. The detective wrote that he was uncooperative and had unrealistic expectations. He regretted not arresting him, but he did have a lead. A corner dealer gave an address off Halsey, an old funeral home that had been run as a rooming house then shutdown. Blood was holed up in the basement apartment.

In his latest entry, Van Meeks was planning to pay a visit, and if he was there, have him arrested. The date was April 16th. It was only two days old. If he was lucky, Ray could get there before the detective did, get Blood to tell him where Lobe's "henchman" was storing his kills. *Because he uses them, because they walk, just like Lenora's friend Kev and the thing that had been Tischer that now lay eviscerated on the floor.*

There was no time to download the files, let alone print them. Ray texted himself the hideout's address, then picked up the replica ax, and cleaved the computer in half.

"Thanks a lot, Tisch," he said. "Hope they have curry in Hell." He gave the severed head a salute and left it where it lay.

48

Ray drove out Broadway with the battle-ax on the passenger seat beside him. The thing was a replica and no substitute for the weapon he'd lost. He knew there had been more to what he and Lenora had done with the dagger than just gratification. The wounds from the weapon had kept him alive. He also knew it wasn't just the blood and the blade he missed. But there was no time for nostalgia over the remembrance of sadisms past.

He began to form a plan. He thought of the angel he'd pulled out of the pool back in Florida in the nightmare's early stages. It had fought with the ant-demon on the Faustina and had massive jaws but lacked speed.

These creatures were immensely strong but had their weaknesses. In the demon's case, it was poor eyesight bordering on blindness. That and the fact cameras could see its reflection added to the possibility he might trap the thing.

He passed Halsey Street and headed further east until he reached Herring Ave. There he made a right and drove between graffiti-laden warehouses until he reached a tilted two-family townhouse covered in a mix of worn white siding and plywood.

The apartment number was 1B. It was more "garden apartment" than basement if you considered the cube of polluted weeds behind the building a garden. Unlike Tischer's cave, only three steps led down to the small courtyard. A door stood at the far end, tucked under the stoop.

But when Ray approached, he found somebody was already there.

"Are you here to see Chris Lansing? I'm afraid you have to wait your turn."

Ray recognized the Hassidic man he'd seen by Tischer's place. The man turned and knocked on the door, calling out, "I just want to talk to you."

A voice from inside hollered back: "I tol' you, come back tomorrow!"

"You said that yesterday."

"I said get outta here is what I said! I'm sayin' now, get outta here, get the hell out!"

The man shook his head and turned to Ray. He wore spectacles and had a full, red-brown beard. Despite its length, he looked very young. Though the black hat and coat were a centuries-old traditional dress, they were also form-fitting and looked somehow kind of hip.

"My name is Isaiah," he said.

He offered his hand and Ray shook it.

"Ray," said Ray.

"I am here to see Chris about a loan," he said.

"Doesn't sound like he wants to see you," said Ray. The hollering continued but sounded further away and incoherent, like whoever was inside moved away from the door. Ray took a step back in the courtyard. There were a pair of plywood-covered windows set into the foundation. Some nails had fallen out of one of them. Ray pulled the corner up an inch, but it was too dark to see inside.

"He should talk to me," said Isaiah. "We could work it out."

"Yeah, well if you don't mind, I'd like to talk to him first. It won't take long." Ray pulled at the wood again, testing its strength.

Isaiah stepped out from underneath the stairs and leaned in close to Ray. "Perhaps I could loan you something as well."

"Don't need money right now, thanks."

"Maybe you don't. Maybe you do. But I'm not talking about money," he said.

"What are you talkin' about?"

"Lenora López. You know her?"

Ray just looked at him. *What do you think?*

"She said I should talk to you."

"How do you know Lenora?" Ray asked.

"We work with some of the same galleries. I own an import-export company."

"What's that got to do with Lenora?"

"She's an art-handler. She's freelances sometimes, you know, pickups, deliveries, appraisals."

The fucking dagger. Of course bartending wasn't her main gig. But he assumed she was just selling a little coke and maybe hooking up escorts like her friend Bobbie and that shit with the video. And if she'd been an undercover cop, he would have smelled it on her right away, and nobody was deep cover enough for what the two of them had done. *But a fucking art-handler?* That was the deepest cut of all. But it also meant another chance.

"So what do you want to loan me?" he asked.

49

Isaiah led him around the block, past the weedy yard to a Cadillac parked along the curb. The thing was old but well maintained and had illegally tinted windows. He asked Ray to get in the back while he sat in the front. Ray slipped inside and pulled a long box over his lap so he could fit.

"Go ahead, open it," said Isaiah.

Ray lifted the polished wooden lid. The sword's three-foot blade shined despite the windows' tint, and it had letters inscribed along its length: +VLFBERHT+.

"It's a copy of sorts," said Isaiah. "But it's not a forgery. Ulfberht blades were crafted in the Rhineland and were prized for their quality during the middle ages. But this particular sword includes another element. It is called *Plutysium*, and it does not come from Earth. You would consider my words those of a madman if you did not see what you have seen. But you know well now that what I say is true. Demons crafted this weapon for one of their brethren who was fighting in Sweden centuries ago. It is rare for something of its kind to fall into human hands, and its value is incalculable. And yet it can be made even more valuable."

Ray took hold of the grip. The weight was heavy enough to strengthen the impact but light enough to avoid fatigue. In his right hand, it felt electric, and for a moment, he felt he was born to wield it and that the dagger had served to prepare him for the weapon he now held.

"You want me to kill the demon with this and give it back to you," said Ray.

"Yes, that is the deal. But first, we need to pay a visit to Mr. Lansing, or Chrissy Blood, as you know him. Think of it as a chance to give the weapon a test-drive."

50

They crossed the courtyard with Ray in the lead. He held the broadsword, and Isaiah followed behind, clasping a pistol. They didn't turn left under the stairs but headed straight for the plywood-covered window. Ray heard a squeak and paused while a woman in a kerchief pushed a grocery cart up Herring Ave, a boy and girl trailing.

"Mira mami! Un cuervo enorme," cried the girl.

Ray held the sword down against his leg. When he looked to his left, he saw the child wasn't pointing at them but at a raven that had landed on the stairs above the apartment door. The woman paid no attention, and the cart squeaked on.

Ray flipped the sword over and pried off the plywood plank. He kicked the already half-broken window and shattered the remaining glass. Chipped shards cut his hand as he vaulted inside.

He landed in a clutter of Styrofoam, cardboard boxes, and tilted candles. The narrow railroad apartment smelled of jasmine, lavender, patchouli, and a dozen other nauseating scents. Only one small white candle was lit. It stood in the center of the floor in a space clear of the clutter. Somewhere down the hall, a fluorescent light flickered.

A scream sounded as a figure lunged from the shadows. By the candle's guttering light, Ray glimpsed a man with blonde cornrows and a black goatee. The bottom half of a tracksuit covered his legs, but he was otherwise undressed.

What might have once been a powerful physique clung to his bones in a bluish web of veins and emaciated muscle. His dark eyes were wide and terrified, and he attacked like a rabid animal. He was taller, and his sword was long, yet Ray's weapon was light and aerodynamic. Their blades clanged and scraped, and sparks flew.

Already Ray felt attuned to the broadsword. He shifted his weight, swung with one then two hands, alternating freely. Blood was strong, but Ray felt his momentum grow.

Despite his bleeding hand, he punched upward with the sword's small crossbar. He clipped Blood's chin, causing him to trip over an old boxy TV and land on the white candle. The man screamed again but managed to get back on his feet. He picked up the candle, poured out the liquified wax, and righted it. The flame sputtered and almost fizzled, causing him to mutter, "No, no, no!"

Ray took the opening and bludgeoned him again with the crossbar in hopes of subduing him. But even in his mortified state, Blood's arm pistoned and swung the longsword. Ray parried the blow, then with both hands on the broadsword's grip, plunged it through Chrissy Blood's foot.

Blood screamed again. "No, damnit, no," he cried. "Please don't!"

"Tell me what I want, and I won't," said Ray.

"Just put it down, please put it down," said Blood.

Ray pulled up the sword and held it in Blood's face. "You drop your blade first," he said.

"Shut your mouth, fool," said Blood. He gave Ray a quick jab to the chin, knocking him back and giving him a taste of his own sword's crossbar. Ray saw that it, too, was a formidable weapon, and the man was skilled in how to use it. He slashed at Ray again, letting him know he could have cut a piece off his neck, then turned away and went on, "Please, just let me have it, let me have it, and I'll talk."

Ray realized then that except for telling him to shut up,

Blood had been talking to Isaiah all along. The man was standing behind them with his pistol in one hand and the white candle in the other. He took a step closer and raised the flame to his lips as if he would blow it out.

"No," Blood cried. "Please don't! Please don't let them come back!"

Isaiah smiled. He handed Blood the candle. "You will talk to my friend Ray now, or losing a sword fight will be the least of your problems."

51

"The demon uses Colborne Hospital as its lair. It goes there at night, fills the old morgue with its pets and prizes."

Blood took a drag on the cigarette Isaiah had given him. He cradled the burning candle like it was his infant child.

"We summoned it so it could hunt and feast, but it never cared about us, never considered us its masters or even its allies. It would just as soon smash us to a pulp or lock us in one of those drawers where it keeps its pet corpses. The thing's made of hatred and nothing else.'

"It toyed with us for a while, a headless monster that laughed from its chest. I never want to hear that laugh again." He paused and sheltered the candle with his hand, glaring at the flame with bloodshot eyes. "Gog and Magog are giants from the void." Blood looked at Ray. "You know nothing about what it is out there. You know nothing about what is in the heavens and the stars."

"I know some," Ray answered.

"Gog and Magog became kings on Earth. They wandered, spread their hellish seed. They were in the east and also in Albion. Those of us who studied learned of their sons. We learned of Magog's bastards and that they can be summoned. They are rare in that they are more than mere imps, but demons of rank. So we brought one of them to us. We were on the rise, and we were high and stupid. Lobe had his club, and we knew some of the families. It was mostly the old Italian families who had done this before, secretly, as part of their power. We wanted some of that power."

Blood stopped to drag on the cigarette, and Ray thought of Crespo, the ace in the hole that Ferretto had used against him. He hadn't understood how vengeance went beyond death, and Ray felt like he could feel the old don, a heavily muscled corpse in gold chains and a suit, shaking his head over Ray's shoulder. *You made a mistake, Ray. Look at you now, look at your family, look at your damn granddaughter.*

"Cut to the fuckin' chase," Ray said, interrupting his own thoughts. "Where's it get in and out of the hospital?"

"We only went there once. That whole building's like a big ol' skull. Its windows are all busted out, three stories, half the top floor collapsed. The morgue's in the basement, though. The demon took us right in the main entrance. It had this homeless dude that night. It smashed some of the poor bastard's ribs, and when we got him inside, set him loose in the old psych ward on the second floor.'

"The vagrant did his best to find his way back down, up to the roof or out the window. But the Son of Magog had closed it all off. The thing used that big ol' hand like a goddamn crane and shoveled the rubble into a whole lotta dead-ends. It chased the man down and broke him one bone at a time until it finally ripped off his head and shoved him down the old elevator shaft and into the morgue."

"How many bodies in there?" Ray asked.

"More than made it in the news."

"What's it doing with them?"

"How the hell am I supposed to know? It stores 'em during the day and goes back for 'em at night. I don't know what the hell it does with 'em."

"Okay," said Isaiah. "You have just made good on this month's payment. I will see you next. Remember, the protection from the candle does not run out, but time might."

52

Isaiah drove Ray back to where he had parked the Crown Vic and gave him a key to a loft owned by a friend. He said to follow him over so he could sleep and prep there.

"What was all that shit about the candle?" Ray asked as they took the freight elevator to the third floor.

"*Ner neshama*, the yahrzeit candle. It is a candle we light for the deceased. Its flame is like a soul, but this one possesses power, like your weapons. This candle protects you from aggressors so long as it burns. And it does not extinguish easily. For the right price, I can obtain them for those who have a spiritual need." Isaiah lowered his spectacles, and his eyes met Ray's.

I'll take half a dozen, Ray thought.

But he remained silent as the elevator door opened. They crossed the hall where Ray's key opened the door to a brick-and-sheetrock cave with a bathroom and kitchenette slapped into the far wall.

"For now, you can rest here," said Isaiah.

Ray nodded, and they agreed to meet up the next night.

He found the fridge stocked and realized the place was kept ready for someone on the lam. He skipped the temptation to grab a beer, eating a hunk of salmon instead and washing it down with a glass of water.

He stepped into the bathroom's skinny stall and took a shower, then lay down on the double bed. The curtains were already closed over both windows, but he could feel the weather changing outside. It was threatening to jump into summer, knocking out spring in the second round like New York preferred.

He remained out for hours in a conspicuously dreamless sleep. At some point, he woke and lay dozing and feeling empty. He felt like Ada was more distant than ever, and what Beth showed him about their life in Florida was just another fancy nail in his family's coffin. He'd never been a speculator but had been a part of enough bad business deals in his life to know when the possibility of getting paid was beginning to vanish.

He tried to will himself to dream of Riel as he lay in the morning heat. He thought if he did, he might cut a new deal with the angel, convince him somehow to let her go.

But it was a child's wish. Payment was contingent upon services rendered. A mechanism more essential to the universe than fucking gravity.

***

Three things now, he thought as he rode the elevator down to his car. *The crew, the gear, and the setup.* After that, only the kill remained.

He drove the Crown Vic south, avoided the BQE, and rolled through downtown Brooklyn. Student types and semi-hipsters in Boerum Hill's more conservative bohemia were in the sidewalk cafés enjoying the strong spring sun. The city hadn't reached its full stink, though it would be close if two days in a row touched eighty.

When he reached Park Slope, he took a left off Fifth Avenue and drove until he reached Windsor Terrace. He was still three blocks from Callaghan's place when he saw them on the school playground. Maribel Callaghan sat on a bench while her son and daughter played on the swings. Ada crouched at the top of a slide beside them.

Ray tried to ignore her as he approached the bench. His shadow stretched across the playground's pavement, driven by the midday sun. He wore a black t-shirt and slacks, all plainclothes cop and not trying to hide it. Maribel looked up at him, hair pulled back, one ringlet hanging loosely along her neck. She was showing off her freckles again in the early spring heat. Her teeth touched her lower lip as she smiled.

"Didn't know you were still in town," she said.

"Still working on the case," he said.

"Door's open if you want some dinner."

She giggled because she wasn't serious, and he'd read her husband well enough to know they weren't that kind of couple. Beneath the giggle was the tiniest bit of resignation as if she saw a ghost come to say goodbye before he finished his business.

"Is Brad at home? I need to talk to him."

"What for?"

Her teeth touched her lip again. *Then again, maybe they were like that.*

"It's related to the case."

She nodded. "You know, I'm gonna put the kids on the bus in a few minutes. Wait with me, and we'll all have a drink."

She stretched her elbows back along the top of the bench, pulling her blouse snug against her skin. Apparently, the quainter flirtation was reserved for Easter.

"Unfortunately, I don't have much time," he said.

Mrs. Callaghan nodded. The sun shone on her cheek and turned her into a curly-haired Madonna, smile a mix of lust and sadness. "Maybe you could use some stress-relief," she said.

"Sure," he said. "But like I said, no time."

"Yeah, okay, I understand," she said. "Lemme try Brad. He'll pick up if it's me." She pulled her phone from her purse and thumbed the screen. She called a couple of times until the smile was fully gone. "He's not picking up. Maybe he's in the basement."

To Ray, it sounded more like *he better be in the basement.*

"If he's home, I could just walk over," he said.

"No, I'll go," she said, "if it's that important. Wait here and watch the kids."

She wasn't asking, and her words had the kind of mother's

231

tone that could make Ted Bundy change a diaper. She gathered up her purse and left, and Ray figured the plan was as good as any. If Crespo was keeping track of Callaghan's movements, it wouldn't be as suspicious to be summoned by his wife, and it was unlikely he had eyes on the playground.

But his satisfaction betrayed him when he turned and found himself face to face with Ada.

The gaunt vulture of a girl sat perched on the slide with her mouth open and her tongue slivered between her jagged teeth. She looked like she was laughing, the way a skull looks like it's laughing when its jaw hangs slack. Her eyes were metallic stones, blanked over like they'd been worn by the wind. Her body was bruised and emaciated, and her clothes were in tatters.

"She says they've had her in a weird cell for twenty years. She says it's like *Little Ease* in the Tower of London, and the angels can bend time when they punish you." Callaghan's daughter Jenny spoke from the swing. She was pumping lackadaisically, and on the upswing, came close enough to whisper into Ray's ear.

Ray looked into Ada's empty eyes as he answered. "I'm almost there," he said. "I'm close, I'm gonna help you, I'm gonna do this, I'm gonna do this for all of us."

"She says people are idiots. She says the word idiot comes from ancient Greek, which they speak sometimes in Heaven and it means *private person*. She says people are private idiots and morons. She says moron's Greek, too. It means *fool*."

"Talk to me yourself," Ray said. He squinted and felt his mouth go dry because Ada crooked her head in that alien way he feared and hated.

"She says she can't talk now, and my brother hardly can, either. She says she helped me when my brother didn't believe me about the golden rods. She made him start singing in choirs. He sings with the angels now in his dreams, and when he wakes up, he can't talk 'cause his throat is so ripped up. If he doesn't sing, they use the golden rods. So they make him sing all night, and they use his throat right until he wakes up. Now he believes me."

The girl hopped off the swing. The bus had arrived, and

she ran for its open door. Her brother followed with slow steps, spittle running from the corner of his mouth. The bus driver honked the horn as the boy stumbled forward.

"I should blame you, but I don't."

Ray turned and faced Callaghan. He had entered the playground through the opposite gate. He lit a cigarette and smoked it by the jungle gym.

"Fuck Crespo," he said.

"How much did he give you?"

"That's the thing," said Callaghan. He took a flask from his pocket and pulled on it. "It's like some Wall Street deal where they brought in the chump new guy. He told me sky's the limit. He said he'd pay off the house and all my other debts. But it was all just a big old shit-pie in the clouds." Callaghan pulled on the flask again. He paid no lip service to moderation like he had that day in the basement. He handed it over and Ray drank deeply.

"Well, I don't know how much you owe, but if you help me out, it's five thousand upfront," said Ray. He handed back the flask, dug a fresh roll of cash from his pocket, and began counting out hundreds.

"I'll take the money, but that's not why I'm in," said Callaghan. "I'm in to beat Tolly."

"You gotta help me kill the demon first."

"You sure? I don't know what to make of that fuckin' thing. Had somethin' to do with that dagger, though, didn't it? That's why Tolly wanted it."

"You could say that. I have a plan though, and I have what we need. You follow my lead, we can take it down. You'll get another twenty-thousand on top and then we take Crespo after."

"Like I said, I'm in."

"And when we take Crespo, I pull the trigger."

"I don't give a fuck who pulls the trigger," said Callaghan. "I just want him to lose. And I want him to see who beat him. All those old assholes—no offense—but all those old assholes, all they do is win and win and win and wanna keep on winning. I want him to lose this time, and I want to see his eyes, and I want

233

him to know who beat him."

53

Ray took one more hit from the flask and told Callaghan that Isaiah would pick him up the next night. He told him there would be two cars, his and Isaiah's, and for fuck's sake, make sure he avoided Crespo in the meantime.

If he had anything left of his ability to read the truth, he read in the young man's eyes that it wasn't a setup. He knew the thirst for revenge when he saw it. If anything, the kid was looking a little too hungry.

He got on the BQE this time and drove north, got off in Astoria, and headed over to Steinway Street. The address on Tischer's receipt brought him to a corner building with a sign that read *Merlin's Oak Games & Gifts*. The shop took up the whole first floor, and in the upstairs window, he saw plump, bearded men sitting around tables rolling dice.

He pushed through the door and headed to the glass counter. One end held dioramas of cemeteries and castles populated with painted miniatures. The other was full of daggers and knives. Larger weapons hung on a pegboard partition behind it. There were swords three, four, and five feet long, and a whole section of maces and flails. Next to these hung a column of throwing axes, along with a single, heavy headsman's ax.

Ray went to the side with the weapons, and the clerk came over to meet him. The man had a long beard and wore corkscrew glasses and a t-shirt with moons and stars on it. He had a belly the size of Tischer's but also had muscular arms built from lifting weights. As he leaned over the counter, Ray caught a whiff of something that smelled like pipe-smoke and Kool-Aid. He glimpsed a stick of incense burning on a shelf behind him. The package beside it read *Cherry Mystique.*

What was it with the damn nerds? Ray wondered. *If they didn't suffocate you with their armpits, they gassed you with burning sugar.*

"Are you looking for something in particular?" the clerk asked. He was staring at whatever Ray had wrapped in a blanket and tucked under his arm.

"I hope so," said Ray. He put the blanket on the counter and unwrapped the sword. "I was wondering if you got anything like this. I got this game I'm playing later and I need another sword."

"You mean a LARP?"

"No, a sword," said Ray.

"I mean the game," said the clerk. "A LARP is a live-action role-playing game."

"Yeah that," said Ray. "I need a sword that looks like this one."

"All right, let's have a look," he said. The man had started drooling into his beard the second he saw the scabbard, and he drew the blade as if he was Arthur pulling Excalibur from the stone.

"This is a beauty," he said.

"Thanks, I got it in Florida. They got nice swords down there."

The clerk frowned then looked back at the blade. "The grain looks authentic. Most Ulfberht replicas are too symmetrical. But I've never seen folded steel quite like this."

"You got anything like it?"

The clerk squinted behind his glasses like he'd been insulted. "Of course," he said. He took a scabbard down from the pegboard, laid it on the counter, then went behind the partition and brought out two more.

"The one in the sheath is hand-forged. The other two are

cheaper, factory-made by a company called *Castlefang.*"

Ray frowned at him, then looked back at the blades. "They're too shiny," he said.

"They're replicas," said the clerk.

"Which one do you think's more realistic?" Ray asked. "Like if you were trying to fool somebody?"

"I don't think these would fool anybody," he said. "You don't have to be an expert to have an eye for authenticity. It's like spotting a fake gamer or a *real gangster.*"

Ray ignored the insinuation. "So then, you don't have anything real, like a real antique?"

The clerk chuckled. "You think I'd be running this place if I did? Hell no. But tell you what, have a look at this." He went behind the pegboard again and came back with a rusty blade five feet long with pointed lugs above the crossbar. *Looks like Lobe's sword*, Ray thought.

"This baby's a replica of an antique. Made to look old, perfect ornament for your medieval feast. They call them *zweihanders* these days, but that's not really the right term. Most two-handed swords are properly called longswords and are Renaissance weapons from southern Germany."

"Whatever. How much?" said Ray.

The clerk grimaced. "Twenty-five hundred."

Ray grimaced back. He only had six-thousand left in the roll after what he owed Callaghan.

"All right," he said. He handed over the bills, then wrapped the blade in the blanket with the broadsword.

"Have fun with your game," said the clerk. "Hey, by the way, you need anything else? I know a guy who can get you a deal on a Glock-9."

Jesus Christ, New York nerds! And what was it with the fuckin' Glocks? "No thanks," said Ray. "And that incense smells like shit."

The clerk smiled as he stuffed the cash in his jeans.

54

Ray drove back to the studio and snatched a few hours' sleep. He woke early, donned the black jeans and hoodie he picked up at the surplus store, then headed out to finish the last of his prep. Traffic was thin for a Friday, and the spring sun had turned merciless.

Brooklyn's streets cooked like bacon on a concrete grill. Ray remembered when he first moved to Florida how surprised he was that the weather wasn't that oppressive. Even in spring, New York City had a cruelty to its heat. The pavement became scorched, and the air didn't move.

He stopped at a deli off Driggs for a coffee before he turned east. A regular meant plenty of cream and sugar, and so today he'd let the drink be as sickly-sweet as the air. The clerks were watching the news, something about kidnapped students from a religious academy off Montrose. The police had found them, and now it was a hostage standoff.

Ray gulped his coffee and headed back out. Only one thing mattered now. Crespo thought he had schooled him, and whoever the hell remained of the Ferrettos thought they had won. But it was Beth who taught him what he owed, taught him the secrets of the world behind the world and what they meant.

I want him to lose this time, Callaghan had said. *I want him to know who beat him.* Ray drove past the old lumberyard off Metropolitan until he reached the furniture warehouse. There were only a few other cars in the lot when he turned in. Its barrenness reminded him of 2001 after the towers came down. The city was so quiet, businesses were open, but people moved around with footsteps like whispers.

He went inside and asked the floor salesman for wall mirrors, no, not vanities, no dressers, just mirrors. He asked for the largest size for the lowest price and as many as they had. When he loaded them into the trunk of the Crown Vic, it wouldn't shut. He had to rope it down so he could drive. He went back into the hardware store to pick up a few more pieces of gear, then returned to the apartment for the final checklist.

On the way, his phone buzzed with a message from Isaiah that he'd come through on the cameras. He had two sets of six he could sync to his phone. It would have to be enough. The afternoon was getting later, and he was going to need a couple of hours in the hospital for the setup. He checked the ammo for the .357, rewrapped the swords, then locked up the apartment.

His phone buzzed again on the elevator. He thought it was Isaiah, but the number was unrecognizable. He read the text:

`got something for you`

Ray felt a flash of hope that it was good news from Beth, or even Riel. Or even Lenora.

`Who is this?`

`Bobbie`

`I'll pick you up`

He met her outside the Mexican bakery on Grand Street. She stood in front of a window filled with colorful cakes covered in gelatinous frosting. She wore a tank top and ripped jeans and had her hair tied back. She had a backpack slung on her shoulder, and her belly-button ring glimmered in the sunlight. When he pulled up, she gave the trademark grin that was both easygoing and all business.

Ray lowered the window and opened the door.

"Get in," he said.

Bobbie slipped into the front seat. "I got something for you," she said. "We thought you could use it, and we could get it done, so we did."

When she said "we," she nodded toward the corner where Ray saw a skinny kid with a wispy goatee and a hoodie. He recognized him from the day he'd bought the gun at the *Bushwick Inn*.

"I know him from the club," she said before he could ask. "Lenora doesn't, but she said bring who I want. She's the one who fronted the money."

"Money for what?" he asked.

Bobbie unzipped the backpack. Ray recognized the saex's bone hilt. "She said you could use it," she said.

Ray drew the dagger. He scraped his thumb across the blade. It had been sharpened.

"I want to see Lenora."

"She's not here."

"Where is she?"

Bobbie shrugged. "Europe maybe. Hey, I gotta run," she said, opening the door. She looked at him like he was already a dead man. He wondered if she knew it was much worse than that.

"Tell her thanks," he said.

"If I talk to her," she said.

She stepped out of the car, swung the door shut, and turned down Graham Avenue. The kid on the corner headed the opposite direction. Neither of them looked back.

55

The sun was setting when he turned onto Lombardy Street and parked in Colborne's gravel lot. The hospital was a husk of pulverized brick and glass, and vapors from the canal blurred its silhouette in the waning light.

The Victorian façade had been "modernized" years before, mixing the gothic cornices with drab minimalism. It looked like the skull of a sick beast waiting for a meal. Ray took the first of the mirrors from the trunk and headed for the entrance.

56

He remembered Colborne from his narcotics days as a part-time crash pad for the homeless and junkies. It had never quite become a crack house because the dealers didn't like it. There was something about its dark immensity that made them uneasy, not to mention the old psych-ward was rumored to be haunted by the patients who had died there.

Yet none made their appearance as he placed his cameras and mirrors along its second-floor halls. The install went smoothly, though it took a little more time to find the old elevator shaft that led to the basement morgue.

Securing an extra rope to its corroded steel frame, he slid down into the gloom. A scrid of waning sunlight shone through a high window as he moved down the hallway and walked around the square room filled with storage drawers. *The bodies in these drawers are not at rest*, he thought.

Yet nothing stirred as he tapped until he found a hollow one. Once his gear was loaded, he went back to the elevator shaft, painstakingly brought down the rest of the mirrors and cameras, and screwed them to the walls. The mirrors made the place look like a demented dressing-room for the dead, and he only had six cameras left, which he had to place strategically. Finally, he wheeled over an old surgical table, stood on it, and fastened his most delicate item to the ceiling. Afterward, he returned to the car in darkness and texted Isaiah.

The car pulled up within minutes, Callaghan got out, and Ray led him to the hospital's crumbled entrance. A few texts later, he confirmed he'd taken up his position, and all was quiet and still.

57

Ray moved to the edge of the parking lot, where he waited between the gravel and the weeds. The hospital loomed before him, lit by the orange glow of the harbor lights along the Newtown Creek. He checked his phone and found a text from Isaiah:

```
it's off lombardy
```

Five minutes passed, then:

```
lombardy again
has body
```

Three minutes later:

```
warehouse roof north
```

One minute after:

```
canal now, upstream
```

Ray ducked into a clump of weeds and looked north. Spools of razor-wire topped a fence that separated the hospital from a row of wretched warehouses along the channel. He saw Isaiah where he had taken up position on a fire escape. The man pointed past an abandoned dock where the channel's surface was foaming and frothing.

The demon was there, rising out of the sludge. Its arms and shoulders came first, then the giant hand, palm pregnant with a corpse. Its fingers clutched the girl like they were strange and swollen veins around some hideously reborn child. It began to move across the lot, body dripping oil and bits of trash.

Before, he would have been tempted to attack it there, would have still thought he could ambush the thing. But he knew better now. *Out here, it'll get behind you. It'll be like the night in the cemetery.*

Ray thumbed a text to Isaiah and Callaghan:

```
heading in
```

He stepped out of the weeds and crossed to the hospital's entrance. In his periphery, he glimpsed the demon's sinewy red limbs as it strode beneath the harbor's amber lights. If he didn't time it right, it was already over. If he ran now, it would rip him apart in the lot. He had to have enough of a lead to get through the entrance but allow the demon to get close enough that it was sure it could trap him inside.

Ray drew the sword, kept it low beside him, and trained his eyes on the broken doors. *Look back, and it knows you've seen it.* He forced himself not to run for the dark opening, and with each step, expected the thing to seize him by the shoulders and dash his brains against the bricks.

I'm on the stairs now, he thought as a reflection appeared in a shard of the doorway's broken glass. It was the corpse held by the demon. The dead girl looked like she was floating, partially obscured by a hand that cast no reflection.

Don't let it know you noticed, Ray thought as he slipped through the door.

He texted Callaghan:

```
inside
```

He climbed the lobby's curved staircase and moved left along the balcony. He headed down the hall, past a bricked over archway. He counted three until he reached one where the bricks had been knocked out, and made another left into the psych-ward. The first of his mirrors hung on the wall to his right. He passed two more, then the nurse's station where Callaghan hid behind the counter.

He waited there at the first intersection, opening the app on his phone and checking the first camera. The demon's reflection appeared on the video as it leaned over to pass through. It dropped the dead girl on the floor, then used one of its claws to pick her up by her hair. For a second, it was like she was looking at Ray with her dead eyes, then the red fingers closed over her skull and ripped her head from her body. It threw the head down the hall after Ray, fanning blood over the floor and walls.

It knows I see it, thought Ray. He made a point of flashing the sword as he crossed the intersection where the entrance to the treatment room stood opposite the elevator shaft. *Let its hunger blind it more*, he thought.

Now it was up to Callaghan. The man was seasoned for his age, but Ray suddenly thought of him as a rookie. He was like a desperate young father trying to feed his family, utterly ignorant of what he faced. *Don't rush it*, Ray thought.

But Callaghan leaped from behind the counter too soon. He made his attack like he was giving the finger to Ray's plan and to the very concept that the demon could be real. It was like suicide by cop in reverse. He let off three rounds with his .40 cal before the demon spun and seized his torso in its hand and held him with his feet kicking in the air.

There was nothing Ray could do. He had told him to wait until he engaged the thing by the elevator, then wound it and run.

But the man had other plans, and now the cavity in the demon's chest opened and the rib-teeth clamped onto Callaghan's kicking legs. The giant hand twisted his torso against his hips, tore it off, and smashed it against a mirror. *News Flash: Officer,*

Husband, and Father of Two Sees Own Body Ripped in Half.

The demon spat Callaghan's still twitching legs on the floor then charged for the intersection. Ray ran for the treatment room. *He didn't even wound it*, he thought. *It's still moving fast.* He entered the room through the door at the end of the hallway. It stood opposite the elevator shaft, which the demon probably knew, but didn't know mattered.

Ray waited by a mildewed bed lined with rusting restraint cuffs. A haze from the harbor lights shone through the pair of broken windows. When he turned, the demon had already ducked through the door and was on him with its wrecking-ball fist. The thing moved with a spider's twisted dexterity. He thought it might be slower in the hospital's confines, but instead it scuttled around him, using its arms as if they were another pair of legs. It smashed with its fist, crumpling the bed, then struck again with the backswing, barely missing Ray's head.

He tried to slash it, but it withdrew its hand and simultaneously grabbed Ray's wrist with one of its smaller claws. Pain shot through his forearm as the claw squeezed and caused him to drop the sword.

Scream like it's more than pain, Ray thought, *like it's trapped you now.* Crying out, he left the replica sword where it lay. Without the weapon, he was able to slip out of the thing's grip. He ran across the room, dodged another bone-smashing blow, and dove into the elevator shaft. The rope burned his palms as he slid down, and he fell the last six feet as the demon broke the knot off at the top.

The bastard isn't wounded, but it still thinks you're unarmed, thinks it has you trapped.

He ran down the hall and flipped on the contractor-lights he'd installed. A crash sounded from the elevator shaft as the demon landed fist-first on the floor. Ray looked over his shoulder and saw it splay its giant fingers like they were legs and scuttle after him. It was toying with him just a little, speeding up and slowing down. Finally, it flipped back over and strode after him, head-hand outstretched, eyes glaring beneath its fingernails.

Ray sprinted. *Maybe Callaghan's sacrifice mattered after all. Maybe he helped make the thing cocky.*

As he burst into the morgue, he heard knocking in the storage drawers. The corpses were thumping and scratching. One of the contractor lights had failed, and the room was darker than when he'd tested it. In the corner, he saw a motion sensor flash. At least the cameras were still working.

The demon's footsteps slowed as it approached the entrance. Ray moved to the north wall and turned the lever on the second drawer from the floor. The slab rolled out, and he crawled onto it. He tugged the rope against the pulley, and the drawer slid shut again as he heard the other drawers opening. He activated the light on his phone, then checked the broadsword in its sheath on his right and the dagger where it lay on his left.

He opened the app for the cameras and saw the room was full of walking, headless corpses. He rolled on his side, clutching the detonator in his left hand and his phone in his right. An array of six images lit the screen. Four cameras pointed at the mirrors, two at the center of the room. Corpses and the reflections of corpses filled the tiny squares.

The images were slightly blurry and suffered from a lag, but in camera two, in the top right, he saw the reflection of the demon's huge red hand reaching through the doorway. It looked ethereal as its fragmented form glided from mirror to mirror. The thing's body followed after, all scars and red sinew, and the corpses raised their hands as if in worship.

Now Ray saw it in three different frames. Filtered through multiple mirrors and the pixilated blur, it was difficult to discern its exact position. He saw its fingers fan outward, and the dead begin searching the room, groping at the old surgical tables and inspecting the shadowed corners.

The eyes on the tips of the demon's fingers looked like dark smudges. It drew upward, close to the ceiling, and made a sudden fist. It had become aware of something, and Ray put his thumb on the button. A few more steps, and it would be directly under the shaped charge. He felt the storage drawer rattle as a corpse took hold of the lever, and the twine around the pulley went taut. One more second and it would yank the drawer out beneath the demon's fist. The thing was already bringing down the blow that would crush him.

Ray pressed the button.

A flash tore through the darkness, and his skull rumbled like a stone in an avalanche. For a moment, he vanished. When he came to, his ears were bleeding and he coughed against the smoke and dust. The storage drawer stuck out a few inches, and the glow of flames accompanied the stench of burning flesh.

He hauled on the twine, and the pulley spun. The drawer scraped against runners blown crooked as the slab rolled out. Ray snatched the sword and dagger and leaped to his feet.

Heaps of scorched bodies lay blanketed in broken glass and chunks of cement. The demon stood in the dusty haze, covered in black blood and shards of mirror. Ray's fragmented reflection swept across its body as he closed his attack.

He swung the sword, severing the head-hand's ring finger. He shoved the dagger upward, piercing the muscles of the thing's wrist-throat. Despite the wounds, the demon's hand closed over him and squeezed, cracking his bones and cutting off his breath.

As their bodies turned in a suffocating dance, he glimpsed a half-intact mirror against the wall. The demon cast no reflection, making it look like Ray was floating in the wisps of dust, smoke, and bits of glass.

Already burning in Hell, he thought.

His strength waned against the hand's crushing force. His oxygen-deprived muscles began to fail. He withdrew the dagger and stabbed the thing's throat again and again, ready to sink into a sea of its black blood.

He realized that he was alternating between stabbing the demon and stabbing himself. A window opened in his crashing brain. A rainstorm was pouring through it, and when he looked through, he saw himself with Lenora, their bodies bare on the floor. They clutched the dagger between them, covered in one another's blood. He stabbed the demon and he stabbed himself, and he did not stop, though he did not know if it was inside or outside the dream.

The collapse brought him back. The demon had crashed to the floor with its wrist-throat severed to the last sinew. As its fingers loosened, Ray sucked a breath into his broken chest. He forced himself to stand despite the pain, drew the sword from where it had fallen among the corpses, and sliced the head-hand from its body.

57

Ray sat beside the thing's remains as if keeping vigil for some twisted and distant kin. He drew one labored breath after another, convinced his own corpse would lay across the demon's before the night was out.

But as light appeared in the basement's broken window, his breath became even, then slowly grew stronger. Like the first glimpse of health after a long sickness, he sat in his shredded clothes and hung onto the smallest increments of relief.

After he had first taken it down, he took photographs of the thing. Then in one immense effort, he stretched its arms out from its torso, slit upward between its rib-fangs, and cut out its heart. He wrapped it in clear plastic like it was a type of exotic victual, then stuffed it in his backpack for the angel.

It had taken everything he had and caused him to collapse again for hours. Now, the morning light and sips of the window's slight breeze were bringing him around. He sat with his hands on his knees, rocking and wheezing as his bones mended and his bleeding slowed.

Riel had given him the weapon he needed, and now it would be returned—but only if he made good on his end and brought back Adu. Would Isaiah let him keep the sword until then? It might matter if Riel had any plans to cross him. A blade that killed demons might be just as good for angels. It was endgame now, and there were only a few more moves to make.

A shadow appeared on the far wall, faint in the morning

light. It grew longer as footsteps sounded from the hall leading from the elevator shaft. Ray made himself stand and raise the dagger and the sword.

Tolly Crespo stepped into the room. He held a Sig P320 in his right hand, almost gently, as if he were bringing a sick man a cup of cool water.

"Might as well put 'em down," he said. "No use bringin' a knife to a gun fight."

Ray kept the blades up, the dagger tucked close, and the sword thrust forward.

Crespo's shadow swung to his left. It got longer and thinner, like the needle of a sundial pointed to some invisible mark on the basement's filthy wall. He gritted his teeth beneath the angles of his mustache. It looked gray in the morning light.

"I'm not gonna tell you to man-up like some gangster in the movies. They assume makin' it quick means no pain. But we know better, don't we? Ferretto taught you that revenge never ends. And as long as he has living kin on this Earth, his family will grow strong again, and you and all of yours will go on suffering, and this is the law of man, not some bullshit about nature and predators and prey, but eternal dominion over the souls of your enemies, on Earth as it is in Heaven, and in Heaven as it is in Hell."

The old detective looked proud of the bullshit he'd concocted behind his overpriced shades. But he didn't get the shot off before Ray flipped the dagger and plunged it into his own chest.

58

Bartolomeo Crespo pulled the trigger and shot Ray in the eye. He wanted to remind him he had been as blind as the demon he'd slain. He wanted to shoot out the other eye, too, and leave him lying with a pair of empty sockets on the floor. Instead, his aim was off, and he blew a bloody hole through his brain.

But Raymond Barrs did not fall. Tolly blinked against a sudden flood of memories, the two of them on the cracked pavement of a Brooklyn basketball court. It was long before Ray had stood up to Joey Ferretto. It was a day when a group of older boys laid into them just for the fun of it, and Ray was still a scrawny twerp who couldn't run fast enough. Tolly had hidden in an alley and watched as they beat Ray bloody.

But Ray had gotten back up. His neck and face had been bruised and imprinted with multiple sets of knuckles. He was eleven years old, and he spat a tooth on the ground. But he had gotten up and even stared them down like *"You got some more?"* before he turned and staggered home.

Now he stood like a statue scraped with scars, a chunk of his head missing, and his arteries pulsing and belching blood. *Why do you think that goddamn dagger is worth so much money?* Tolly's finger moved on the trigger a fraction of a second after Ray swung the broadsword. Ray had been blind to the depth of Ferretto's revenge, but Crespo had underestimated Ray's endurance, and in trying to score the dagger, his own goddamn greed.

59

Ray's chest heaved and wheezed, and his skull hissed and hemorrhaged as blood ran down the broadsword's blade. It flooded the groove, gushed over the hilt, and drenched his hand.

He moaned as he saw figures in a hazy half-light, a gruesome committee he assumed was welcoming him to the afterlife. They clawed at him like ushers for some immense and wretched theater.

But as the dagger's wound bled down his chest, the images fled. He saw the sun's rays growing stronger and that he had sliced off Crespo's arm. It lay on the floor, still clutching the pistol. His body had fallen against Ray's, and his remaining hand was grasping for the dagger as he bled out.

He was trying to take it away, as if it could heal him, too. But he had neither the strength nor the time. Ray dropped the sword and held Crespo against his shoulder as his friend finished dying. If he had any curses for his wife's family, he did not utter them. For all Ray knew, he'd already sold his soul and would soon join them for Hell's feature presentation.

60

That afternoon, April felt like August. The sun choked the city's streets, using smog like a gaseous garrote.

Ray called Riel from the BQE, and the angel gave him the address of a Korean church in Jackson Heights. The place was upstairs from a diner on Roosevelt Avenue. The marquee read *Bulgogi Sikdang* in bright blue letters, and the whole building smelled like a barbecue. He entered through a side door and climbed a sliver of rickety stairs. When he reached the second floor, he heard a warped mix of voices singing hymns, some with perfect pitch, others grossly off-key.

A door opened at the end of the hall, and the angel popped his head out. His salt-and-pepper hair looked feathered and combed. He wore a suit that passed for a banker's and even straightened his tie as he led Ray into the room like they were about to sign loan documents.

But the seven-foot-tall figure in plate armor belied any semblance of normalcy.

"Is this the mortal?" he asked. He stood by the window, sun shining on the sheets of steel capping his shoulders. They overlapped his breastplate seamlessly. The gauntlets on his hands flared out from his forearms, and when he pointed, his finger looked like a shining claw. "That is a rare weapon," he said.

Ray glanced at the sheathed broadsword.

"How do you know?"

"I can tell by the hilt alone. It was forged in the Rhineland by some who are neither angels nor demons, nor are they human. And I despise them more than either."

Ray ignored him and spoke to Riel. "I brought the demon's heart. It's in the trunk of the car," he said. "I kept my end of the deal."

"Where did you get that weapon?" asked the tall angel. He stepped forward from the window, sun dancing over his armor as he moved. "Perhaps I should take you to Heaven. Would you like to go to Heaven? It is a beautiful place where you will serve without question. It is a place where all can play their proper roles."

"Enough!" snapped Riel. "We have a covenant," he said to the angel, then turned back to Ray. "Give your keys to Jo Han-Ul. He will retrieve the demon's heart from your car. When he's done, you can take the girl."

As he suspected, there was no talk about the final installment. That's why the glorified thug in the armor was there, to make him feel lucky just to get the girl. That's when Ray realized there was someone behind him. He turned to the doorway and saw Ada standing beside a young Korean man. Her blonde hair hung in matted cords, and dark circles pocketed her eyes. Yet there was an alertness he hadn't seen since he'd pulled her from the ocean. Her mouth was slightly open as if she tasted a little energy on the tip of her tongue and was happy just to breathe.

She is alive, and this time they're never getting her back.

She stepped forward, but the man kept hold of her arm, sending Ray's hand instinctively to the broadsword. Riel frowned, but the angel grinned and put his hand on his own blade.

After a moment, the man checked his cell phone, then spoke: "No need for the keys. Hong-San got into the trunk. We've got it."

He released Ada's arm, and she ran to her grandfather. Her embrace was weak but warm. He held her though they had no time. *And even if this is all we have left, it was worth it.*

"I'd run now if I were you," said the angel. He didn't draw

his sword, but he did widen his smile. "Every demon in Hell wants to rip you to shreds."

Ray looked out the window and realized that the burning smell wasn't just the barbecue. It came from a troop of figures in hooded robes making their way up the avenue. The crowd parted as they advanced. Some stared as they stumbled back, some cut and ran. Two of the figures held swords, one of them a whip. Wisps of smoke rolled from their hoods and sleeves, and their footsteps scorched the ground.

They were half a block from the Crown Vic.

Ray clenched Ada's hand, and they bounded down the stairwell, the girl gaining speed and pulling him along. He let her go as they neared the car, and the robed figures closed in.

He glimpsed one of their faces, barbs of a black beard against red flesh, fangs uncovered by a snarl. It swung its sword, and Ray stopped to parry with his own. He slashed low, cut the thing's ankles, then leaped over the hood, opened the door, and slid into the driver's seat.

He heard a whip crack as he started the engine. One of the demon's snagged the rear wheel and pulled the cord taut. Ray pressed on the gas, and the car began to lurch into the lane. Another hooded demon clasped the whip's handle, and smoke billowed as the wheels spun.

Ray tossed the dagger in the back seat. "Cut it," he cried.

Ada grabbed the weapon, leaned out the window, and slashed the whip. The car jolted forward, and they coughed against the smoke as they sped east toward the LIE.

Tires screeched, horns blared, and cars swerved. A black Impala appeared in the mirror, pursuing them. A muscular, red arm reached out the window and hurled a spear. It smashed through the Crown Vic's rear windshield and grazed Ada's ear before piercing the glove compartment.

The girl's face contorted with pain, but she did not scream. Ray kept his foot on the gas and hands on the wheel.

"Light the candle," he cried. "It's in the backpack! Lighter's in the pocket!"

Ada dropped the dagger and unzipped the pack. Blood flowed through her hair as she rummaged around and pulled out the candle. The Impala was gaining on them. It made a weapon of itself and aimed to ram them from behind. He saw the fiend's face in the rearview mirror, its wiry beard and teeth streaked with black blood.

"Hang on," he said as he took a hard right. They were nearing Elmhurst, and on his left, he saw the ramp to the LIE.

Now it was only Ada's face in the mirror. She pinched the candle between her knees and lit it as gently as if it were on a birthday cake. When the flame appeared, she looked up. The soft glow spread over her chin and cheeks.

She looked more alive than he had ever seen her. She was pale but didn't have the mechanical twitch to her neck like when he'd pulled her from the ocean the first time.

"You did it," he said. "Thank God, you did it." Ray gulped against a knot in his throat. Who was he thanking again? He thought of Mari Callaghan's words—*Even if there was a place like that, it wouldn't really be Heaven would it?*

61

Ray checked the mirror as they pulled onto the LIE. The Impala had slowed down but was still following them. A Chevy Suburban swung in alongside it. He saw more creatures inside.

These did not wear robes and were crammed into the front seat, a jeering mass of flab, fangs, and muscles. The other traffic on the expressway ignored them even though their windows weren't tinted. Ray wondered if it was infernal magic or just New York. Another half dozen black cars swung into the lane and formed a convoy of demons that snaked along behind the Crown Vic.

Every demon in Hell wants to rip you to shreds, the angel had said.

It was getting later, and the sun was going down. He drove east on the LIE, back window smashed, hot wind whipping through the car. As he looked for an exit, he caught a glimpse of Ada. She was staring blankly, her expression worn but alive.

He slowed down as he swung onto the ramp and connected to the Meadowbrook Parkway. The demons matched him but didn't come close. He drove southeast now, the sun flashing in his mirrors, and followed the signs to Sligo Beach.

Warm salt air and the smell of the ocean filled the car as he exited the parkway. Sligo Beach was a narrow sliver of dunes between Jones Beach and Gilgo Beach further to the east. Napoli Ave swung around to the left toward South Oyster Bay, then cut back across the parkway to a row of once trendy bungalows facing the North Atlantic.

Ray parked the car beside one of their splintered walkways and opened Ada's door. He took the yahrzeit candle then gave it back to her once she was out of the car. "Hold it with both hands," he said.

The row of cars that followed them lined up along Napoli Ave. The closest parked about a hundred yards off. He saw the driver's face, pink flesh with a slash across it, and maggots crawling from his lips into his mouth.

"Let's go," said Ada, looking up from the shadows around her eyes. He knew she was more than older than him. She was time-ravaged. Whatever humanity they'd given her back as part of the bargain, her memories could be nothing but an abyss.

They followed the walkway to the bungalow's porch, where Ada ignored the door and pushed up the broken window. She slipped through, then came around and let him in.

They moved into an open room that stank of mold and bat urine. Rotted rafters hung from its slanted ceiling, and the sunset leaked through cracks in the roof. The side windows were boarded up, but through the broken front window, he saw the demons' cars had moved closer. They were just behind the Crown Vic now, and he heard their doors opening and thumping shut again as they emerged.

They moved as if in a procession, some robed, some naked. He made out their hoods and horns silhouetted against the dying light as they surrounded the house. Ray moved back to the middle of the room and crouched on the floor with Ada. They put the candle on the floor, and its light cast shadows on the walls.

His phone buzzed in his pocket. *Lenora*, he thought. *She wants the dagger.* He wasn't fooling himself that she was calling for anything else. He just knew she had to call.

But when he looked at the screen, he saw it wasn't her.

It was Beth:

tell ada i'm coming

Ray turned to his granddaughter. The candle's glow lit her face. Its reflection flickered in her eyes as she read her mother's text.

"She's gonna come get me now," she said. "I knew she would."

Ray didn't answer. The wind had risen and whipped the waves against the beach, and beneath their churn and crash, he heard the demons circling the bungalow. Their hooves thumped the sand, and their claws scratched the walls.

One of them looked through the broken window. The corners of its eyes slanted downward like it was permanently weeping, and its jaw quivered like it couldn't stop laughing. Though its flesh was all wrinkles, its teeth were white and square like a goat's. It bit off a shard of glass and its tongue bled as it chewed.

"I was other places more than I was here," said Ada. "I hardly remember being a kid. They hurt me in Hell and they hurt me in Heaven, and now it's like I'm *ancient*."

Ray nodded. He looked at his phone and wished for another text.

"Now my mother's coming. Wherever I was, I thought of her. And I know she was thinking of me. That's why she joined the reverend and learned to walk the dreams. Because she never gave up, because she learned the truth, and because she made a plan."

The demon in the window reached inside. The yahrzeit candle flared, and its hand steamed and puckered. It withdrew, took another bite of the glass, and glared at Ray.

"Don't feel bad now, Grampa. They were disgraceful men who did this to us. And you did what you had to do. You helped."

Ray squeezed her hand. "Are you sure she's coming?" he asked.

But what he meant was that he understood his part was finished. He was out, the way Beth had been out, and Bonnie had been out. He had set the feud in motion, and as far as they were concerned, he had now paid what he owed.

"This is a good place to wait," she said. "I can hear the waves. I still like the waves."

Through the window, Ray could see the black water beyond the demon's face. The waves she spoke of weren't rolling and crashing in the way lovers liked. They ripped and slashed in the relentless wind. They scoured the land in the unnatural spring heat. But for Ada, they were still of the Earth and a balm the way mold-ridden bread was a feast to those who starved.

The phone buzzed. *It's Lenora*, Ray thought, knowing it was Beth.

i'm outside

But it wasn't Beth, either.

It was Isaiah.

When Ray looked up, the demon was gone. Instead, he saw the Hassidic man standing on the porch in his black coat and hat. He was holding another yahrzeit candle in his hands, flame guttering in the wind.

"Come in," said Ray.

The hinges squeaked as Isaiah twisted the knob. The force of the storm caused the door to fly open, and he stepped inside. Ray saw the hooded and fanged figures behind him, and behind them, Isaiah's Cadillac parked among their cars. It was sandwiched in close and untouched because another candle, set into a metal case, burned on its hood.

Isaiah moved to the center of the room, where his shadow blended with Ada's. "So you've succeeded," he said.

"You could say that," said Ray. "This is my granddaughter, Ada."

Isaiah smiled. "Pleased to meet you, Ada."

"Help my grampa, if you can," she said.

Isaiah nodded, though his face fell. "To business then. You have some things that belong to me that you must return. And I have one more thing for you."

"I have your sword," said Ray. He looked at the blade he held in his right hand as if he just realized that it didn't belong to him. His grip tightened on the hilt as he spoke. He saw the demon had returned to the window, eyes weeping, jaw laughing.

"Yes, I must collect the Ulfbehrt blade," said Isaiah.

Ray's grip was still tight as he handed it over. The steel shined softly, letters obscured by dried blood. When Isaiah's hand clasped the hilt, he let go.

"I must also have the Frisian saex," he said.

Ray started. The dagger was Lenora's.

"Look at your phone," said Isaiah, knowing his thoughts. "You'll see it is mine."

Ray glanced at his screen and saw there was a new message. This time it was Lenora:

word

Ray shivered. He was supposed to want the dagger, but what he really wanted was to know why the hell she hadn't texted him before.

Because it's over.

Ray drew the saex from his boot and handed it to Isaiah. He stood between his friend and his granddaughter in a house surrounded by demons, crosshatched with bloody wounds, and unarmed.

"I have something for you," said Isaiah. He reached in his long coat's pocket and pulled out a banded roll of cash. He handed it to Ray and said, "An advance on your share of the sale."

Ray took the money. It was oddly reassuring.

He dug in his pocket again, and this time produced another yahrzeit candle. It was larger than the other two and contained in perforated metal housing like the one that stood on the car's hood. The housing had a small hinged door, and when he opened it, Ada used her flame to light the candle inside.

"Here," she said. "You can take it with you."

"But I'm staying with you," said Ray.

"No, Grampa. You have to go. You'll run out of time. When the candle burns down, you won't be safe."

Ray looked at Isaiah, whose face fell again. "It is the best I can do."

"What about her? What about her candle?"

"She doesn't need it. Your covenant with the angel protects her. But she will keep her candle for when her mother arrives. And I will stay here tonight, until they've all gone, to be sure."

Ray looked at the broken window. The demon's face was there, but it had moved back. Its weeping eyes were on the candle he held in his hand, and its quivering jaw was full of pain instead of laughter.

Isaiah handed him a set of keys. "Take my car," he said. "I'll return yours to the garage and pay for the damage. You can keep the Cadillac. Consider it part of your advance."

"Where the hell am I supposed to go?" Ray asked.

"As far as you can," said Isaiah. "Keep the candle burning while you drive."

Ada looked up at him and nodded.

"So what, I'm just gonna leave you here? I did all that to leave you in a goddamn abandoned bungalow?"

"It's not damned," said Ada. "And it has nothing to do with God." Her eyes flashed in the candlelight, and then she turned away. "My mother's coming, so I'm staying here. You have to go."

62

The demons stuck to him like a drunken sweat, following the Cadillac all night and into the scorching Brooklyn morning.

Whenever the black suburban came close, he saw the jeering faces in his rearview mirror and glared back. He had sixteen-thousand bucks in his pocket, which was enough to buy quality firepower if he saw fit. *I may not have the sword or the dagger, but I've watched bullets drop you and make you bleed. If they can't kill you, that's okay. I just want you to suffer.*

They stayed with him as he got on and off the LIE, then the BQE, then rolled up Flushing Avenue. Whatever advantages they had, he knew the candle would protect him for now. He thought of the first day Ada's ghost had appeared in the waves, how little he had known or understood. And even now, he believed he had only the smallest glimpse of understanding. To learn anything of the truth and use it meant accepting this little piece of humility.

As for Crespo and the Ferrettos, fuck them. He'd come back to Brooklyn and dealt with their asses. The suffering they promised his family would be eternal was handed back in the proverbial handbasket with a note that posed the question, *how 'bout them motherfuckin' apples?*

There was a part of him that still wanted to check his phone. There was something in his heart that still wanted Lenora to call. But he let that be and let it burn like the candle in the cage, knowing that at some point it had to melt away.

He had made his way back up to Grand Street, where he drove past *La Vela Roja*. The building was half-charred and covered in plywood. It looked like they dressed its corpse up just enough to keep the cops from making trouble, then left it alone. An ending that was not without grace in a business that was nothing if not pragmatic.

But as he moved west down Grand Street, it was as if the rest of Brooklyn danced on its grave. Merengue blared on the stoops where men sipped beer and played cards. Cars parked along the curb thumped and rattled with slow grooves that blended with the merengue and added a certain cackling menace.

He thought of the weeping-laughing demon he'd seen outside the bungalow and wondered if it had been a demon at all, or just a high and horny drunkard hell-bent to suck down a summer full of filthy, blood-boiling nights.

Passing Union Ave, he made his way toward the Williamsburg Bridge. A girl in combat boots with red and black hair who could have been fifteen or thirty-five stood smoking outside a bodega. She glared as he passed like, *"The fuck you lookin' at?"* She wore thick black mascara that made her eyes a pair of dark, glassy pools. Her lips snarled as she shook her head. She tossed her cigarette and ducked into a dive bar next to the bodega.

Ray pressed on the pedal and drove on. The Cadillac's engine roared as he accelerated onto the bridge. He didn't see the demons in the mirror, but he knew they were there.

He would drive north now, as far as he could go. The wind from the open windows caused the candle's flame to flicker in its housing, but it didn't go out. Shadows from the bridge's girders cut across the rising sun, and among them lurked another shadow, one that told him to check his phone.

Instead, Ray swung onto the ramp and headed north on 95. He didn't look back for the angels, the demons, or anything else, for he knew that before he left the city, the city had already left him.

About the Author

Carl R. Moore lives in upstate New York with his wife Sarah and two daughters, Maddy and Izzy. He is the author of Slash of Crimson and Other Tales (Seventh Star Press, 2017) and Mommy and the Satanists (Seventh Star Press, 2018). His fiction has also appeard in Rymfire's Heavy Metal Horror and Rymfire Erotica anthologies, as well as magazines Thuglit and Macabre Cadaver.

News and contact information can be found on his website, www.carlrmoore.com

www.ingramcontent.com/pod-product-compliance
Lightning Source LLC
Chambersburg PA
CBHW021003260626
47169CB00006B/1926